THE CULLING

THE CULLING BOOK ONE

RAMONA FINN

D1413432

THE CULLING_

The Culling

The Authority

The Ferrymen

RAMONA FINN

THE
CULLING

CONTENTS

BLURB_

In a solar system where The Authority decides who lives and who dies, only one of their own executioners can stop them.

Glade Io is a trained killer. Marked at a young age as an individual with violent tendencies, she was taken from her family and groomed to be a Datapoint—a biotech-enabled analyst who carries out the Culling. She is designed to identify and destroy any potential humans that threaten the colonies: those marked as lawbreakers, unproductive or sick. But when she's kidnapped by rogue colonists known as the Ferrymen, everything Glade thinks she knows about the colonies, and The Authority that runs them, collapses into doubt.

Pulled between two opposing sides, and with her family's lives hanging in the balance, Glade is unsure of who to trust—and time is running out.

ABOUT RAMONA FINN_

Ramona Finn writes about courageous characters who fight to live in broken, dystopian worlds. She grew up sitting cross-legged on her town's library floor - completely engrossed in science fiction books. It was always the futuristic world or the universe-on-the-brink-of-extinction plot lines that drew her in, but it was the brave characters who chose to fight back that kept her turning the pages.

Her books create deep, intricate worlds with bold characters determined to fight for their survival in their dystopian worlds - with a little help from their friends...

P apa fell down and he didn't stand up again.

I'd seen Papa jump the tallest fence in our colony. I'd seen Papa laugh and dance with Mama in the living room when I was supposed to be asleep. And I'd seen Papa run alongside me, so fast. But I'd never seen Papa fall down until that morning.

I puzzled it out as I sat with Mama in our front yard, one of my twin sisters on my lap. "But where did he go?" I asked her.

"I don't know." Her voice didn't sound like Mama's voice.

I looked at the place where he'd fallen. The red dirt was pushed around like something had been dragged through it. I tried to understand. "But those men took him somewhere."

Mama stood up quickly then, one of the twins on her hip. "They took him away. With the rest of the culled, Glade."

I frowned. I didn't know what that meant. All the grownups had been talking about the Culling, but no one had told me what it was. And then Papa had fallen down. And hadn't

1

moved for hours. Mama had gone out to him. Just once. Just for a minute. She'd leaned down over him and shook and shook. It had looked like she was talking. But she hadn't let me go outside. Not until men had come by on a truck and picked Papa up and driven him away.

"And he won't come back?" It didn't make any sense. Papa always came back. He was the kiss on my forehead before I fell asleep. Papa made breakfast for all of us. Of course he was coming back.

"No. He won't." Mama was standing, and then she was snatching up the baby from my arms so that she held one twin on each hip. I thought she was going to say more, but instead she went into the house.

When she came back out, she'd put the girls down for a nap and she didn't stop walking until she was almost on top of me.

"Mama!" I cried when she hugged me so tight that I gasped. She was gasping, too.

"You have to promise you won't be like your father, Glade," she whispered into my ear.

"The way I look?" I asked, trying to pull free of her grasp. I didn't know how to change that. Everyone said I looked just like Papa.

She laughed, but it sounded like broken glass clinking at the bottom of a trash can. "No. The way you think. You can't be like him. You have to blend in, Glade. You hide in plain sight, okay?"

"I'm good at hiding. But I don't like it," I said, trying to pull myself from her arms again. "Papa can never find me when we play."

"It doesn't matter if you don't like it. You have to do it,

Gladey. You blend in. You hide. But here." She pressed a dry palm to my forehead. "You have to hide here, too."

"Mama." I was gasping because she was hugging me too tight again.

"If they can't see you, they can't find you," she whispered, over and over into my hair as she rocked us back and forth, and after a while, I just sat perfectly still.

———

Clicking open the small screen at his wrist, the man studied the readout of the little girl's brain. Even now, he could barely believe what he was looking at. Finding her profile had been like taking a handful of sand on the beach and finding a perfect, polished ruby.

Someone else might have looked at this same image of brain-waves and seen a cloud of colors surrounding a brain. But Jan Ernst Haven looked at the image and saw only potential. A tremendous capacity for greatness. She was the key for him. She held the future of their society within her.

He looked up from the image projected from his wrist and caught sight of the child herself. She sang a song with no melody, lying on her stomach in her yard, her feet making circles in the air behind her.

Haven looked down at the boy standing next to him on the sidewalk. Just a few years older than the girl. "Do you see how calm she is, Dahn?"

Dahn nodded, with his dark hair long but scrupulously neat.

"Her father has just been culled, and her mother made quite the scene, but still, the girl is calm."

Dahn nodded again. A thought struck his nine-year-old brain. "That's what a Datapoint would do in this situation. Stay calm."

"Yes. Exactly. Very good." Haven's eyes moved back to the girl's brain readout. He still couldn't believe it.

Dahn's small chest swelled at Haven's praise and the little boy thought the man might put a hand on his head or his shoulder. But Haven just kept staring down at the tech on his wrist. Trying to push down his disappointment, Dahn studied the little girl. She had hair that fell around her shoulders like a blanket. And when she rolled over, Dahn saw that she had dark eyes to match.

Her father had been culled that morning, and there she was, playing in the dirt yard. He glanced up at Haven. Dahn thought of the day his own father had died. The way he hadn't been able to get the tears to stop. How his chest had been made of ice for weeks. He hoped that Haven didn't know about that.

He was going to be a Datapoint someday. He just knew it. And as he watched the little girl playing, he knew in his gut that she would be, too.

ONE

CHAPTER ONE_

Ten Years Later
~The Asteroid Belt~

I've always hated hide-and-seek.

But if you had to play it, like I did right now, so much better to be the hunter than the hunted.

I cracked my knuckles in front of me as I stepped into the simulator, and the door slammed behind me. I was instantly plunged into darkness – a blunt darkness, as can only happen indoors. Two points of light opened up in front of me, one on the left and one on the right.

I bared my teeth in a feral grin as my eyes bounced from one point of light to the other. They were throwing two colonies at me at once. I waited, tense and ready, as both points of light started spiraling open, focusing. They were forming not just into images, but into my new reality.

Within seconds, I was straddling the line between two

worlds. I could see the images with my eyes, but when I closed them, I could see the images projected across my brain, as well. The computer implanted in my arm and head was cool like that. There was almost nothing I couldn't do with it.

I scanned the two landscapes on either side of me. Glacially icy on one side, offering all the blues and grays of an icy planet. And on the other side, the black sky met the umber sand of a red planet. I looked back and forth between them. Two colonies at once. I knew it was just a simulation, but still, a bead of sweat rolled down my back as I planted my feet on the floor of the simulator.

Come out, come out, little citizens.

Using my computer, my integrated tech, I zoomed in on the icy landscape first. I felt the frigid wind, the brisk scent of ozone filling my nostrils, and soon I was close enough to see the roofs of dwellings. And yup. There the people were. I ignored the heavy furs that covered all but their eyes. I ignored their varying heights and weights. I ignored the way some of them held hands or rode on one another's backs. I ignored the laughter that rang out from a group of citizens who had to be just about my age. I ignored the familiar admonishing tone of a mother at her wit's end. The only thing I saw were the reddish glows that emanated from each person's brainwaves.

The integrated tech computer that had been implanted when I'd been chosen for this job was designed to detect brain patterns. The computer in my brain could see other people's brainwaves, and it presented the information in a way that allowed my eyes to see it, too. It had taken a long time to get used to it. But now it was almost like second nature. I let the

reddish blurs around each person's head remain just that –
blurry.

Shifting my attention to the red planet now, I gave my eyes a
second to adjust from the blinding white of the ice planet to the
burnished, sunburned bake of the second colony. The black sky
was a rich dark, the kind of black that had depth. With the Milky
Way splashed across the skyroof of the red planet, I gave my
eyes a second to adjust as my tech zoomed in on the colony, the
red planet rushing past in my periphery. Soon we were there.
The thick canvas tents that the citizens used as dwellings
flapped in the constant, stinging wind. Each person wore white
garments to reflect heat, but they were all dyed a deep, dusty
pink from the red sand being flung in every direction.

This was a busier colony than the ice planet. People bustled
past one another, balancing baskets of wares on their heads. The
streets were narrow and craggy, lined with red rock walls that
gave way to the canvas dwellings that stood every ten feet or so.
So little of this planet was hospitable that the people had to live
on top of one another like bees in a hive. The simulation raced
me down one twisting street and to the next, so that I was
coasting past grannies in doorways who were sorting seeds into
one basket or another. Past children huddled around a game of
skipping rocks on the ground. Past a ratty dog, everything but
his eyes covered in red grit.

And then I landed in the main square. A place I'd only seen
photographs of in the past.

People haggled over prices in the canvas booths that lined
the square. Eggs and bread were traded and bartered. A group
of unwatched children ran screaming from one end of the
square to the other, adults scowling after them. A line of people

800 feet long wrapped around the square. Everyone held empty chalices. It was the line for water. A group of citizens shouted over one another as they crowded around a small wooden platform where an ox stood. The animal's age was shown in its milky eyes and swollen joints, but still, the farmers shouted and scrapped for the auctioneer's attention. On a planet as hard to farm as this one, any help was highly sought after.

I pulled my attention from the details of the two worlds and back to the task at hand. This wasn't a sightseeing simulation. I was a trained Datapoint. This was my job.

This was a Culling.

Using every bit of training that had been pounded into me over the last two years, I began to block out all of the sensory details of the two colonies on either side of me. The slate gray clouds and the pale icy sun melted away on my left. On my right, the baked red became nothing more than a neutral background. Like I had a hand gripping a knob on a radio, I guided my integrated tech into turning the volume down. The noises of the market on one side muted, and the noises of the children playing on the other side did the same.

Soon, all I was left with were the citizens and the halos of red around their heads. I brought each red blur even further into focus. Starting with one alone and then moving to each citizen individually, I read their brainwaves with practiced ease.

My integrated technology and my brain worked in perfect, synchronized tandem as I identified the citizens I was looking for. In the simulation, they were scattered about, as they'd be in their worlds. But in my mind's eye, it was as if all of the citizens were standing neatly in a line before me. Using my technology to organize them, I saw about a quarter of the citizens stepping forward. These were the ones I was about to cull. The ones with brainwaves indicating violence and aggression. The ones with the capacity to commit murder. The ones who were inclined to bring down pain on the citizens around them.

There were hundreds of citizens about to be culled, and another bead of sweat traced down my spine. This was almost as many as I'd culled in the last simulation, and I'd ended up in the infirmary for two days after the strain of that Culling. And I still hadn't even readied the icy planet yet.

Sure, it would be easier to cull them in groups. Do a hundred here or a hundred there. But that wasn't what this simulation was for. This was mass culling.

I could almost hear Haven's voice in my ear. *"Push yourself, Glade. You have the capacity for greatness. Yet it's almost like you're trying to blend in."*

I took a deep breath and turned my attention to the next planet, zooming in on each citizen's brainwaves, pulling forward all the ones to be culled.

Between the two colonies, there had to be at least a thousand that needed to be culled. My vision blurred and I realized I'd stopped breathing. The way I would if I were lifting something heavy. I felt my brain stuttering as I attempted to combine the culling groups from the two colonies. It didn't matter that they were across the galaxy from one another. It didn't matter that I was attempting to separate each citizen from the next, to cull some and not all. It didn't matter that each citizen was moving about, talking and laughing and pulsing. I had to cull all at once, and with vicious accuracy.

Within the simulator, my knees trembled. My hands clenched open and closed and, for a horrifying second, I lost grip on my tech and all the sensory stimuli flooded back in. Red dust and jutting glaciers of ice. Children playing, women hugging, the dusty dog digging in a pile of refuse.

No!

My brain wove itself into the integrated tech and took control again, zooming in on the citizens waiting to be culled. I ignored the faces, and I ignored the voices – all I saw were the reddish blurs of their brainwaves.

Ruthlessly separating them in my mind, I realized my mistake. I was going too slowly. I'd never been a long-distance runner. I was a sprinter. My knees shook again and I knew that I wasn't going to make it more than ten or fifteen more seconds before I collapsed and ended up in the infirmary again; my brain couldn't take the strain.

My vision blurred as I huffed air in and out of my lungs. I was losing the groups. The culled were mixing in with the regular citizens. I couldn't hold the line. Couldn't tell the difference. With my heart stuttering in my chest, the computer in my arm felt foreign and angrily sharp. I was failing. I was failing again.

Clarity raged within me even as every single brainwave of every single citizen melted into the next. Their brain patterns were a single, cacophonous blur.

I gripped the sides of my own head and screamed into the strain of it. It was useless. I was too exhausted to distinguish them.

Mass Culling.

I could all but feel the breath of Jan Ernst Haven in my ear. *Mass Culling.*

Individuals didn't matter.

The red blur of their pulsing brains seemed to cloud around me, bearing down on me. They were so close. Everywhere. I lifted one hand in the air – the arm where my integrated tech had been implanted. My brain warred for dominance with the computer that had been implanted in me. The integrated tech strained, searching for just the cullable citizens. My own brain strained for silence, for this to be over. I felt the familiar feeling of my tech's grip on the brainwaves of a citizen. I always visualized a hand gripping a giant plug. This was bigger than any plug I'd ever pulled before. But there was no looking back now. The red of each citizen was about to collapse on me. I couldn't hold them all. It was me or them.

My brain and my tech synchronized and, in one crystal clear moment, we, as one, yanked the red brainwaves together. The citizens, such a large group, resisted at first. Pulling one citizen's brainwaves was easy. It was like plucking a hair from a head. But pulling thousands at once was like yanking out a whole handful of hair.

But my brain was strong. And so was my tech. With a scream like a warrior, I gritted my teeth and gave a final yank. I felt the brainwaves come loose from each citizen, blinking instantly into blackness. Into silence. My tech immediately stopped blocking my senses. And there were the two colonies. One icy and gray-blue. The other baked red and blistering hot. Both of them silent as a tomb. And not a brainwave to be found.

———

I sighed as soon as the door to the simulator creaked open. I knew exactly who was standing on the other side and I knew exactly what he was going to say.

"You've got to be joking, Glade."

Apparently, he always thought I was joking. I merely raised an eyebrow at Dahn as I pushed past him, out of the simulator and into the training room. Everything was gray metal and brown upholstery – even the command chair where Dahn had just been sitting. For one brief second, I thought wistfully of the two gorgeous landscapes he'd just shown me in the simulator. And then I thought of the vacuous silence I'd left in each of them. I shoved that thought away.

He let me brush past him, but immediately chased after me. When I didn't show signs of stopping, Dahn slid his stocky frame in front of mine, blocking my way. His dark hair stood out starkly against his pale skin as he stared down at me, his arms crossed over his chest. It always annoyed me in moments like this that he was so handsome.

"All of them, Glade? All of them? Every single citizen?"

I shrugged, acting as if I wasn't sure what was so wrong about the choice I'd just made. "You heard Haven. He wants us to focus on *mass* culling."

"Don't play dumb. You know he wouldn't have meant for you to cull *every single citizen*." A piece of his long dark hair fell forward across his forehead and he elegantly tied it back with the rest. "I don't even know how you manipulated your tech to cull the citizens who didn't require it."

That gave me pause. Actually, now that he mentioned it, that part hadn't been hard at all. Even though my tech wasn't designed for that purpose, it had been surprisingly easy to cull everyone.

I cleared my throat and gave the only answer I could think of. "It was too many people. My sensors were completely fuzzed over. I couldn't tell one from the other." I tried to step past him, but he smoothly moved right along with me. After years of knowing Dahn, this behavior didn't surprise me. He'd been smoothly putting himself in my way since pretty much the day I'd met him.

"You're telling me that you had trouble distinguishing between them in the simulation?" he asked, a line of worry forming between his eyebrows.

That was Dahn for you, always balancing frustration and worry.

"So what if I did?" Not an answer, exactly, but not a lie, either.

Dahn narrowed his eyes in that way of his. The way he did when he thought he was hiding his temper. "Let's go through this one more time."

He waved his hand through the air like he was wiping something clean between us. A glowing projection of a human brain appeared where his hand had just been. I envied the ease with which he was able to manipulate his own tech to do what he wanted.

I'd been selected to be a Datapoint – just like all of the other Datapoints – because apparently, I was naturally inclined to be one. And sure, give me a computer, no matter how archaic, and I could make it stand up and dance for you. But the integrated tech they installed when you started your training as a Datapoint? Well, even after two years, it still felt unwieldy.

I traced my own hand over the shimmery, clear motherboard that lined my left arm like crystal jewelry. As my fingers

15

brushed the tech, I felt the shivery corresponding buzz in the tech on the left side of my face, also illuminated by iridescent crystals.

Dahn's own tech pulsed with light at his temples as he almost carelessly rotated the projection of the brain to face me. A flick of his fingers, and the brain lit up red in a few different zones. Dahn raised one of those imperious eyebrows at me. His soft gray eyes shone with frustrated expectation.

I sighed, surveying the projection, knowing exactly what he was asking of me. We'd only done it about a thousand times before. "It needs to be culled, of course."

He flicked his fingers and the red zones on the brain shifted, but infinitesimally.

"Culled," I repeated, almost bored.

The red zones in the projection shifted again, this time indicating a person who shouldn't be culled.

"That one's to be left alone."

Now the projections went faster and faster, showing different zones each time.

"Culled, left alone, culled, culled, left alone, culled."

Dahn snapped his hand closed with barely disguised frustration and the projection disappeared, leaving behind only a slightly black spot in my vision.

"Explain it to me then, Glade," he bit out. "How you can score with one hundred percent accuracy on the projection tests, and fail so catastrophically in the simulations?"

With a strange tug in my stomach, I thought of the strain of distinguishing between the citizens, how unnatural it had felt. And then I thought of how relatively easy it had been to pull the plug on all of them, rather than just the ones needing to be culled. But I said nothing. Instead, I did what I pretty much always did around Dahn. I shrugged.

His temper flashed bright in his gray eyes for only a second before they dimmed. "This isn't something you can shrug off, Glade. This is the *Culling*. The glue that holds our entire society together for God's sakes. And the decade is up. It's coming. Around the corner, and you're not ready for it!"

Shame sliced through me for just a second, white hot. Dahn was right. Frustrated with my inability to do well in the simulations, I'd begun treating my training with disdain and indifference. "I know."

His look softened, but Dahn Enceladus had never been one to pass up the opportunity to make a point. One of his graceful hands floated back to gesture at the simulator. "You just culled people who shouldn't have been. Instead of concentrating and ferreting out the citizens with violent or murderous tendencies, you culled every single one of those people. Including the people with attributes that *strengthen* our society."

I cleared my throat and tossed my long black hair back over my shoulder. I shifted my weight onto my good leg; even so, I felt the tremor in my knee. I was exhausted from the simulation, but I'd be damned if I showed weakness in front of any other Datapoint, even Dahn. "I know what I did, Dahn. Now, if you'd get out of my way for a second…"

Instantly, his soft gray eyes went from boring into mine to scanning down my body. The black workpants and tight black t-shirt that every Datapoint was required to wear didn't do much to hide the trembling in my muscles.

"You're exhausted," he said, stepping back, and a look came over his face that I couldn't interpret. I'd seen that look before

17

from him and it confused me every time. It was… soft. He reached one arm toward my elbow.

"I'm fine. I just need to—"

"Glade Io."

I tried not to wince at the reedy voice that always seemed to be speaking directly into my ear. There was only one person who consistently called me by my full name. I'd hoped that he hadn't taken it upon himself to watch that particular simulation, but he always seemed to be keeping an eye on me.

"Sir Haven," I addressed him, turning on my heel and nodding once to show respect. As a member of the Authority, Jan Ernst Haven was one of the seven most important people in our solar system. Each of the seven members of our government served for a lifetime, working together to uphold the laws and rules of our solar system. He was the only member of the Authority I'd ever actually met, and he lived on the Station with us. Really, it was an honor that he'd taken a personal interest in my development as a Datapoint. But one look at the subtly disappointed expression on his face and his interest once again felt like an additional burden.

"Perhaps you'd like a private word with me?" He always spoke like this, softly and in question form. Thing was, they were questions that had only one answer. Whatever answer he wanted.

"Yes, sir."

Without even acknowledging Dahn's presence, Haven turned, and I dutifully followed him through the training room and toward the private office he kept.

———

The Station, where all us Datapoints trained and lived, floated in the middle of the asteroid belt between Mars and Jupiter. Because it had to be of a fairly indestructible nature (given all of the asteroid collisions it was dealt), everything was built for durability, not design. It gave the entire place more the look of a glorified jail than a space station.

When I'd first come here from my sweltering, volcanic planet, I'd been shocked by the lack of color. Where there'd been glowing streams of red hot lava in my past, here there were only gray and brown hallways. Where the sun had burned yellow through our navy sky at home, here I saw only slivers of black universe through the rare and tiny windows. The only light we ever got were the pinpricks of the distant stars and the synthetic florescent lights that lined the ceilings.

Two years later, and I was mostly used to it. The only room that still turned my stomach was Haven's private office – and, oh look, there we were.

He sat in his royal blue armchair, the way he always did, and I sat on its twin across the room from him. For a long minute, Haven said nothing. He merely looked at me across the office. Everything about him seemed to be silver. His hair was like gossamer spider webs, perfectly metallic in color. His eyebrows and eyelashes the same. Even his eyes looked as if they were two silver coins in his perfectly symmetrical face.

I'd heard plenty of the other Datapoints going on about how handsome Jan Ernst Haven was, but I couldn't see it. The strange lightness in his eyes, the unblinking stare… I found it all to be the opposite of attractive. Repellant, even.

"How long have you been training here, Glade?"

What was the point in asking a question he already knew the answer to? "Two years, plus a month or two."

"So, at sixteen, that would make you on the older end of our fifty or so trainees now, wouldn't it?"

He knew exactly where I fell amongst my peers.

I nodded.

He nodded.

I resisted the urge to sigh.

"Glade, tell me, what's the first thing any Datapoint is taught to do after their tech is integrated into them?"

I tossed my long hair back over my shoulders. Dahn and I once saw footage of an old movie from Earth where a black horse did the same thing with his mane. Dahn had teased me about it for days after that. I pretended to be annoyed at the time, but since then I've come to like the comparison. The creature in that movie was proud. Confident. Doing exactly what it was born to do. I channeled those feelings as I answered Haven.

"To sync with the Authority Database."

It was the one thing I hadn't done during the simulation. And it's the one thing I definitely should have done. Most likely, it's the whole reason I'd failed. I knew this; Haven knew this.

Haven rose from his royal blue chair and stepped gracefully over to a steel panel on the wall. He touched the corner of the panel, and it recognized his fingerprint, lighting up immediately. The screen that appeared was something I'd always admired. A beautiful piece of technology. As usual, my fingertips itched to explore it. I desperately wanted to know how it worked, the intricacies. I wanted to learn how to use it. I was confident that, given twenty minutes or so of free rein, I could learn to use it. Yeah, I was that good. It was likely the reason I'd been chosen to train as a Datapoint. My fluency in all things computer. It was also likely the reason that Haven was so constantly disappointed in my performance as a Datapoint these days. Frankly, it just didn't make sense that a computer genius like myself would have such a difficult time wielding the integrated tech on my arm.

Haven waved his hand in front of the screen, scrolling idly through parts of the interface he didn't care to see – until he got to the Authority Database homepage.

"Square one," I muttered.

He nodded, ignoring my tone. "Exactly. The very first thing any Datapoint trainee sees when he or she comes through the doors of the Station." He stroked one hand against the edge of the screen and I wondered if he realized he was doing it. "It's a lovely interface, Glade. Wouldn't you agree?"

I nodded. Because I really did agree. Everything about the interface between Datapoints' integrated tech and the Authority Database really was user friendly. Fun, actually. It was designed perfectly. Syncing to the Database was a joy for a Datapoint. A physical joy, even, considering our tech was a physical part of us. I absently brushed one hand over the tech on my arm, feeling the corresponding shiver over the tech that lined my left cheek.

Haven turned to me, his arms crossing loosely over his chest, his silvery head cocked to one side. He reminded me, for one second, of the winking of a distant star. "Then why do you resist it so fiercely, Glade Io? Every other Datapoint relies on – no – *rejoices* in the interface with the Authority Database. But you resist it. And to what end? Failing your simulations."

He uncrossed his arms and turned back toward the screen,

staring at the Database home screen almost lovingly. Behind his back, I tossed my mane of hair again and thought of the horse.

"The Database is here to help you, Glade. To guide you. It is impossible to do your job as a Datapoint without it. The strain you felt today?" He turned back to me and his silver eyes both tugged at me and repelled me. "If you allow yourself to sync with the Authority Database, it does the work *for you*. Takes that strain off of your shoulders, Datapoint. The Database identifies those to be culled *for you*. And then, all you have to do is the actual Culling."

Pull the plug. All I have to do is pull the plug.

It's true that, as Datapoints, we had been scrupulously trained on how to identify who was to be culled and who was to be left alone. But we were also simultaneously trained to rely on the Authority Database to complete the identification of those citizens for us. It had never made sense to me until the idea of mass culling was introduced. Until I'd realized that my simple human brain and the tiny tech on my arm couldn't possibly handle a load of data that large without the Authority Database.

"So, tell me, Glade Io, why do you resist?"

It was a simple answer. Simple enough that I knew Jan Ernst Haven already knew it.

I didn't trust the Authority Database. I would never give that kind of control to a piece of technology I didn't understand.

"If I could just explore the Database, Sir Haven, understand a bit more about how it works, then I'm sure I could sync with much more—"

"We've been through that, Glade." And for the first time, his tone was clipped, non-indulgent.

I snapped my mouth closed.

"There are things you simply do not have access to. And I have no intention of changing those rules and regulations. Rules and regulations which are there for good reasons that a child cannot understand."

He turned back to the screen and flicked it off with his fingertip. When he turned back around, his temper had flared out. He was calm and quiet, as he normally was. "I have a theory that you're actually very much like me. That you understand the language of computers much better than you understand the language of people. Your Datapoint entry testing shows that clearly enough. Not as high on the sociopath scale as some of your Datapoint comrades, sure. But high enough to be selected."

He sat back in the royal blue chair across from me, crossing one leg over the other and leaning his silver-stubbled chin on one hand. "Humans aren't computers, no matter what the Authority gifts them with." He nodded toward my integrated tech. "And even if your brain is as devoid of empathy as we could possibly find, there are still… complications within you. Thoughts and emotions that make you impossible to program."

It was almost as if he'd forgotten I was there, as if he were talking to himself, leaning on one hand, his eyes riveted to mine.

"Communication with humans has always been a personal frustration for me, though I find myself better at it than most. For words are not pure information. They're inadequate. No matter how hard a human might try to communicate a thought or emotion, there is always a disjunction between what they say..." He lifted one hand, and then the other. "And what they feel."

I tossed my hair back again and Haven followed the movement absently with his eyes before continuing on. "Glade, you say that you have trouble syncing with the Authority Database because you don't understand it. Allow me a humble attempt at translating for you. What you really mean."

His posture hadn't shifted, yet I sensed a change coming over him. Something rigid was lining each word that came out of his mouth. He was lazy in turn, but somehow his words sliced through me.

"You are, basically, telling me that you *won't* do what we're asking you to. Despite your levels of technological intelligence. Despite your score on the sociopathic scale. Despite the fact that, on paper, you are a perfect Datapoint. Despite the incredibly high hopes we had for you when you were selected at the age of thirteen. Despite it all, there is something within you, some flaw in the human design, that makes you very difficult for us to work with.

"I find myself wondering. If only I had access to a version of Glade Io who had almost all of her attributes besides the thing that makes her resist. If only such genetic material existed… But, oh, it does, doesn't it?"

My sisters. He must have been talking about my sisters. Still, his leg was crossed, his chin propped on his hand as if we were discussing what we'd like on the menu for dinner. But there was nothing casual about his words. Nothing casual about his threat to my family.

"You're considering bringing my sisters in for Datapoint training?" A memory burned through me, almost making me wince. *Florescent lights sting my retinas as steel hooks hold my eyelids open. I'm straining against chains at my chest and arms; even my feet are pinned down. I can see nothing but the blue light above me,*

24

but my mind is racing, my thoughts jumbled, confused, terrified. My left arm and the left side of my face experience searing pain where they've opened the flesh, implanting the computer tech into me. But that's not the most painful part. The most painful part is the fact that now they're programming that tech to interact with my brain. Some technician sits behind glass and fiddles with the settings on the computer that's connected to my brain through the side of my head. My thoughts are not my own. My brain tries to understand, to right itself. But the computer toggles with the information. My legs jump as the motherboard in my arm tells them to. No! My brain screams, grappling for control. The integrated tech doesn't control me. I control the tech. Pinwheeling into pain and the brightest, most excruciating darkness I've ever experienced, my body thrashes against the intrusion.

The integration of my tech. It took three days for my brain to accept it. Longer than most, shorter than some. And that was the easy part. The harder part was the years of practice, of simulations, of constantly straining to sync my brain with the computer implanted inside of me.

Haven wanted to bring my sisters here. He wanted to do that to them.

Haven shrugged, acknowledging my words and changing his posture for the first time since he'd sat down. "We're running out of options, Glade. I'd rather not start from scratch, of course. We have invested a great deal of time and money into you, Datapoint. But the bottom line is that we're not interested in creating Datapoints that only fulfill seventy-five percent of their duties." He pointed at the screen behind me, and just the movement of his hand commanded it to turn on. He scrolled through the air and brought up what he was looking for. "You might be interested in seeing your sisters' Datapoint scoring, which we only recently performed on them. A preliminary testing, not the official testing, of course. At eleven, they're a touch young for it, but, as you know, I've always been a curious man."

He'd had preliminary testing done on them? I'd never even heard of that before. I gripped the armrests as my world tilted. Apparently, there were fewer rules in this game than I'd thought.

I focused my eyes onto their two names at the top of the screen. Daw Io and Treb Io. Identical twins.

My stomach sank as I read their scores. Their intellect was high. Though technology had never naturally interested them, the technical fluency would be easy enough to teach. Across each scoring category, they looked more and more like the perfect candidates for Datapoint training. *Creative problem solving: High. Tenacity to accomplish a task: High. Speed of decision making: High.*

My heart leapt when I read the most important category, though.

Exhibition of sociopathic tendencies: Non-existent.

Thank God. They were ineligible. No Datapoint was without at least some sociopathic score.

"Don't their scores on the sociopathic scale render them ineligible, Sir Haven?"

I'd carefully kept any trace of hope out of my voice.

"Normally, yes."

He resumed that lazy Sunday posture. "Except, in their cases, the rest of the Authority and I found that their low scoring there was offset by these scores." He scrolled his hand again in the air and brought up another screen with their testing results.

Acceptance of rules: Extremely high.

Mental malleability: Extremely high.

My stomach sank again. Translation? Daw and Treb did exactly what they were told to do. This was no fabrication on Haven's part. I'd seen this quality exhibited in them since they were old enough to understand English. If they came here, if they were integrated, trained as Datapoints, they'd follow every direction given to them. They'd learn to cull. And they'd do it well.

And it would destroy them. I had no doubts in my mind of that.

Halfway through tossing my hair, I froze. I thought of the footage of that horse. The glossy beast. Its haunches bunching and rolling as it raced through an earthen field. A horse that was broken and owned, but could never really be subdued – not if it had a field in which to run. The sun on its back.

Burning light in my eyes. Hands tied. Pain of an indescribable measure at my temples. The computer makes my fingers curl. I fight back. Open my hands and make the computer bend to my will. I can't see. I can't hear. I can only feel my heartbeat, every beat of my pulse slicing through me like teeth made of ice.

"It's not necessary to waste the resources on replacing me," I heard myself say, ignoring the pleased glint in Haven's eye. "I understand that my efficacy has been subpar. I'll work harder." I paused. "I'll sync with the Database."

————

She didn't see him as she stepped out of Jan Ernst Haven's office. She tossed her glossy black hair back over her shoulders, took a deep breath, and headed toward the trainee's section of the Station. Dahn watched her go.

It didn't surprise him that she hadn't looked back and seen him standing in the hall. She barely even saw him when she was looking right at him. They were friends, sure. Had been for years. But as he watched her disappear down the hall, exhibiting that funny little gait of hers, he realized that he had absolutely no idea what she was thinking. He had no idea what she'd been thinking when she'd stepped out of the simulator, he had no idea what she'd been thinking when Jan Ernst Haven had singled her out yet again, and he had no idea what she was thinking now as she disappeared around the corner.

It surprised him that he wanted to know, though. *That* was fairly new. He'd always been intrigued by her, interested in the fierce little Datapoint who was somehow different than all the others. But recently he'd found himself drawn to her. It was just curiosity, he was certain. He'd always had an annoying amount of it. And he knew that, like any thirst, it could be quenched. But Glade Io was just so damn close-lipped. There was no getting to know her – not even for someone who'd been her friend for two years.

So, his curiosity about his friend who held him at a distance... lingered. It was a feeling he wasn't comfortable with. Just like he wasn't comfortable with the rising desire to follow her down the hall. To ask her what had happened with Jan Ernst Haven. To sit with her at dinner.

He took one step in her direction before he paused. When she'd been in the office with Jan Ernst Haven, Dahn hadn't felt any confusion about where he was supposed to be. But now, one of the two reasons he was standing in this hallway had just turned the corner and walked the other way. And now Dahn found himself staring at the gray steel door in front of him and pausing.

He pushed the feeling of hesitation down. He never paused. And he'd be damned if he started pausing now. No matter how shiny her hair was. Or what the sight of her perma-frown did to his pulse. That didn't matter. The only thing that mattered was being the best Datapoint he could be. The only thing that mattered was excelling. The only thing that mattered was being one of the seven one day. The Authority. Dahn couldn't imagine a higher honor than being one of the seven whom every other citizen looked up to, admired, and trusted. The Authority made life safe for the entire solar system. And one day he'd be a part of it. That was the only thing that mattered.

Dahn knocked on the steel door and it rang hollowly in the hallway. The same way it always did when Dahn knocked after lessons.

"Come in." Jan Ernst Haven's reedy voice was so soft that it could barely be heard through the closed door.

Dahn swung it open. "Evening, Sir Haven. I was wondering if you had a few minutes to talk about my simulation from yesterday."

Jan Ernst Haven chuckled as the young Datapoint stepped into his office. "Always so eager to improve, Dahn Enceladus."

"Yes," Dahn agreed, a warmth washing over him as, for the first time that day, he was finally being seen.

CHAPTER TWO_

"You're driving me insane," Sullia snapped, looming over where I lay on my back on the barracks floor. Her carved, beautiful face was narrowed in annoyance, and her brown hair, lined with the navy blue she'd just highlighted it with slid off her shoulders and into her eyes.

"That's unfortunate." I smirked at her.

Cast, a Datapoint two years younger than I – and the person I usually spent time with after dinner in the barracks – snickered his usual laugh and held his hand up for the ball we'd been bouncing at one another.

"If you bounce that ball one more time, I swear on Scorpio's stinger that I'll—"

I cut off Sullia as I noisily zinged the ball across the large room, letting it bounce twice before it smacked into Cast's outstretched hand. The rest of the Datapoints were scared of her, because her admissions scoring indicated that she was a true sociopath, incapable of any form of empathy. But she didn't scare me. She had no power, just like the rest of us Datapoint trainees. So the worst she could do was bitch and moan.

Shooting a completely neutral look my way, Sullia stalked across the barracks and dropped to her knees next to where Cast sat, with his messy thatch of blond hair spilling into his eyes. He froze, his eyes as big as moons as he watched her lean into him, her chest pressing into his shoulder.

I watched in half chagrin and half amusement as he fell instantly into her spider web. Her lips, half an inch from his ear, whispered something that had his eyes growing even wider. When she reached up to brush the hair out of his eyes, I sighed deeply. There went our game of catch. Without hesitation, Cast handed the bouncy ball over to Sullia.

She instantly snatched it from his hand, bounded gracefully to her feet, and shoved the ball down the refuse shoot before she sashayed back to her bunk in the far corner and plopped down with a satisfied expression on her face. She didn't spare Cast another glance as she pulled the curtain around her bed. He, on the other hand, stared at her closed bunk with a dumb, open-mouthed look on his face.

A low chuckle from behind me had me rolling onto my side.

"Poor kid never stood a chance," Dahn muttered, shaking his head as he leaned against the wall, arms crossed over his chest.

He'd changed into our more comfortable evening uniform, loose athletic pants and a baggy white t-shirt. His hair was wet and clean, and it fell around his shoulders instead of his usual style, where it would have been scrupulously pulled back.

I rolled backward and looked over at Cast, who had gone rosy red. He shrugged at me sheepishly. "I don't get it," I said to Dahn. "Why do they fall for her crap so easily?"

"It's not her crap they're falling for, Glade," Dahn replied, pushing off the wall to come sit next to me on the floor. Technically, as a graduated Datapoint, he wasn't supposed to spend time in the trainee barracks, but our after-dinner time wasn't highly monitored. He fished in his pocket and tossed something to me.

I snatched it out of the air, hissing in a breath when I realized what it was. "Hell yes," I murmured under my breath. My night had just gotten a lot more interesting.

I studied the small screen in my hand. It was about the size of my palm and had an archaic keyboard attached to the bottom. A few years ago, Dahn had fished it out of one of the refuse shoots. It was an artifact from Earth, back when the planet had been inhabitable, from when people had still lived there instead of among the cols spread across our solar system. It was some sort of gaming device, as best as we could tell. And it was positively primitive. Ever since then, Dahn and I had passed it back and forth. We programmed and reprogrammed it, coding in puzzles and traps for one another, trying to see if we could outsmart the other. So far, each of us had a perfect record, though he occasionally had to work on his puzzles for a few days longer than I did.

I fiddled around with it for a second, trying to figure out what kind of puzzle he'd left for me until the gaze of his eyes on the side of my face had me instinctually looking up.

Dahn had piercing gray eyes that seemed to reflect light. His gaze was always very noticeable. In a training program with a bunch of sociopaths, strange eye contact was a pretty normal occurrence. But recently, Dahn had been looking at me a lot more often than usual. And the way he was looking at me?

Honestly, it was the exact same way he looked at the gaming device whenever he was trying to crack whatever puzzle I'd left for him.

"What?" I asked him, raising an eyebrow. I liked using my eyebrows. They were thick and dark against my olive skin. My brown eyes, slightly tipped up like my dad's had been, were nothing to write home about. But my eyebrows were commanding. And they said more than my words ever could. Whenever I could, I wielded them.

He shrugged, looking away from me and breaking our eye contact. The second my eyes went back to the gaming device, though, I could feel his gaze back on my face.

"Seriously, Dahn." I slammed the device down and sat up on the palms of my hands, my hair slipping down my back. "What the hell are you looking at?"

He held my gaze for longer this time, his eyes narrowed as they bounced between my left and right eye. "I'm wondering what Jan Ernst Haven said to you about your simulation."

I looked away from him, glancing at Sullia's curtained bunk. We were talking too quietly for her to hear, but even if we hadn't been in a public place, I wouldn't have told Dahn what we'd talked about. Talking about it would mean I'd have to admit that I hadn't been syncing to the Authority Database. And admitting that would mean that Dahn would know exactly how disobedient I'd been. And worse, how resistant I'd been. Neither of those traits were things to be proud of. And both of them were already on the verge of getting my sisters admitted to the program. There was no way I was rocking the boat anymore tonight.

"And," Dahn continued, "I also know that there's no chance

you're ever going to tell me. Not if I asked outright, or even if I tried to manipulate it out of you, like Sullia would. Nope. I'm just looking at you and trying not to get too frustrated that everything I want to know is just inches away from me." He leaned forward and gently knocked a knuckle against my forehead. "And it's all locked up tighter than that puzzle I left for you." He cocked his head to one side, his eyes narrowed, his temper on a tight leash. "You're the one encryption I can't break, Glade."

I raised both eyebrows in tandem, and repeated something that Haven had said to me just a few hours before. "Humans aren't computers, Dahn."

"I know," he said, looking at something only he could see. "It's freaking annoying."

I grinned, the expression as brief and rare as a shooting star. "Tell me about it."

"Did you find out yet, Dahn?" Cast called too loudly as he crossed the room toward us.

As I expected, Sullia's curtain flung open the minute she heard Dahn's name. She had some sort of interest in him that I didn't trust. It wasn't romantic, which I could have understood since Dahn was very handsome. No, it was something much more centered in her own self-interest.

"Find out what?" I asked him, trying not to laugh as Cast took the long way across the room, giving Sullia quite a wide berth before he came and sat with us.

"If he's been chosen to be a mentor." Cast plopped down next to me and reached for the gaming device in my hand. He was as interested in the puzzles as I was, but I almost never let him work on them. They were a rare spot of fun for me, and besides, Dahn always designed them specifically for my brain. I slapped his hand away, but shifted so that he could watch the screen as I worked my magic.

"Oh yeah?" I asked, my eyes still on the screen. I could feel Dahn's gaze on the side of my face again. "I didn't know you were eligible so soon after graduation."

"Most people aren't," Cast said, a sort of pride in his voice. "But Dahn excelled so much in the program that there was a rumor he'd be a mentor."

"For one of us?" It seemed strange to me that they'd group such a young mentor with someone our age. Dahn was only three years older than I was. There was usually a much greater age disparity.

"As far as I know, it's just a rumor," Dahn said in a quiet voice, those gray eyes still on me.

I shrugged, my focus shifting back to the gaming device and the particularly frustrating puzzle he'd left for me. Dahn and Cast kept talking, and after a minute Sullia's voice swirled in, as well. But I ignored them. It was a skill I'd had for as long as I could remember. I had the ability to singularly focus on any task at hand, regardless of what was going on around me. It used to drive my mom crazy. She'd call me ten times for dinner while I was reading or messing around on the old desktop I'd dragged from the junkyard and hot-wired. It wasn't until she'd shake me by the shoulders that I'd even realize she was in the same room.

When I'd come to live at the Station, I'd become hugely grateful for the skill. We were living on top of one another, surrounded by each other all day long. This willful solitariness of my mind was the closest I ever got to privacy.

The rise and swell of their voices faded even more, and I let my mind wander between the puzzle in my hands and my sisters.

Daw and Treb were identical. Even my mother had trouble telling them apart sometimes. But not me. I think my unemotional eye was always better at seeing the things that made them different. Daw was a worrier, her eyes always bouncing from one person to the next, trying to figure out what was going to happen next, or why someone was laughing or why they were yelling. Treb was a hider. If things got loud or exciting, she was gone in a flash. And if for some reason she couldn't leave a room, she had this amazing ability to hide within herself. It was like the lights were out. Nobody home. She'd be deep in her own brain, doing whatever the heck she did in there.

They made a good pair. Looked out for one another. With their identical shoulder-length blonde hair and brown eyes, they even did that twin switching thing every now and then. After I'd been selected to be a Datapoint and had had to leave Io and my family behind, it had reassured me to no end that Daw and Treb still had one another.

My eyes slid around the bleak barracks, all steel bunks and thin brown sheets, and the blank cavernous spaces between our beds. If they had to come here, they'd definitely be split up. The first part of Datapoint training was reinforcing that the only thing that any Datapoint should rely on was their own intellect. The second their trainers got a whiff of them leaning on one another, they'd be sent to opposite ends of the Station for the rest of their training.

Blue light in my eyes. So tired, my heart is stuttering in my chest. I don't think I've slept in two days. The only sustenance I've had is some water they splashed over my mouth hours ago. I'm still fighting the computer surgically implanted into my brain, into my arm. I can feel the tech trying to dominate me. My brain surges up, fights back. I'm refusing to work with it. Refusing to sync. Refusing to integrate. The pain of warring with the computer makes my skull feel like it's going to split in two. I don't remember my life beyond this. I don't remember a life without pain. I need to be soothed. Anything. Before I crack and dissolve into thin air. "Papa." The word sneaks out of my lips, my voice a foreign croak to my ears. The image of him swirls into my mind. His deep frown and laughing eyes. His shocked face when I did the Mongolian jigsaw puzzle at age four. "Syb, we got ourselves a little genius!" he'd crowed at my mother, tossing me straight into the air. I can even scent the way his shirts used to smell. Cool, like shade.

"Your father cannot save you from this, Glade Io," a reedy voice speaks right into my ear and, for a second, a face eclipses the blue light above me. My eyes struggle to see. All I see is silver, a glinting gaze. "Your father was a murderous, violent man who was culled to save the rest of us. Thank the Authority that you never had to witness the despicable things he would have done to other citizens. Maybe even to you, or your mother, or your sisters."

Something cracks in my heart and I try to bring up the soothing image of my father again, but all I can see is silver.

"Let that feed you. You will save people from that very same danger. You will cull. You will have that power. But you have to save yourself first. Your mind will not crack under this pressure. You will not fight it. You will sync. You will integrate."

That had been the last morning of my integration process. I'd tried to think of my father once more after Haven had retreated. But the word 'murderous' kept getting in the way. It would be months before I could remember the good parts of my father, but always, *murderous* was there, tainting every memory.

My thoughts had shifted to my mother then, and her soft blonde hair.

"*Hide in plain sight. They can't find you if they can't see you.*" How many times had she said it to me in my childhood? A thousand?

It was with those words in my brain that I'd finally bent, some door in my mind opened. And I'd let the computer in.

Yes. They break you down to make you. And then, when you think you can't take another second of it or you'll die, they find the very last thing you are using to soothe yourself. And they take that too. Until the only thing you have to rely on is your own intellect and the computer they splice into your being.

"Can you believe how close we are to the Culling?"

Cast's voice pulled me out of my reverie. My hands paused on the keyboard of the gaming device and I looked over at him. He sounded like a kid on the night before his birthday.

"Do you remember the last one?" I asked him, curious about the note of excitement in his voice.

His eyes shifted over to me as he reluctantly shook his head. "I was only four or so, and my parents kept it pretty well under wraps. I didn't know anybody who got culled."

I brought my eyes back to the gaming device, my face flat and frowning as usual. But my ears felt hot. I knew what was coming next.

"Didn't someone in your family get culled, Glade?" Sullia asked, a sickly-sweet syrup in her tone.

"Yeah. My dad." I answered her in as bored a voice as I could manage, my fingers playing quickly over the buttons of the keyboard.

Cast froze beside me. We'd been friends for a year, since he came into the program, but I'd never mentioned that information to him.

I could feel Sullia's disappointment at my lack of reaction and I knew she was still hungry. Sullia was always hungry for the emotion of others. Maybe because she didn't have any herself. "What was it like to grow up with a murderer?"

I thought involuntarily of my dad's laughing eyes. Of him kissing my mom on one side of her neck while he snuck a slice of bread out of the basket. I thought of sitting on his lap while he showed me how to tie complicated knots in a piece of old rope.

Murderous.

It still didn't make sense to me. Murderous. My father. I felt, lying there on the floor of the barracks, my brain struggle against my integrated tech for just a second before it all synced up again.

I shrugged. "He seemed just like any normal dad, I guess. But then, the Culling shows you who people really are."

"That's why it's so important," Dahn said from beside me. I looked up in surprise. He was sitting closer to me than he had been a few minutes ago.

Sullia frowned at him. And then at me.

Dahn pulled one knee up to his chin and those gray eyes burned into the side of my face. "Because, like Glade said to me a minute ago, humans aren't computers. You can never really know what someone is capable of. But the Culling shows us."

"The Culling keeps the rest of us safe," Cast chimed in. His fingers played in one of his shoelaces.

I looked back and forth between the two of them. They hadn't said anything I hadn't heard a hundred times before from our trainers. From Haven. But hearing Dahn and Cast speak it out right now, it hit me how much both of them truly believed it. I wondered idly how many days their integrations had taken, whether or not the sync had been a struggle for them.

Sullia was studying me. I could feel it. So I dropped my eyes back to the gaming device and tried to focus my mind on something safer. The puzzle Dahn had made for me. The secret was in the way he'd coded it. I wasn't going to be able to solve it as a user. I'd have to alter the—

BAM.

The Station juddered and lurched beneath us, and I slid a full eight inches across the floor, slamming into Dahn. One of his hands came to steady me as the startled cries of Datapoints erupted up and down the hall.

"An asteroid?" Cast asked, coming up to his hands and knees, his blond hair in his eyes.

Dahn's eyes narrowed to slits. "I don't think so, that was way too—"

A blaring siren cut off the rest of his words. A flashing green bulb lit up over the doorways, swinging its light in time with the siren.

"An attack?" Sullia exclaimed. The green light sliced across her face, illuminating her strangely gleeful expression.

Dahn was on his feet a second later, dragging me with him. The gaming device slid out of my hands and ricocheted across the floor. I automatically started to chase after it, but Dahn's hand was tight on my shoulder.

"Battle posts." His words were laced with command. For the first time, I realized how much more training Dahn had had than I. Three years went a long way in a situation like this. "Now."

40

The four of us raced out of the barracks and down toward the perimeter of the Station. I raked my memories for the classes I'd taken on Station-based battle. A green light meant that we were still dealing with a perimeter attack. Whoever it was, they hadn't breached the Station yet.

Another deafening boom exploded in my ears and the hallway tilted. Cast ended up in my arms and I ended up in Dahn's. Sullia gripped a door handle and righted herself. I grabbed Cast by the scruff of his shirt and helped him stand, and then all of us were sprinting down the hall again.

I pictured my battle chair and ran faster. I was vulnerable and exposed without it. I needed to get to my post. We swung a left down the perimeter hallway that ran the length of the Station, almost there.

"Glade!"

I looked back and saw Dahn behind me. I realized, with a strange sinking in my chest, that he wasn't going with us. The trainees fought in a different, more protected part of the station. Dahn was headed off with the rest of the graduated Datapoints.

Five steps away from me, he opened his mouth as if he were going to say something. He paused, though, shifting his weight forward, towards me. But a few seconds passed, his eyes shuttered, and his weight shifted back. He said nothing else before he turned and sprinted away from us, toward his post.

Another explosion had me following suit and running toward my own post. I slipped and slid down the perimeter hallway until I hit the doorway to our battle chairs. The battle rooms were divided by bunk room, so just the three of us would be in this particular post. I could hear the other trainees slamming through the doors of all the rooms down the long hallway.

Our room was small and dark and had three chairs side by side. Just like all of the trainee posts lining the perimeter of the Station. Three small windows sat in front of the chairs, showing slices of the black sky, currently innocuous and revealing nothing about our attackers. Cast and Sullia were already sliding into their chairs.

The trainee battle stations lined the outside of the Station, located behind the thickest layer of artillery proof steel. Even though we were on the edge and closest to the action, we were actually in the safest position. The Station, shaped like a donut, was most vulnerable on its inside edge, where the Datapoints who manned the battle chairs there were in danger of hitting the Station itself as they attempted to pick attackers out of the sky.

Our battle chairs were old and rickety. I slid into mine, between Cast and Sullia, and belted myself into the brown harness that x-ed over my chest. Without pausing, I plugged my left arm into the column next to me. I felt a shivery buzz skitter across me as my integrated tech synced with the Station's battle mainframe. Now I could talk to every other Datapoint plugged in, not even having to use words. Not to mention that I could also talk directly to the Gatling gun that connected to the bottom of my chair and extended outside of the Station. Where I swiveled, so did the gun.

I felt better already.

"There!" Cast shouted, and I heard his voice both with my ears and in the interface between his computer and mine.

I swiveled to the left, just as he did, and saw just the sun-bright trail of the attacking ship's aft thrusters.

Arm. My Gatling gun armed itself. *Aim.* My inner eye and the scope on top of the gun circled into focus. *Engage.* The lasers let loose from my gun in a gorgeous arc of jet black venom. The Station vibrated with the juddering of the Gatling guns firing from every side of me. But the attacking ship was gone, having slipped around to the other side of the Station.

"Ferrymen," Sullia growled from my right.

"You saw?" Cast exclaimed, whipping around to look at her.

"I didn't have to," she bit out. "Who the hell else can move that fast?"

Sullia swiveled her chair all the way around and reached into the chest beside her for a different type of ammo. She plugged the fuel pack into the back of her gun. It was a different type of ray – less destructive, but much faster.

"Good idea," Cast muttered, and did the same. "You're not gonna change your ammo, Glade?"

I adjusted my chair to face the window again. "You guys slow them down, I'll blow them up."

Cast answered my grin before he sobered, his eyes scanning the sky. "You guys really think that those are Ferrymen?"

Ferrymen were a rebel group from the lost colony on Charon. They'd tried to separate from the Authority years ago, and hadn't been able to survive on their own. The Ferrymen were all that was left of the off-shoot group, and they had a score to settle. They pillaged and stole any supplies that they could and, in their spare time, murdered just about any citizen they came across. They hated the Authority, and did everything they could to destabilize it.

I watched in horrified fascination as the Ferrymen's skip sped through our line of sight again. It was a blur of black metal and burning trails of streamlined fire. It was faster than any skip I'd ever seen.

43

The skip dipped out of sight again and all three of us craned our heads to find it. Seconds later, it appeared from the opposite direction.

"Holy smokes!" Cast yelled. "Did it circuit the Station in that time?" He didn't bother waiting for an answer to his own question before he began letting loose with his Gatling gun again.

The Ferrymen's skip easily dodged the line of rays, rolling onto its back before speeding straight toward us. Was it going to...? No way. That was suicide. But it kept coming, not stopping.

"Prepare for collision!" I screamed the words and also sent them through my integrated tech and into the computer mainframe. The Station's battle computer, receiving the message, turned the green blinking light to a red blinking light just seconds before the Station was knocked clean off its axis.

My skull clanked onto the metal back of my battle chair, my teeth rattling in my skull. I blinked stars out of my eyes and frustratedly shook the buzzing from my ears. The three of us were askew and tilted, mine and Sullia's hair starting to float around our faces.

"They've disrupted the gravity simulator!" she shouted in annoyance as a loose pack of ammo lifted into the air.

Ignoring the new distraction with fierce precision, I simultaneously scanned the sky for sight of the skip and scanned my tech for any signs of damage.

Nothing on either count.

Until the steel underneath my feet began to squeal.

My brain barely had time to process the noise before a half circle of flame and heat sliced through the flooring of the Station. It wasn't a clean line by any means, but I could see

44

exactly what was happening. Something was cutting a chunk out of the bottom of the Station. Any guesses who?

"They didn't collide!" I screamed. "They docked!"

I smacked the release on my harness and flung myself out of my chair seconds before the dangerous circle was completed and the chair itself was sucked away. Cast grabbed my wrist, tugging me down from where I'd been floating, and I made somber eye contact with him. Both of us waited for the vacuum of space to suck the air from our lungs and collapse our blood vessels. To pummel our hearts into their very last beats.

But nothing happened. There was a dark, jagged circle cut out from the bottom of the Station, and we weren't being sucked into space. My brain was still struggling to make sense of what was going on when a light flicked on from under the dark circle. Two shiny silver hooks were tossed out of the hole and into the ship, and two people immediately followed.

They were ragged and strange looking, and I barely had time to take in anything about them other than the looks of pure hatred burning on their faces.

Sullia released her harness and pulled a hand ray from its holster on the side of her chair. She got off one good shot before the two Ferrymen pulled weapons of their own. One of them held his arm, singed from Sullia's ray. But they both managed to point their guns first at Sullia, and then at me and Cast.

I expected a laser blast. A bullet. Poison.

What I got was worse.

A strange pulsing magnetism shot out of their guns. It looked only like a disruption in the air. Like heat. But it wasn't heat. It was sound.

I wished for death as a sound wave rolled over me like water in a sea. It was too loud, too much; my brain was on the verge of bursting. My hand involuntarily reached for the motherboard on my arm. My fingers tightened around it. I'd rip it out. The sound coming from their guns was targeting our integrated tech. It was scrambling the sync between our brains and our tech. It was making me want to tear the computer straight out of my brain.

My body was tight, even floating in the air. A rictus of excruciating torture. I think I was screaming, but I couldn't be sure. I felt nothing and everything. I wouldn't have been surprised if the skin had been peeling from my body, my bones getting crushed to dust. I scrambled for the motherboard in my arm. I didn't care if it killed me. The thing was coming out of me if it was the last thing I did.

My fingernails scraped my skin as a hand closed over my mouth, and another clapped down over my eyes. Darkness fell, and then, blissfully, silence. I struggled against the black for just a second before, inexplicably, I thought of the horse, that defiant toss of its mane. And then there was only black as I tumbled into nothingness.

CHAPTER THREE_

I awoke at the bottom of a pit of water. And with about three seconds worth of oxygen left in my lungs.

My long hair tangled in my fingers as my panicked brain searched for a way out. My hands hit nothing, and my eyes were wide and saw only black. I was completely submerged and had no way of knowing which way was up. If there even *was* an up.

My body rolled in the dark as my lungs screamed. I was going to drown. I was going to drown in the dark and quiet and that was it. The end of Glade Io. Dead and drowned in the dark.

"Breathe." A voice bit its way through the darkness and I startled, my lungs convulsing in my chest as they begged for air.

"You can breathe," the voice said again.

I didn't have a choice but to try. I was going to die either way. I gave up. Breath exploded as I reflexively released out and in, taking a deep, desperate gulp.

I was greedy, lusting for air as I took huge drinks of it. The burn in my lungs subsided and my brain stopped swimming.

I realized three things all at once. One, that I wasn't in the complete darkness. There was a dim light maybe ten feet away from me. Two, that I wasn't in water, though it rather felt like it. I was floating without gravity and the air had a strange quality to it, slippery and disorienting. Three, that three people were lining a wall ahead of me, and they were staring at me.

Two of them were Cast and Sullia. On their knees with their hands tied in front of them. The third was a girl, tall, thin, and with no hair on her head. She stared at me with undisguised hatred as she held a gun toward Cast and Sullia.

"Let her down," the girl said in a surprisingly low voice. Husky.

There was a buzzing, a click, and half a second later, I was tumbling to the floor. The strange air that I'd thought was water had receded and I was subject to gravity once again.

"Get up," a voice said from behind me.

Still gasping on my knees, I looked behind me to see a boy of about Cast's age. He was stocky and wide. He had a sturdy look about him that was offset by the pale, fragile blue of his eyes. I eyed his gun as warily as I had the tall girl's, but the boy didn't have the same ringing hatred in his expression.

Allowing myself one more gasping second, I sat back on my haunches. It wasn't more than a moment before I felt cold metal at my wrists and realized I was being shackled in the same way that Cast and Sullia were.

The boy, pressing the gun into the side of my neck, dragged me up by the shackles and over to Cast and Sullia.

"Up," the tall girl said to all three of us.

We followed them out of the strange, dark room and into a blindingly bright hallway. I hissed against the light and had to wonder how long I'd been out for if my eyes were taking this long to adjust. Still disoriented, my eyes burning, I gasped in surprise when the boy's hand gripped my shoulder and shoved me sideways into a room not much bigger than a closet. I stumbled, barely getting my footing before the door slammed behind me, cutting out most of the light. Only pinpricks of stars from the tiny window at the top of the room illuminated anything.

I heard two more slams just seconds later and realized these were holding cells for the three of us.

Two sets of footsteps disappeared down the hall and a distant door slammed.

"Glade?" Cast's voice whispered in the dark from my left.

"Yeah." My voice sounded like it had been shaved to the bone. There was almost nothing left of it. Just sun-bleached feathers.

"I-I," his voice sounded years younger than he actually was. I thought involuntarily of my sisters. "I can't feel my tech. My tech is dead. It doesn't look damaged, but it's quiet."

My brow furrowed as I looked down at my own tech. My hands were shackled at the wrist, so I tipped my arms to one side to get a better view. The motherboard in my arm. It was as iridescent as ever, looking for all the world like it was working. I twisted my hands in the shackles so that I could just brush my fingers over it. But I felt no corresponding buzz in the tech on my face. I let my joined hands trace up to my cheek, something I almost never did. I gently slid my palm over the tech that was implanted there. I could feel its cool edges against my skin, but it was ominously quiet: no information, no attempt to sync. Nothing.

I closed my eyes and attempted to sync. Nothing. I huffed out a frustrated breath. Again. Nothing.

I froze, my blood turning to ice as I put the pieces together. For the first time in over two years, there was silence. There was no tug of war. There was no tech. There was only me. Only Glade Io in this skull of mine. I was both dismayed and relieved. Free and terrified. I hadn't realized how much I'd relied on the tech – the constant whisper of it guiding me, informing me – until it was silent. Just a dead synthetic thing stuck in my skin.

"It was a dampener," I said.

"What?" Cast's voice was getting more and more anxious.

"That thing they put us through," I explained. "That thing where you felt like you were drowning? Part of you kind of was. Our tech was drowning. Even if our bodies weren't. It's a kind of machine that Ferrymen use. A weapon."

"Is my tech... dead?" There was a note of grief in his voice. I wasn't sure why that disturbed me so badly.

"Not permanently. They can hardwire it again in the Station."

There was silence then, and I imagined that the other two were probing the dead zone where their tech had been, exactly the same way I was.

"Why?" Cast asked after a few quiet minutes.

"Christ!" Sullia griped in frustration. "How your intellect scores got you admitted to the Datapoint program, I'll never know. Don't be an idiot, Cast! They're disabling our main weapons. If we have our tech, we can talk to their skip, commu-

50

nicate with their guns, their computers; hell, we could even communicate with the Station."

"We're blind this way," I finished for her.

"What the hell would they want with a blind Datapoint?"

It was a good question he'd asked, and I had no idea of the answer. "I haven't spent a ton of time pondering the thought process of a Ferryman, Cast."

It was an hour before any of us spoke again. I crouched in the corner, my back against the cold wall, still unnerved by the silence within me, the silence without my tech. Honestly, I could only think of two reasons why they'd want to kidnap Datapoints. Either we were hostages that they were going to use as leverage for something they really wanted. Or we were a statement waiting to be made. The Ferrymen were always trying to stir up dissent in the colonies. I could only imagine the reaction of the colonies to a televised execution of three Datapoints.

I was glad that part of our training had included hand-to-hand combat. I thought of the two Ferrymen that had brought us to our cells. Neither of them had looked like pushovers. But I also didn't think they could take me, Cast, and Sullia if we hadn't just had our brains scrambled by the dampener.

I sighed and ran my hand over my tech one more time. When it was dead like this, it felt so foreign and intrusive. When it was on, it was integrated into my nervous system, and I could feel its response when I touched it. It was like another part of my body. But this way, in the dark of the Ferrymen's skip, it was as clunky and alien as the gaming device I'd left behind at the Station.

"He called for you," Cast's voice came out of the darkness.

"What's that?" I asked as I watched the light of the stars filter in through the thin slats of windows at the tops of our cells.

"Dahn did. Right after the skip docked onto the Station. You disengaged from the mainframe to jump out of the way of the hole they were cutting. But Dahn was yelling for you through the computer, across the Station."

My brow furrowed. "What did he say?"

"Just your name."

I couldn't think of a single thing to say to that, and so I stayed quiet for long enough for Cast to continue on. "I think the rest of them realized what was happening before we did. That they were docking and about to either take us or kill us. They must have had a better vantage point."

I might have pondered that for longer if something hadn't caught my attention. The skip we were on wasn't traveling – I knew it from the way the light patterned across the ceiling of our jail cells, looking oddly familiar. It was a rising and falling of light, like a ship on the ocean. Slowly I rose up, leaning my back against the wall. My wrists still shackled, I felt along the walls of the cell for any kind of foot or handhold. *There!* I grabbed the edge of a small shelf at about eye level. My bad leg twinged beneath my weight, but I ignored it, used to it at this point. Boosting myself up just high enough, I could just barely peek out of the thin slat of the window at the top of the cell.

"Hey," I whispered to the other two as I let myself down. "We're still in the Asteroid belt."

"What?" Cast whispered back excitedly.

Sullia said nothing.

"I just looked out the window and saw Teros," I said, naming one of the major asteroids that the Station stayed downwind of, so to speak. Teros took the brunt of most asteroid collisions and generally cleared a path for us.

"From what angle?" Sullia asked sharply.

"About 30 degrees sunwise from our normal view," I guessed. "Though it's harder to tell without the tech."

"That's travelable in a short-range skip!" Cast whispered excitedly.

Why the hell the Ferrymen were docking so close to the Station I had no heavenly clue, but either way, Cast was right. It might be our ticket out of here.

"Alright," I whispered, mostly to myself. "We gotta get the hell out of these cells."

"Are you joking, Glade?" Sullia's voice cut through the dark. "That's idiotic. You're gonna get yourself caught."

"I'm already caught," I answered dryly, one eyebrow halfway up my forehead.

———

I hated everything about not having my integrated tech. Including how much I hated it. I didn't like the realization that I'd completely relied on it. But here, in the dark, belly-crawling down one of the dimly lit Ferrymen hallways in the back half of their skip? Well, I really wished I had my tech to tell me if there were any warm bodies in the vicinity. I wanted my tech to pull up a blueprint of the skip. Without it, I didn't know where we were in the asteroid belt, or which direction we were traveling; I didn't even know what time it was for God's sakes.

Sneaking around the skip without my tech was like having

my ears stuffed with cotton and putting a patch over one eye. I felt clunky and useless without it.

And that made me angry.

I dragged myself along the floor of a silent hallway. My leg hurt, but I ignored it. There was a doorway spilling out dim light up ahead. Screw the Ferrymen who'd taken away my greatest tool. I could escape from this broken-down piece of tin with or without my integrated tech. I laid one cheek on the floor and slid myself forward. Just my forehead and one eye peeked through the door.

A storage room, it looked like. Pilot suits and helmets. In one corner was a box of what looked like replacement burners. Hopefully, that meant we were somewhere close to the landing pad. But I also didn't fool myself into thinking these idiots were anywhere close to being organized. I moved on, sliding past the door almost silently.

"Why didn't she come with us?" Cast asked from behind me. For probably the thirtieth time since we'd left Sullia behind in her cell.

His voice was just the husk of a whisper. I knew he wasn't asking me as much as he was asking himself. It didn't make sense to him at all that she would have chosen to stay in her cell.

It made perfect sense to me. All you had to do was integrate one piece of information into the equation. Sullia didn't care about the Authority. She didn't care about getting back to the Station to continue her training as a Datapoint. Sullia cared about Sullia. And the best move for her immediate safety was, admittedly, not potentially getting caught by Ferrymen as we tried to sneak out.

I understood it as well as I understood that I was currently sliding along a rusty floor, a thirteen-year-old kid at my feet, as I peeked in one doorway and then the next, searching for the landing pad of the skip.

I figured a craft this size had to have short-range skips. And yeah, sure enough, twenty minutes after we'd left our cells, here we were. My wrists ached from yanking them free of the shackles. I'd thought I'd break a finger from all the tensile strength it had taken to twist my cuffs into the shape I'd needed to pick the lock of our cell doors. But, it turns out that staring into almost certain death can make a girl freaky strong. I'd jimmied my cell door and then Cast's. Sullia was still caged up like a chicken in a coop. *Good luck.*

"Found 'em," I whispered back to Cast, whose eyes shown in the dark, his hair flopping across his forehead.

I thought of my sisters for one tight moment and I realized that I had to get Cast the hell off this craft. Ferrymen were dangerous, unpredictable, and were known throughout the cols as murderers. Of citizens and of Datapoints. Whatever they wanted from Cast, they were not gonna get it – not as far as I was concerned.

I peeked back in the doorway of the landing pad, making sure there wasn't anyone in there. A light burned in the far back corner of the cavernous garage, making the three small skips appear shadowed and dinosaur-like.

One of the skips was obviously out of commission. It rested on its side, its rear door ajar and a smattering of tools laying on the floor around it. The second was just a lander. Skips like that were used for lunar landings, or on the cols, not for going skip to skip or back and forth among vessels in space.

But the third? Bingo.

A short-range skip. It sat all the way across the landing pad, fifty feet from our door. The cockpit was tiny, but Cast and I could fit if we half sat on one another. Sullia's sullen face flashed across my mind's eye and regret lanced through me. Maybe I should have tried to talk her into it.

But no, Sullia didn't listen to anybody. Least of all me. *Well, then, maybe I should have knocked her out and dragged her away.*

I sighed, scanning the room one more time. In the opposite corner from the short-range, there was a – surprise, surprise – makeshift command station in one corner. Made up of a few ancient desktops wired into what looked like keyboards from an old station. The whole thing was dusty and lilted to one side, a pile of dirty laundry in the chair next to it. These Ferrymen were a bunch of slobs.

My eyes narrowed on the short-range skip we were aiming for. A light pulsed inside the cockpit, dimly, blue and then green. A corresponding light on the command desktop's control panel did the same.

Even from this distance, I could deduce the first three moves I'd have to make on the panel to get the skip up and running. Damn, I was good.

"Okay." I slid back down, out of the doorway, and dragged Cast's ear over toward me. I whispered so quietly it was more air than words. "We're both going in. There's no one in there, but there might be alarms. You need to get into the cockpit and get the skip kicked on. I'm going to get to the control panel and sever the connection with the skip so that even if they discover we're in there, we're still going to be independent."

Cast nodded, his eyes wide, and I hesitated for just a second.

"You passed your pilot's training level one, right?"

He nodded again. "In the simulators."

I bit back a curse. *Great. Grand.* "That's fine. Look. I'll be there to do the flying, but if I'm not—"

"Glade!" he protested, cutting me off.

I ignored him. "If I'm not, just fly it exactly like you would a simulator, okay? It's not different except it'll feel heavier when you steer. It doesn't have to be pretty; you just have to get the hell out of here. When you're close enough to the Station, their landing beam will do all the hard work for you, okay?"

He nodded, his rabbit eyes giving way to determination as thoughts of the Station crossed his mind.

Fatigue clawed at my muscles, turning my eyes scratchy. My stomach was a cavernous pit of hunger. And I really, really wanted to brush my teeth. Would I have considered this an ideal time to try and steal a short-range skip from a band of murderous Ferrymen?

Well. Now or never.

I peeked into the skip room and then back toward Cast one last time. "I'm not even gonna ask if you're ready," I told him.

He nodded, but I only saw half of it because I was already on my feet, scuttling into the room and directly toward the control panel. I could feel Cast behind me, but I couldn't hear him. The kid was silent, just like all Datapoints. It was the first thing they taught you in training. Well, besides the whole computer-surgery-surrender-to-your-tech thing.

I didn't bother watching him as I skidded up to the control panel. I heard a loud click and knew he was entering the cockpit.

Two lights started blinking on the control panel in front of me. The damn thing was so old that nothing was labeled. Lord.

They even had twist buttons. I hadn't seen those in anything but a museum. Well, looked like I was going to have to do this the old-fashioned way.

I cracked my fingers and flicked on the screen. I said a silent prayer of thanks to Dahn for every one of the puzzles we'd solved together. Compared to those, this would be like changing the settings on an alarm clock.

The screen was old, but I was surprised when it blinked on and showed a fairly new operating system. How the hell had they integrated that with this archaic board? I fiddled around with the keys in front of me for a second and then realized the trick. None of it corresponded the way it logically should; they used this board as a way of inputting commands in binary, not directly commanding the desktop.

Easy enough. I resisted the urge to crack my fingers again. No need to get cocky. But again. D.A.M.N. I was good.

I heard a few more clicks from behind me and one small grunt. I knew that Cast was getting the skip ready for takeoff, though it hadn't been powered on yet. In a second, it would hum to life.

I was going to have to do two things in the following seconds. One, I was going to have to sever the connection between the skip and the main craft. Two, I was going to have to do so with reckless precision, considering that the short-range skip was still going to have to talk to the craft long enough to open and close the lander doors to the outside.

I didn't let my mind dwell on the logistics as screens showing code, binary, and schematics streamed past my eyes. The only sounds in the rusty cave of the landing pit were the soft sounds of my fingers on the control panel and Cast scuffling around in the cockpit behind me.

I ignored everything as I pulled up blueprints of the skip. My fingers hovered over the keys that would disengage it from the main craft. All I needed was for Cast to—

FOOOM.

"Holy shit!" Cast whisper-yelled across the garage as light, heat, and sound practically exploded around us.

Both of us had been expecting the stealth mode of the short-range skips that we'd practiced in at the Station, but this baby was old school. Twin thrusters burned blue fire and the engine inside of it grumbled and purred.

I cursed and started engaging the code. I hoped to hell those landing doors were quick because we had definitely alerted somebody to our presence here.

My fingers were just brushing the final keys when something hard and vicious tangled in my hair, yanking me unexpectedly backwards.

I didn't let myself get deterred as I held on to the control panel, finishing the last key swipes required to sever the short-range skip. There! Thank God. And now I could concentrate on this – I shifted and avoided another blow – the bald giant was trying to claw my eyes out.

It was the girl from the dampening room.

I easily ducked the blow she sent my way and landed a quick jab to her ribs. I was thrilled that my dead tech wasn't hindering my ability to beat the hell out of this girl. It was frustrating enough that she'd been able to sneak up on me. If my tech had been functional, it would have warned me a hundred different ways that Baldie was on her way to try and tear my hair out. I dodged another blow from the girl and swept her feet out from under her, sending her plummeting to the ground just as I heard Cast engage the main thrusters on the skip. Good kid.

All I needed to do was get into the skip and we'd be fine. There was no way for them to stop us if we were in the skip.

I bolted toward Cast, but slipped when the bald chick grabbed the ankle of my bad leg. Pissed and frustrated, I kicked her in the face and she howled, rolling away. Problem solved. Now I just had to sprint the fifty feet across the landing pad and swing up to the cockpit.

But I wasn't more than two steps on toward the skip before another set of hands was grabbing me around the neck, slamming me to the floor.

Quickly assessing my situation, I realized that there were two more Ferrymen bearing their weight down on me, as well as the bald chick moaning on the floor, and three more coming through the door. There were too many for me to fight on my own, and even if Cast came down to help us, our chances of getting away were narrowing by the minute.

As far as I knew, they hadn't even realized Cast was in the skip at all. The kid was so small, they probably couldn't even see him over the dash. *Go, Cast. Leave!* I cursed myself as I tried to use my integrated tech to talk to his. How many times was I going to have to learn that it was off?

I was going to have to do it the old-fashioned way.

Elbowing one of the dummies above me in the gut and slamming the other's head into the ground, I jumped to my feet and screamed at the top of my lungs. "Go! Don't hesitate! Go!"

I saw Cast's eyes and knew that he'd listen. There was a moment of fear. For me, I think. But I saw the second his training took over. The fate of the Datapoints, the fate of our program, was more important than my life. One of us needed to get away and back to the Station.

My words must have made the other Ferrymen realize that there was actually a kid in the short-range skip, and they hauled ass toward Cast.

Heck no. I heard the tell-tale sound of the cockpit clicking closed. *Good kid.*

Launching myself after the three jerks trying to get to Cast, I scattered them like bowling pins. We were a kicking, rolling mess as I heard the bald chick scream out in rage. I caught a glimpse of her jamming her hands down over the control panel. She was probably just now realizing that the skip wasn't going to listen to a damn thing she had to say.

I couldn't control the feral grin that ripped across my face as I head-locked one of the struggling Ferrymen below me.

The landing door shot up from the floor of the garage, exhibiting itself as a surprisingly sleek collaboration of glass and steel. We were sealed off from Cast's skip then, and I watched in suspended glee as the second set of doors spiraled open and the black of the sky dilated into view. Cast didn't waste time as the skip took off from the pad, hovering unsteadily in the air for just a second.

I held my breath and flipped a Ferryman off of my back, relishing his grunt of pain. *Come on, Cast. Engage the thrusters. Get out of dodge.*

And just like that, the main thrusters burned from red into blue into light, electric purple. And the kid was gone. Into the asteroid field and searing toward safety.

CHAPTER FOUR_

Dahn Enceladus swallowed fiercely against the tight feeling in his throat that had been overwhelming him for hours. It was annoying. He sat alone in one of the Station's main control rooms, an echoing chamber filled with computers of all kinds. At any given moment during the day, it bustled with technicians who attended to all aspects of the Station's operations. The defense shields were controlled here, but so were the bells that marked the end of class periods. Hell, the timers on the coffee machines were controlled from here.

But that wasn't why Dahn had chosen to come here. It was for the windows. The largest windows in all of the Station; they lined up along one exterior wall. He could see one arm of the asteroid belt on the left side and the whole yawning maw of the universe on the other side.

It had been hours since the attack now – almost half a day later, and the Station had finally gone quiet. The technicians, the Datapoints, and everyone else had finally exhausted themselves.

But not Dahn. Dahn couldn't imagine sleeping right now. Not after what had happened. He shifted in the technician's chair closest to the windows. He'd been among the first to realize that the attacker's skip was docking. And he'd been the very first to understand why.

He'd known that Glade was either going to be dead or captured in less than a minute, and that there was nothing he could do about it.

Yeah. Sleep was non-existent since that realization had hit him.

Not to mention the fact that he'd screamed in Jan Ernst Haven's face not an hour after the three Datapoints had been taken.

Dahn shifted in his chair again and let his forehead fall into his hands. God. It was like a knife of electricity through his chest when he thought of it. He'd stormed into Sir Haven's quarters – without knocking – and demanded to be given a skip to follow the Ferrymen.

Haven had calmly rejected the idea and attempted to send Dahn away.

"Don't you get it?" Dahn had screamed, an inch from Sir Haven's face. "They'll murder her!"

The older man hadn't even blinked. "No, boy. It's you who doesn't understand what will happen to her. And if you think I'm going to send a single Datapoint to further enrage her captors, then you don't have the logical brain I always thought you had. Use your intellect, Dahn Enceladus! And go back to your quarters."

Dahn had never been so thoroughly dismissed from Sir Haven's presence before, and the shame of it burned through his blood like the dark brown liquor that his father used to drink.

Unable to look at the vast expanse that rolled out in front of him, Dahn swiveled in the technician's chair and faced the screen again.

The blackness on the screen was even worse.

An hour and a half after the three Datapoints had been taken, three sensors had blinked on that screen. Their tech had been alive and pulsing, tracking. And then, one by one, the sensors had gone dark.

Intellectually, Dahn knew that the sensors going black could mean any number of things. That the attacker's skip had gone through an artificial black hole and ended up out of range. That the Datapoints' tech had been dampened and immobilized.

But he couldn't stop the voice in his head from telling him it was because they were dead.

A decade ago, Dahn had sat in a different control room, staring at a different screen, and had watched a different sensor blink out of existence. His father's. He'd been eight years old when his father, also a Datapoint, had been captured and murdered by Ferrymen.

Dahn knew he couldn't blame himself completely for the emotional reaction he was currently trying to swallow down. The attack the Station had endured today was startlingly similar to the one that had ended in Dahn's father's death. And it was a known truth that even the most controlled and trained of Datapoints were often subject to the echoing emotions of their childhoods.

But even knowing this, the intensity of his reaction embarrassed him. His throat burned, his heart raced, and he'd screamed in Sir Haven's face.

God. Years of careful training. Of never doing anything wrong. Of excelling in comparison to every single one of his peers. And he was pissing it all away.

Dahn rose up from his tech's chair. He shouldn't be sulking in a technician's chair, staring out at the sky. He should be resting so that he could be at the top of his game tomorrow. Either Sir Haven would decide on a plan of attack, and Dahn would do his part, or Sir Haven would decide that the lost Datapoints were collateral damage in the war against the Ferrymen. And Dahn would have to play the long game.

He was going to become a member of the Authority. And it would be from that lofty position that he would make the Ferrymen pay. Dahn knew that then, and only then, would he be able to dismantle their skips, culling each and every one of them. Hell, he'd even bomb Charon into the next galaxy if he had to.

But there was nothing else to be done tonight.

He was already turning from his view out the windows when something caught his eye. A comet? A rogue asteroid?

No.

That was a skip. A short-range skip. And it was incoming. Dahn raced to the window and his tech tracked the skip at the same time as his eyes did. One life form aboard. Headed sixteen degrees sunwise toward the landing dock. The skip was ancient, but fast.

There was no doubt in Dahn's mind that it was a Ferryman's skip.

There was one thought in Dahn's mind as he turned and

sprinted, hopping clear over the technician's chair he'd just been sitting in. No. It wasn't a thought. It was a single word.

Glade.

––––––––

Jan wasn't disappointed, per se, when it was the boy Datapoint that tumbled out of the Ferrymen's hijacked short-range skip. But he did allow himself one gem-bright moment of frustration.

With Glade Io.

He felt that he knew the story before the boy, Cast Europa, even told it.

Jan, who'd been awoken by Dahn Enceladus' incessant banging on the door of his chambers, had practically sprinted down to the landing dock to greet the skip.

Dahn, the dear boy, had insisted on checking it out first, though. After all, the boy was a trained weapon, and Jan could admit that he'd be a sitting duck out there on the landing platform.

But it wasn't a renegade Ferryman springing out of the dumpy skip, guns blazing. And it wasn't Glade Io, returning to the Station. To, as far as Jan Ernst Haven was concerned, her destiny.

It was new trainee Cast Europa. And now, here he sat in Haven's office, covered in the blanket Dahn had tossed over his shoulders and practically vibrating with nerves and leftover adrenaline. Jan cast an eye over the young boy. He made a mental note to check Cast Europa's file the first chance he got. The boy was exhibiting high levels of excitement and emotion. He'd been admitted to the Datapoint program with flying colors, but mistakes were occasionally made. And, occasionally, it was hard to know a child's true nature until they were exposed to the rigors and realities of the program.

"She saw that we were still close enough to the Station to escape on a short-range skip. And she decided we were going to get out of there," Cast explained, pulling the blanket around him even tighter.

"Glade or Sullia?" Dahn cut in, but Jan already knew the answer.

"Glade. Sullia didn't want to get caught. She thought we'd get killed if we got caught."

Jan nodded and Cast continued.

"It took a long time for us to get out of our handcuffs, but Glade figured out how and talked me through it. And then she used the pieces of her cuffs to pick the locks on our cells. And even then, Sullia still wanted to stay."

Jan couldn't blame Sullia. The girl was extremely practical. She made decisions based on what was good for her and her alone. He didn't trust her as a Datapoint, but he was able to anticipate her next move. Which made her strangely malleable, and which in turn made her very valuable.

"We snuck through most of the skip," Cast continued. "We were both really surprised because it's big. Really big. But we didn't run into anybody. Like, there weren't very many Ferrymen aboard or something. And Glade couldn't believe how old some of the tech on the skip was. She kept exclaiming and stopping to look and stuff. She said it was like they'd patched together ten different skips from ten different eras."

Jan watched as something soft came over Dahn Enceladus'

face at the boy's words. He knew the boy had taken an interest in Glade. But that soft look was… surprising.

"We made it all the way to the landing dock before we got attacked by a Ferryman. It was the girl."

"What girl?"

"Oh, sorry. It was this tall, bald girl who put us through the dampener." Cast gripped at the tech on his arm. "She attacked Glade. I was already in the skip, getting it turned on, but Glade was disconnecting it from the control panel. She and Glade fought hand to hand. And Glade was… really something. She'd have had the girl beat if more Ferrymen hadn't shown up. By then I had the skip up and ready. I was going back for her when she told me to leave. She screamed at me to go."

Cast looked down at the dead tech on his arm and scratched at it absently. Jan knew that the boy was waiting for an indication from someone that he'd done the right thing in leaving Glade. And, in fact, according to his training, he'd done exactly the right thing. Datapoints were told over and over again that two Datapoints should never be sacrificed where just one could be. The future of the program was infinitely more important than any single Datapoint's life.

But Jan surveyed the shivering novice in front of him and he wished, unabashedly, that it had been Glade Io who had made it to the skip.

CHAPTER FIVE_

The place was a dump. No question. Every ventilation grate I'd seen was rusted and ill-fitting. Every quadrant I'd been dragged through looked as if it had been bolted together with nothing more than a welding gun.

It was fast, though.

I had to admit that much. I hadn't been even remotely prepared for the warp the skip had jumped into seconds after Cast had gotten away. It was more than light speed. More than a jump into an artificial black hole. No, this was a different kind of space travel that I'd never experienced before.

And half a breath later, we were floating idly past a grouping of stars I didn't even recognize. It didn't take a genius to realize that we weren't in the asteroid belt anymore. I'd only had time to hope that Cast had made it safely back to the Station before something very heavy landed on my head. I'm pretty sure it was the bald girl's foot.

When I'd woken up, my ankle had been chained to an

armchair, here, in the main room of the Ferrymen's skip, directly outside of the cockpit. It was definitely the most impressive room I'd been in yet. This section of the skip was obviously all part of one continuous design. It didn't have the awkward, cobbled together look of the other parts of the skip that I'd seen. The room was tall and spacious, and there was a humongous window on one side that showed a breathtaking sweep of the sky all at once. I'd never seen such a large swath of space – almost 180 degrees. Most of the windows in the Station were port windows, smaller than my head and only allowing just a bite of the sky to be seen at once.

I refrained from being impressed.

I'd been left alone for hours and I'd been dozing, my stomach grumbling and my head aching. But now I heard footsteps coming down the hallway and immediately switched my position in the chair. I tried adjusting my ankle, but these shackles against the leg of the chair were considerably more substantial than the ones I'd wiggled my hands out of earlier. I shifted uncomfortably. It just had to be my bad leg that was smashed in this uncomfortable position. Of course.

The lights flickered, the way they often did in this piece of crap skip, and when they came back on, the door slammed open.

That's when I first saw him. Caught in a flicker of light, halfway between shadow and light. He wore a pilot suit, rolled up at the elbows, tattoos showing at his wrists and one creeping up out of the collar of his jumpsuit. And, jeez. Was everybody around here bald? The expression on his face was hard to read, though. He studied me, but not in a wary way – in an almost fascinated way. Like I was a lost creature from Earth.

I thought of the horse, channeled the energy, and tossed my black mane of hair back over my shoulder.

He grabbed a folding chair from against the wall and dragged it over to the center of the room. He flipped it open and twirled it backwards, sitting in it with the practiced ease of someone who knew exactly how to get comfortable.

It wasn't until he was sitting three feet from me that I realized how young he actually was. God. He must have easily been under 20. I studied his face. It was sturdy and almost plain. A pronounced brow shadowed a nose that was just a touch too big, and there were deep lines on either side of his mouth – whether from smiling or frowning, I wasn't sure. His head was shaved and so was his jaw, but a shadow of new hair lined all of it. The only thing that was notable about this man's face were his eyes. They were the bright, startling blue of Earth's sky. I'd only seen photos, of course, but the color wasn't something you easily forgot.

As he watched me watch him, something hardened in his expression. "So, you're a Datapoint."

I raised an eyebrow and leaned further into the armchair, ignoring the wince-inducing pain of my shackled ankle. I caught sight of myself in the reflection off the great window and saw that I was sitting in the exact same position that Haven had sat in earlier that day. Chin lazily on my hand, one leg crossed over the other. I was relieved it looked as lazily disdainful on me as it had on Haven. I suddenly understood it as a power move.

"So, you're a Ferryman?"

There was unmistakable disgust in both of our voices, though his was also laced with something else. Something I couldn't quite put my finger on.

71

"You don't look like I thought you might," he said almost casually, as he tipped his head to one side and surveyed me.

"I could say the same for you." I raised an eyebrow even further. "Are you even old enough to have a pilot's license? Suddenly the Ferrymen don't seem so menacing, now that I know they're led by a child."

"Funny, because the Authority seems a hell of a lot scarier now that I know they're training children to do all of their dirty work."

My eyebrow fell flat back down and I kept my face as closed as I could.

The Ferryman's leg bounced and his fingers drummed the back of the chair, like there was a flock of birds beating at the bars inside of him. Suddenly he was up and off the chair, tracing a rough palm over his shaved head. "God," he chuffed out to no one in particular. "I knew that most Datapoints were teenagers. But to actually see it with my own eyes..."

He turned back to me and something old showed out of his young face. "How long have they been training you?"

"Two years." I wasn't sure why I answered.

He swallowed hard. "So, they spliced you with that weapon when you were, what, thirteen?"

His eyes were raking across the tech on my cheek and over my arm. I thought again of the glossy, proud horse and refused to trace a hand over my tech. I held perfectly still.

"You think of my tech as a weapon," I guessed blandly.

"Of course. You murder people with it, don't you? Even under the loosest of definitions, I'd say that qualifies as a weapon."

The girl recoiled from Kupier as if he'd slapped her, and for a second he felt a wave of guilt.

Good one, Kup.

He swallowed back the urge to apologize to her. There was no place for that kind of softness in this war. He sought for what to say next.

He wasn't perfect – he knew that better than anybody. And he was off kilter. He'd swaggered into the room expecting to come face to face with an android. He'd known that Datapoints were humans, technically. But he'd also known that their technology was integrated so deeply into their brains that they could barely function without it. He'd expected a shell of a person. He'd expected to interface – he hadn't expected to converse.

And he definitely hadn't expected this girl.

Maybe a few years younger than him, and kinda cute. Except for the frown that could have blown a crater in the moon. Oh, yeah, and the hate lasers coming out of her eyes.

Looking at her, the whole of the dang universe spreading out in the window behind her, and seeing how young she was, all of it came crashing down over him, the way it did every once in a while. The immensity of the atrocities the Authority was committing. This girl didn't deserve to be turned into a weapon. To be brainwashed. The whole thought of it horrified him. Exhausted him. And Kupier was suddenly overwhelmed with missing Charon. His home planet. The one he hadn't seen in three months.

If he'd been on Charon, maybe he'd have been eating an early supper with his mother. Maybe he'd have been on his way out to see if he could flirt with that girl Sira who used to live a few streets over. Maybe he'd have been hot-wiring ancient four wheelers and trying not to crash them.

Maybe.

But what did it matter, really? He wasn't on Charon. Shit, *Charon* was barely even on Charon anymore. Things had changed. The Authority had seen to that.

Kupier's colony, once a place where troublemakers and 'criminals' had been sent when the Authority didn't know what to do with them, had slowly evolved to be something the Authority could never have predicted.

Charon was the only completely self-sufficient colony in the solar system. It was filled with people who'd been sent away to die, and damn if they hadn't survived. Nope. In fact, Charon had thrived. Innovated. Adapted. Invented.

But those had been the good old days.

The good old days that Kupier would have done absolutely anything to get back.

Forward, Kup! Don't look back. Learn from the past, but don't go back there. Move forward. Always be moving forward. It was his older brother's voice in his head. And words in his memory were all that was left of Kupier's brother. Luce was gone. The real leader of the Ferrymen. And now Kupier was all they had left.

Kupier shifted for a second in his chair and traced one hot palm over the leg of his jumpsuit. How could someone feel too young and too old at the same damn time?

Of the million-and-five things he was teaching himself these days, though, letting go was one of them. He figured it was the first step in *moving forward*. So, he took a deep breath and concentrated on the little black-haired computer girl currently trying to set him on fire with just the look in her eyes.

She cleared her throat and sat up a little straighter in her chair. His murderer comment had obviously plucked a chord for her.

"If you think I'm so dangerous, then where are your bodyguards?" she asked.

Kupier tipped his head to one side. "I don't think you're dangerous after your tech's been dampened. Now, you'd have to kill me with your bare hands." He let his eyes sweep over her, appraising. "And in hand-to-hand combat? ... Now that you mention it, I think we could give each other a run for our money. You sure gave Aine a hard time. And she's no pushover."

Kupier was still in shock that one of the Datapoints had been able to escape. He'd inspected the jimmied cells himself and been inordinately impressed that they'd been able to pick the locks using their own handcuffs. He'd also been very, very impressed that this girl had been able to hold off four of his best men for over three minutes while her friend had gotten away.

He'd also been confused about why they hadn't tried to take the other one, the taller girl Datapoint, with them.

The black-haired girl stared him in the eye, her frown deepening even further. "Why am I here?"

Kupier rose from his chair and strode over to the huge window that sprawled out behind her. He leaned his back against it. "What's your name?"

"Why am I here?"

"Do they even let you keep your names there? Or is it just Datapoint 1, Datapoint 2, and so on."

"Why am I here?"

75

"Or maybe it's a lettering system, then? Datapoint A? Datapoint B?"

"Why. Am. I. Here."

Kupier pulled a small blue marble from his pocket and bounced it in one hand – an old habit. She was fully facing him now, and her eyes followed the path of the marble.

Unfortunately for her, it was gonna be a long time before she learned why she was there. Kupier didn't need just any Datapoint for this whole thing to work; he needed a *cooperative* Datapoint for this whole thing to work.

The girl's eyes flicked up to his. He saw the fire there. She was a far cry from cooperative at the moment. He got the impression that she would shove broken glass down his throat the first chance she got. Just his luck.

"Do you know who I am?" he asked her.

She pulled her lips into her mouth for just a second, then let them out. "You're a murderer."

He tossed the marble into his other hand and held her eyes. "Come again?"

The girl flung her hair back behind her shoulders and it caught the light. It reminded Kupier of something – he just didn't know what. She wore all black, her horrifying tech glinted in the light, and she glared at him like a sullen child. But somehow, she still looked kind of... regal. She had that I'm-in-charge thing that Luce had had. That Kupier sincerely hoped he himself had.

"You're a Ferryman, no?" she asked him, her chin tipping down.

He grinned, slow and lazy, at her words. After all these years of looking up to his brother, looking up to the stars at night, praying he could do *something* about the Authority, it still gave him a thrill to be identified as part of the Ferrymen. "That's right."

Her eyes flicked back to the marble in his hand. "Then you're a murderer."

Kupier laughed, turning his back to her for the first time. He watched the endless black of the universe rolling out before him. "Is that what they're telling you in Datapoint school, DP-1?"

He looked over his shoulder and saw that she was furrowing her brow at the nickname.

"DP-1," he explained. "Datapoint 1. Since you won't tell me what your real name is."

"Yes," she ignored him. "That's exactly what the Authority has informed us of regarding Ferrymen. They're pirates. Anarchists. Misguided rebels who want to bring the entire system crumbling down. They – you – kill any citizen who stands in the way, between Ferrymen and the Authority."

Kupier laughed again, pressing the heel of one hand against his eyes for just a second. He laughed because what the hell else could he do? It was ridiculous – insane, even. The Ferrymen murdering innocent citizens?

"Right. Yeah. That's exactly what we do." He flung his hand out toward the haphazard ship. "We run a real tight genocide operation around here. You can tell from all the weapons we have."

Her eyes flicked around the main room, where he knew she wouldn't see a weapon in sight. His own eyes stayed glued to the tech on the side of her face.

"The Authority sure has a real convenient definition of 'murderer.'" He'd said the words softly, when he'd really wanted to spit them out like razor blades.

Her hands tightened in her lap. "Culling is not murder."

"Sure isn't trial by jury, either."

"Trial by jury is a flawed system. Archaic and subject to human error."

Kupier raised both eyebrows. "Yeah, I read that textbook in school, too." That Authority-issued textbook that explained the exact reasoning why the government-sanctioned mass killings were justified. They'd studied those textbooks on Charon as evidence of why the Authority needed to be brought down.

He flicked the marble between his knuckles while he crossed the room and plopped himself back down in the folding chair across from her. "So, you're telling me that the Culling *isn't* subject to human error?"

She smirked, one eyebrow raising halfway up her forehead in a way that Kupier recognized as very practiced and very effective. "Of course, it isn't. Culling is scientific. It's an exacting practice. It's the whole reason why Datapoints have integrated tech."

She lifted her arm and Kupier felt a corresponding shiver race down his back. Even though her tech was neutralized right now, he knew exactly what she could do with it if it were activated.

"The integrated tech shows us the brainwaves of each person. That's how we know who gets culled. It's scientific," she repeated. "It's *medical*."

"So, you think that the Culling isn't subject to human error because Datapoints are trained to work with their integrated tech. And the tech is what decides who gets culled and who gets left alone?"

She nodded once, tersely. But he saw the look on her face. Suspicious, hate-filled. She knew he was leading her into a trap. He did it anyways.

"Well, tell me, DP-1. Who programs the tech?"

She said nothing.

Kupier stood and shoved the marble back into his pocket. "The tech wasn't born. It didn't spring into existence after its two tech parents decided they loved each other and wanted to make a family. This tech wasn't a gift from God. It was designed. Engineered by humans. Maybe they were scientists, sure. But they sure as hell were humans. So ask yourself if something designed by humans could *possibly* be subject to human error. And now ask yourself this." He held up two hands, a foot apart. "On the killing scale. How far apart are murder and culling?"

He clapped his hands together, just once, loud enough to echo off the steel and glass in the room.

The girl didn't jump. In fact, she looked almost bored. She still said nothing.

Kupier hoped he'd made his point, however, because his heart was racing, he didn't think he had much more of this conversation in him.

He faced her, his hands in his pockets again, his fingers finding the marble. "My name is Kupier." Her bored look intensified. "And we don't have to be enemies."

————

Kupier wasn't surprised when he left the main chamber, the

79

Datapoint scowling after him, and found Aine waiting in the hallway.

Aine's black eye had intensified in color, and he noted that she walked with a slight limp as she fell into step beside him. "We don't need her," Aine growled, tipping her shaved head back toward the room that held the black-haired girl.

DP-1.

Kupier also wasn't surprised that this was the way his tall, tough friend felt about DP-1. DP-1 had beat the crap out of Aine not more than five hours ago. This was not something that Aine was just going to take on the chin, so to speak. Aine was a warrior, a fighter, a pilot. Honestly, she was the most loyal member of the Ferrymen, and some days, Kupier didn't know what he would do without her.

On other days, like right now, he wished that her pride would give it a rest for a minute.

"And why's that?" Kupier asked her as he gripped the roll bar at the top of a hallway and swung himself down into the makeshift kitchen.

Aine followed suit, wincing at some hidden bruise.

"Because you said so yourself, Kupier; we need a cooperative Datapoint. And she's not only tried to escape, she's done battle with your crew!"

Kupier lifted an eyebrow as he tore the end off of a loaf of bread and tossed it on the countertop. He dug around in the cabinet for the jar of nutbutter they'd picked up from the last stellar port. "'Done battle' might be a little strong, Aine. I know she was fierce, but it was a barroom scuffle and you know it. She wasn't trying to kill you. She was trying to distract you long enough for her friend to get away. And it worked."

Aine clapped her mouth closed for just a second, but opened it again. At six feet, she was almost as tall as Kupier. The closest she ever got to him was when she was angry. And now she was toe to toe, almost nose to nose.

"You're insane if you think you can talk her into your point of view, Kupier. She's never going to work with us."

Kupier slowly lifted a spoonful of nutbutter in between them, popped it into his mouth, and spoke around it. "Maybe. Maybe not. But all I know is that I'm not making decisions based on hurt pride, Aine."

The words had her stepping back a full two steps. She was NOT doing that and he was an ass if he thought so. Well. Maybe she was doing that a little. But he was still an ass for pointing it out.

He wasn't an ass, though, she told herself. He was a good man. And a good leader. The thought had Aine deflating. Sometimes it killed her that he always, somehow, ended up making the right decisions, because they were almost always the opposite of what she herself would do.

"I spoke to the other one. Sullia."

Those words had Kupier narrowing his eyes, studying Aine. "When I was talking to the black-haired one?"

Aine nodded.

Kupier, still studying Aine, tore himself a piece of bread, dipping it in the nutbutter. "And?"

"And she's willing to cut a deal with us."

Kupier scoffed. "Is that right? She just came out and said it?"

"That's right," Aine snapped, her stance widening. "She told me that she had no love for the Authority. She'd do whatever we

81

wanted if it meant her getting out of here in one piece. She'll cooperate, Kupier. She's the one we want."

Something that looked sickeningly like disappointment crossed Kupier's eyes as he gently pressed half of his sandwich into Aine's hands and took the other half over to the sunken doorway of the kitchen. He reached up to pull himself out.

"If she doesn't have any loyalty to the Authority, Aine, why the hell would you think she'd have any loyalty to us?"

He gripped the bar then, and was up and out of the kitchen in a flash.

Aine's mouth opened, like she was about to call something after him. But she found herself with nothing to say. Nothing at all.

CHAPTER SIX_

W e don't have to be enemies.
          Yeah, sure. I knew what that meant. We didn't
have to be enemies as long as I did whatever he wanted me
to do.

It had been three days since they'd jacked us from the
Station. I guess they'd put two and two together, figuring that
Sullia and I weren't going to murder them while we were in
deep space. Not with no idea where we were and no idea of
how to navigate this sea monster they called a spaceship. They'd
stopped chaining me to any surface available, and they'd let
Sullia out of her cage.

Most of the Ferrymen were keeping a wide berth between
themselves and us. Except for that Aine chick who pretty much
knocked into me every chance she got.

Kupier, on the other hand, was being weirdly... nice.

At the moment, for instance, he sat across from me, this
Kupier guy, and ate a sandwich. His boots were up on one

corner of the table where we sat and his chair leaning back on two legs. He took a humongous bite of his sandwich.

"You sure you don't want any?" he asked through about three inches of bread.

Seriously? This guy was the leader of the Ferrymen? It still didn't compute to me. With his ratty cargo pants, his oversized t-shirt, and a blue stocking cap on his head, the guy looked more like a stuffed animal than a hardened gang leader. But I'd seen the way the twenty or so Ferrymen on this skip treated him. With ultimate respect. Even now, three of them, shaved heads and all, stood scattered around the kitchen, playing bodyguard. Kupier was casual, beguiling eyes and feet on the table, as if he didn't even notice them.

I raised an eyebrow at him. "We just ate."

It was true. Sullia and I had just had soup from a can that we'd heated ourselves. We didn't trust anything that the Ferrymen made for us.

Aine had confiscated the can pretty much the second I'd finished emptying the soup, of course.

"Yeah, I'm sure that bowl of warm water with two pieces of celery floating around in it really tided you over," Kupier scoffed before holding his sandwich out to me yet again. "Come on. There's tinned meat in here…"

Honestly, the salty smell made my stomach grumble, but I'd be damned if I showed him that. Ever since our first, very disconcerting meeting, my goal had been to remain completely aloof and distant since there was absolutely nothing I could do to escape while we were still traveling. Cast had escaped in the only short-range skip, and I had no idea how to fly or land a skip of this size.

When we docked, wherever we docked, my behavior would be an entirely different story. Get me on land? Then I'd have coordinates to send to the Station. I'd have a hundred places to run to and hide. Hell, I'd have access to any computer I could steal or borrow. I'd be able to communicate with the Station.

I just needed to make it to some colony. Any colony.

"I'll have a bite."

The voice over my shoulder bothered me. Even more than it usually did. Sullia leaned her body across the table toward Kupier and accepted the part of his sandwich he'd just broken off for her. The three bodyguard Ferrymen exchanged glances, though Kupier's expression didn't change. Aine appeared in the doorway and scowled at Sullia like she wanted to break her fingers off.

I knew how she felt.

"Captain, we've got a message from home for you."

Kupier was up and out of his chair, following Aine in a heartbeat. He was almost out the door of the kitchen before he paused, looked back, and shot a grin in my direction. Then he pulled himself up out of the sunken kitchen and was gone.

The other three Ferrymen disappeared after Kupier. I couldn't tell if it was because they wanted to be where he was, or if they were nervous to be so close to two Datapoints. Besides Aine and Kupier, the other Ferrymen aboard were pretty skittish. They kept their distance from us, and that was fine by me. I had no interest in making friends with these lunatics. I was happy to continue minding my business on one end of the ship.

Sullia, though? Apparently, she had other plans. I turned in her direction, seeing she still chewed at the sandwich he'd shared with her. My eyes narrowed.

"What's your problem, *DP-1*?" Sullia sneered without looking up from the bread she picked at. I could tell she hated the nickname Kupier had given me, and I wondered why she hadn't given up my real name to them. I was sure that it made sense probably because she didn't want them to trust me more than they trusted her own head, some sort of strategical decision that I couldn't work out. She wanted any leg up where she could get it, as evidenced by the sandwich ridiculousness that had just taken place. In her mind, giving up her own name had been a tactical choice. Just like withholding mine was.

"I don't have a problem, Sullia. I mean, besides the fact that we're captives here on a Ferrymen skip that's about a week of travel away from home, with no way of knowing what they want or what they'll do to us. And weirdly, that doesn't seem to be a problem for you."

Sullia narrowed her unusually pretty face in my direction. Her hair, still navy blue in places, was braided back off of her face. "Just trying to make friends."

I scoffed. "Sullia, you and I both know you don't give a shit about friends."

"Fine." She rose and tossed the rest of her sandwich in the trash. "But I do give a shit about surviving."

"What are you saying?" I asked her back.

She didn't reply before she yanked herself out of the galley and was gone.

"She's a treat."

The voice was one I recognized. It was the youngest member of the Ferrymen, the one who'd held a gun to my head after putting me through the dampener. Oh joy.

"A real fountain of cheer."

He laughed as he slid down into the kitchen. A short burst that seemed almost involuntary. He kept one eye on me as he skirted his way around the kitchen. His eyes flicked to the loaf of bread that sat on the counter directly behind me. I sighed and tossed it over to him.

"I'm not gonna skin you in the kitchen."

He laughed again, but this time it seemed forced. "I know that. I've just... never been around a Datapoint before."

"I've never been around a Ferryman before."

He shrugged like he was conceding my point.

"Even a junior one," I finished.

A frown erupted over his face as he tore off a hunk of bread. "I'm not a junior Ferryman. We're all equals. On the same level. No matter our age."

I eyed his small, stocky frame. He didn't look delicate, but he sure didn't look like he was done growing either. I pegged him at twelve, maybe thirteen years old. I thought back to where I'd been when I was thirteen.

Drowning in blue light. My integrated tech interjects itself into my thoughts. 'No,' it tells me. 'That's not the fastest way off this table. The most logical way off this table is to integrate. Sync,' it tells me. And still, I fight.

"I've got two sisters about your age." I wasn't sure why I'd said it, but he just looked so young, standing there in holey trousers and a t-shirt with the neck hole pulled to one side.

He took a bite of the bread and looked at me like he was trying to figure out what the trick was.

"What's your name?" I asked him.

He eyed me a second longer before shrugging again. "Oort."

"Oort," I repeated, completely deadpan.

He shrugged – something I was coming to recognize as a bit of a tick of his. "Oort."

"I'm gonna go ahead and guess that's a family name?"

Oort huffed, his cheeks going pink, but there was the slightest trace of humor in his eyes, as well. "At least my name is better than being just some numbers and letters the government assigned me."

I rolled my eyes. Kupier's precious little nickname for me had apparently caught on. And as I'd yet to give up my name to any of the Ferrymen, that's what they all called me.

"That's not my name, you know."

"I figured."

The skip juddered underneath us as it shifted directions, and I found myself wheeling forward as cans of goods slid to the other ends of their shelves.

"Damn it!" I shouted as we wheeled back in the other direction and I was forced to grab outward and steady Oort before he brained himself on the counter. "How the heck this God-awful skip is even airtight, I'll never know."

"It's not a skip," Oort replied, his eyes on my hand on his shoulder.

"What?"

"The Ray. She's not a skip."

"What are you talking about?"

"The Ray is a full-on ship. A real one. We don't use artificial blackholes to jump space."

"You're kidding." I looked around at the rusted patchwork of bolts and metal all around me. Real spaceships were practically a myth at this point. They were expensive and hard to maintain. Skips that utilized artificial blackholes to jump from one place to another had come into the market about twenty years before. I'd never been in a real ship before.

"Artificial blackholes are traceable," Oort said, answering my unspoken question. "We're not covert in skips. But in ships, we're untraceable. For the most part."

I stood, an unstoppable curiosity fueling me as I swung myself out of the galley.

"Where are you going?" Oort called out from behind me.

"I want to look around a little bit," I answered, pausing instinctively. "I've never been on a ship before."

Oort laughed as he followed me up and out of the kitchen. "You've been on a ship for the last four days."

"Yeah," I said over my shoulder, a grin hot and quick on my lips. "But I didn't know."

I'm not sure why, but the ship was different to me, once I knew that it wasn't a skip. That it wasn't mired in what I'd always thought was a pointless technology. Skips were designed to jump from one artificial blackhole to another, but in short-range distances, or any kind of space-based battle, they were utterly useless, slow and clumsy. In order to skip through artificial blackholes, their designs forewent a lot of the technology required for speed. Sure, they could jump great distances, but skips couldn't fly half as well as a ship could.

I took a few steps down one of the hallways, peeking into one of the control rooms that was locked manually. I knew there wasn't a chance in hell they were letting me in there. I turned halfway back to Oort. "What if I let you tie my hands behind my back – any chance you'd let me in there to look around a little bit?"

Oort's mouth dropped open.

"Is that Europa?"

I flipped around as I heard Kupier's deep voice from behind me. He was stealthy, that one.

"Where?" Oort asked, looking automatically out of the small port windows that lined one side of the hallway.

"No," Kupier laughed, stepping fully into the hallway and locking the door he'd just come through. "I meant in DP-1's accent. Is that Europa I hear?"

I frowned at him. Always with the questions with this guy. "No."

"Ah," he nodded, a small, knowing smile coming over his face. "Io, then. I always get those two accents confused. They're so similar."

I said nothing.

"DP-1 Io," he said with that same annoying smile on his face. He was fishing for my first name again.

"I don't have to guess your last name," I told him through a frown. "I know you don't have one."

His smile only grew, even though I'd just insulted him. Ferrymen went without last names of any kind. Most of them were from Charon, but plenty of them were recruited from the other colonies. They went without second names to symbolically shake off the customs of a solar system they didn't want to be lumped in with. But they also did it to remain as covert as possible. None of them wanted their families to be connected to their activities as Ferrymen. I realized, though, that this wouldn't be an insult to him. This lunatic was actually *proud* of being a Ferryman.

"You really thought Europa would be out the window, Oort? You know for a fact we're lightyears away." Kupier laughed, leaning back against the wall and eyeing the young Ferryman with amusement.

"It was knee-jerk!" Oort insisted, leaning against his own wall in exactly the same manner.

I looked back and forth between the two Ferrymen. One of them was tall and thin, lean muscles lining his arms, an amused and nearly disdainful expression on his face. The other was short and square, looking like a battleship couldn't knock him over. But there was something there. Something very familiar in both of them.

"Wait…" I began slowly. "Brothers?"

Oort looked up at me in surprise. "No one ever guesses."

I shrugged. "It's in the facial expressions."

Kupier said nothing, but his eyes didn't leave my face. I started to shift on my feet then, but I froze instead. I wasn't going to let this guy with his freaky blue eyes and annoying smile make me uncomfortable.

The human in me made me want to say something as I turned to walk away. The Datapoint in me had me turning on my heel and heading back down the hallway.

I could feel two sets of eyes on my back as I stalked down the hall.

It wasn't until I was back on my side of the ship, where the doors were actually unlocked, that I let out a breath. I closed the door to the small chamber they'd given me. Sullia's was just next door.

There was a cot, a port window no bigger than my hand, and a single blanket. This was the only place on this ship that I was safe, I reminded myself. Everything else was an illusion.

Kupier watched DP-1 head down the hall with a thoughtful expression on his face. "You making friends with the Datapoint?" he asked his brother.

"Shut up." Oort's ears went red.

"No," Kupier teased. "I get it. She's cute."

"*Shut up, Kup.*"

Kupier snickered, and had to admit that it felt good to clown around with his brother. Especially after the call he'd just gotten from their home base on Charon. Things were bleaker than ever there. Kupier thought guiltily of the sandwich that was filling up his belly. They were bringing as many supplies back to Moat, the main city on Charon, as they could, and it still wouldn't be enough. And now those supplies sat useless in the belly of the Ray. Because everything was grinding to a halt, what with these two Datapoints making everything so confusing.

He needed a willing Datapoint for this plan to work. He'd thought the abduction was the hard part. *Yeah. Right.* The hardest part was trying to figure out these two Datapoints.

DP-1 was prickly and righteous. Dangerous as hell and ready to slit his throat the first chance he gave her. But it was the other one he really didn't trust. Sullia. With that sultry smile and her constant hints that she'd take any kind of deal he had to offer. He had absolutely zero doubts that she'd stab him in the back in a second.

If he had to choose between having his throat slit and being stabbed in the back, he'd choose the blade to his throat. At least he'd know who his attacker was.

Kupier sighed, suddenly very, very tired. He dragged a hand

over his face. "Seriously, Oort. You think there's any chance she comes around on us?"

Oort lifted his eyebrows. "Would you if you were in her place?"

Kupier eyed his little brother as he walked down the hallway toward the cockpit, Oort easily falling into place beside him. "Good point."

Kupier came back to the image of her striding down the hallway just then. Proud, angry, suspicious, that slight limp in her walk. And there was something else mixed in, too. She'd held one hand over the dead tech on her arm. She often did that. He wondered if she even realized that she did it.

An idea fluttered down like a feather from the sky.

CHAPTER SEVEN_

"He wants to see you," a stiff voice said from the doorway of my bleak little chamber. I'd found a ball the day before and I was currently taking great pleasure in bouncing it on the wall between mine and Sullia's chambers, but the interruption brought me to look up, and instantly frown.

It was the bald chick, Aine. I thought she might be narrowing her eyes to match the pursing of her lips, but it was hard to tell with the black eye I'd given her. She crossed her arms over her chest and stood as still as a photograph.

"Who?" I asked from where I sat with my back against the wall, my fingers tracing over the ball in my hand.

"Who do you think?" she asked, the look on her face telling me that she thought I was the biggest idiot in the world.

For a second, I considered refusing to go, just to screw with this chick. Because we both knew she couldn't make me.

"Christ, Glade," Sullia spoke from behind Aine, her eyes

rolling so far back in her head that I couldn't even see the brown in them. "Stop being so difficult."

I glared at Sullia, bouncing the ball hard against the wall and snatching it from the air with one hand. I was very glad to see a muscle in her cheek twitch. I knew the sound must have been bugging the crap out of her for the last hour.

"Glade?" Aine asked, disdain dripping from every letter. "So you actually have a name."

I ignored that, sending a glare toward Sullia. I hadn't intentionally been keeping my name from the Ferrymen for any reason in particular. But it had made me feel like I had the upper hand in some small way. With the secret out, I felt yet another shred of power dissolve into thin air.

"Why do you act like he's the king?" I asked Aine as I rose and joined them in the hallway.

"Kupier isn't a king," she said quickly. "He's the captain of this ship and—"

"Well, you act like he's some sort of all-powerful ruler. Like he can do no wrong. Like a god or something."

"I do not." Her words were as stiff as her steps, and Sullia and I exchanged glances when the back of Aine's neck started turning pink, but we followed her just the same. "I value having a leader who is fair and smart."

"Smart?" I scoffed. I thought back to his mouth full of sandwich, that annoying grin, and him sitting backwards in a chair. Smart was not exactly the first adjective I would have chosen to describe him.

Aine stopped dead in her tracks. "You don't know anything about him."

"I know that he sent an underling to fetch the Datapoints for him."

"He didn't send me." She scowled and picked up her pace again. "I asked to come get you."

Another glance to Sullia. "And why's that?"

She was practically speed-walking through the halls now. "Because I don't trust you. And it's best if *I* spend time with you, because I'm not in danger of succumbing to one of your little games."

What the hell was this chick talking about? "Games?"

Aine's eyes traveled Sullia's body from head to toe. Ah. Okay. Well, fair point. Sullia was definitely playing some kind of a game. One I didn't quite understand either. But me? I wasn't playing a game. I was just trying to keep to myself.

Aine's hands scraped over the circles tattooed on her wrists. All of the Ferrymen had them. "Both of you are so brainwashed by the Authority that you're acting like this whole thing is a game. An inconvenience. You don't give a shit that we've worked for years to get here. To get *you* here. That we've all lost people in this struggle. That our last leader was murdered by the Authority before Kupier's eyes. That we're thanklessly fighting for every soul in the solar system, *including yours*." Her eyes were narrowed into hateful slits as her words slammed into me. "And you don't care. You see our ship and think, 'stupid Ferrymen with their cobbled together technology.' You don't even see the innovation and intelligence and determination it took to make all this! And I'm not just talking about the ship. I'm talking about the entire movement. You have no idea what each and every one of us has been through, personally and as a group. You have no idea. You just sit there with your fancy tech feeding you every comforting lie in the galaxy and wait for a way to sabotage all of it!"

I stared at Aine's back when she turned away again, absorbing her words. Glancing over at Sullia, I saw that she looked wholly bored. But I wasn't bored. I was unsettled.

"I could say the same for you, Aine." I spoke quietly on purpose. "That you're brainwashed by the Ferrymen and that you're doing everything you can to destroy a good system. A system that works."

She stopped still at that, right outside the doorway of the room where I'd first talked to Kupier. She breathed slowly through her nose and turned to look me in my eyes. "It's not brainwashing if you're given *all* the information. Asked to choose for yourself. If it's okay to leave at any point. My life is *harder* because I've chosen this side. I haven't been given any fancy technology, or three square meals a day, or privileged status throughout the solar system. I agreed to live my life in constant danger, to be an outcast. Because I believe this is right. I have no question that this is what is morally right."

I refused the urge to step back from her. She couldn't know that I'd questioned the role of Datapoints. That I'd refused my tech at first. That I'd wondered about the process and gotten zero answers from Haven. That our roles as Datapoints were shrouded in secrecy. I thought of her view of the life of a Datapoint. *Blue light in my eyes. My brain fighting to keep out the intrusion. Haven's voice in my ear. Sync. Sync. Sync.* She thought that becoming a Datapoint was easy. Luxurious. The path of least resistance. "You think we're weak."

Her eyes searched mine. "I think you were chosen to be Datapoints for a reason."

Aine swung through the door and into the room with the huge glass window. I didn't look at Sullia. I knew what I would see. Her bored expression morphing into an attractive, affable expression. I didn't want to see that right now.

————

Kupier watched DP-1 step into the room, her eyes wild and her hair that glossy black. He wasn't sure why she always drew his eye so quickly – well, scratch that. He knew exactly why. She was cute. Not in a cuddly way. No, no, no. But in a looks-like-she-smells-good kind of way.

He frowned at himself. He shouldn't be thinking this crap in a moment like this. So much rested on his shoulders, and he couldn't afford to get lost in la la land. Kupier forced himself to look away from DP-1, but he didn't like what he saw. He saw Aine looking like she'd swallowed astral dust and, more disturbingly, Sullia giving him quite a sultry eye.

Kupier sighed. He knew that sending Aine to get the Datapoints had been a bad idea, but he'd done it anyway because he was learning to delegate. When he'd first become leader of the Ferrymen, he'd wanted to do everything himself. That attitude hadn't lasted more than a month before he'd realized he'd have a heart attack before he hit twenty-five if he continued on such a path. There were lots of ways to show competence. Doing everything on his own wasn't one of them.

"Everything alright?" Kupier whispered to Aine as she came to stand beside him. The Datapoints didn't come any further than the doorway. The rest of the twenty Ferrymen stood in a circle around the edges of the round room, as they'd never show

98

their backs to the enemy. Kupier knew that he and Oort were the only ones who'd softened toward the Datapoints at all. None of his Ferrymen had even shared their names with Sullia or DP-1. In fact, they were mostly avoiding the Datapoints, scared of being noticed, observed, singled out. His Ferrymen stood tall here, though. By his side. None of them flinched or shifted. Kupier was proud of them.

Aine scoffed at his question. "Just peachy."

"Anything I should know?"

Aine opened her mouth to say something nasty, if the expression on her face was any indication, but at the last second she changed tack. "Her name is Glade."

Kupier's eyebrows shot up to his hairline as he turned the name over in his head, like a stone in his hand. His eyes found their way back to the black haired Datapoint. Glade. It suited her, he decided. There was something fluid and natural about it. But also, it rhymed with blade. And that *really* suited her. The thought made him smile to himself as he watched her frown and stare broken glass directly into the face of anyone foolish enough to look at her.

He wondered how Aine had figured it out, knowing that DP-1 would never have given it up herself. Kupier slicked a hand over his buzzed head and tried the name out.

"Glade." He wasn't sure if he was just getting used to the sound of it or trying to get her to look at him. She didn't look, though, and Kupier wasn't particularly surprised.

"Well?" Oort offered from next to him. "We might as well get this over with."

Oort was not excited about what was about to happen. None of the Ferrymen were. It hadn't been a long conversation he'd had with them, but it had been pretty eventful. He couldn't remember a time when his comrades had objected so strongly to an idea of his. But he'd been proud of them. They'd spoken their thoughts, showed a little emotion, and then stood behind him when they saw he'd thought it through.

It didn't mean they had to like it, though. And Kupier could respect that. He wanted to make this process as painless as possible.

"I'm not one for ceremonies," he called out, and the group quieted. Though, several Ferrymen chuckled at his words. They were probably remembering the day he'd become the leader of their group. He'd taken his brother's dagger in his hand, raised it up in one hand, and said, *I'm not my brother. But I'm gonna get good at this. Let's get started.*

Yeah, ceremonies were definitely not his thing.

"So, let's make this as brief as possible."

Kupier took a step forward, a step toward the two Data-points. As he did, he planted one boot on a huge tin chest that sat before him. He launched the chest forward, into the middle of the circle of people, and as it screeched to a stop, the top flung open.

"We stole you from your world. It's not a world we respect. But that doesn't mean we don't respect you."

Kupier spoke the words, and he meant them, but he could feel the tight, unbridled strain of each of his loyal Ferrymen. He was speaking for them, and they were not in agreement. But they understood why he was doing this. And he could also feel the skepticism practically dripping off of DP-1. Glade.

He could understand that, too.

"So," he continued on. "As a show of peace. And, hopefully,

of friendship..." Kupier offered as he looked right at Glade. Without pausing, he strode up to the open tin chest and pulled the dagger from the holster at his hip. His brother's dagger. The same dagger he hadn't gone a waking second without wearing. And he tossed it into the chest with a monumental clank. Next came the two small knives in his boots and the brass knuckles he kept in one pocket. Last were the three sleeper darts he kept in his breast pocket at all times.

He didn't look at the Datapoints as he strolled back to his place in the circle, palming his blue marble in one hand. He looked at his Ferrymen. And they looked grim.

Oort was the next to step to the chest. His two throwing knives and the mace he wore at his belt went directly into the chest. One by one, each Ferryman stepped to the chest. Some of them threw guns, some threw poisons, and all threw knives.

Kupier stood across the circle and felt a swelling of pride at the loyalty of his people. His eyes settled on Glade and Sullia. Sullia looked pleased and awed, friendly. Kupier didn't trust her for a second. Glade looked skeptical still, but less than before. Her eyes followed the movements of each Ferryman who stepped up to the chest. Kupier imagined she was memorizing the placement of where each weapon had been held on each person. In case she ever had to fight them, she'd know where all their tools were kept.

And then there was just one more. Aine.

She stood stiffly next to Kupier, both his and Glade's eyes on her. Kupier didn't reprimand her. He didn't prompt her. He wouldn't do that to her. He wouldn't embarrass her like that. But he could feel her internal struggle. She wanted so badly to defy him. And yet, she wouldn't. They both knew it.

Seconds passed, and then a full minute, and still, Kupier waited patiently.

He was rewarded with the quick, stiff steps that Aine took toward the chest, her hands already tearing the twin daggers from their holsters at her wrists. She looked at no one as she rid herself of each weapon with deadly efficiency. She kicked the chest shut when she was done, and stalked back to Kupier's side.

"It's done," Kupier said, his deep voice falling heavily in the room. "We're holding you here, yes. But while you're with us, we won't keep you vulnerable. We won't threaten you with weapons or violence by holding weapons which you don't your-selves have."

Sullia looked quickly back at Glade, as if trying to verify that she'd just heard what she thought she had. And when she looked back at Kupier, it was with a different expression on her face than he'd ever seen from the pretty Datapoint. It was calcu-lating. Kupier had just changed the game on her and now she was reassessing her strategy. The sight of it sent a chill down his back.

Glade, on the other hand, didn't look away from Aine.

Kupier moved through the crowd of Ferrymen, speaking quietly to them. Thanking them; dismissing them. By the time he made it to the two Datapoints, the room was mostly cleared.

"Quite a show," Glade said, her eyebrows high and dark on her forehead.

"It wasn't for show," Kupier said, his voice low and honest. "But it was to send you a message."

"That you won't be violent toward us?" she asked, her voice laced with disbelief.

"You don't buy it?" Kupier asked, turning the marble in his hand, and her eyes fell to it.

"Of course not," she scoffed. "That little display showed nothing more than that your people are loyal to you."

"So I guess the question, then, is whether or not you think I will order them to be violent toward you." He paused. "Glade."

Her eyes seemed to stab into his own, and Kupier was momentarily rocked with the emotion he felt coming off of her. It wasn't hatred, but it was just as hot. She was vulnerable right now, he realized. And pissed off about it.

"Don't ask questions you don't want to hear the answer to," she said, nearly biting off the words before they could make it all the way out of her mouth.

"I don't think you *know* the answer, DP-1."

She didn't look away from him, but he saw the snap of surprise on her face at the fact that he'd reverted back to her nickname. And perhaps the moment she'd registered just a hint of affection in his tone.

"It's fine if you don't trust me," he continued. "It's fine if you don't trust us. But tonight, you're going to sleep on a ship where no one is armed."

She took a step back from him, her eyes sweeping to his feet and all the way back up to his face.

"Why don't you sleep on it, Datapoint? And tell me how you feel in the morning."

CHAPTER EIGHT_

"Glade!"

Someone was whispering my name and, for a moment, my dream mixed with my reality. It was my sisters calling my name. But they were young again. Sweet and blonde and four years old. And then it was Dahn, the way he'd been when I'd first met him. Younger and so serious, whispering my name in admonishment when I was doing something he didn't approve of.

But then I came just a touch more awake, and without even opening my eyes, I knew none of that was my current reality. I wasn't on Io with my sisters in the bunk next to me. I wasn't on the Station, a new trainee with a new friend. I was on the Ray. A hijacked prisoner on a Ferryman's ship. In a cold room with a tiny window and a bed jammed in its corner.

"Glade."

And someone was whispering my name in the dead of the night.

"Don't you know better than to wake a Datapoint from sleep?" I couldn't help but whisper back.

There was a weighted pause that gave me a clue as to who was doing the whispering. There was so much young wonder in that pause.

"Why?" the whisperer asked fearfully, his voice slipping into my room from the cracked door. In my sleepy state, it was almost like his voice rode in on that small triangle of light that splashed across my floor from the hallway.

"Because," I grumbled, tossing my feet over the edge of the bunk and grabbing my clothes from the ground, given that I only slept in my underthings. "When we first wake up, we're thirsty for blood."

Another weighted pause, and then a whispered, "Really?"

I couldn't help but let out a sharp bark of a laugh as I yanked on my shirt and then my pants. "No, Oort."

"Oh." His voice had brightened considerably with that one syllable.

"Why are you waking me in the dead of night?"

His shadow shifted in the slightly cracked doorway. "I wanted to show you something."

I considered turning him down, just because I could. But a deep voice flashed through my head. *But tonight, you're going to sleep on a ship where no one is armed.* Kupier had insisted it would make a difference. And as I followed Oort out of my room and down the hall, I wondered if it had.

Oort tossed me a bottle of water and gestured to the bathroom down the hall. "We don't have much time, but I can wait."

"Gee, what a gentleman," I muttered as I passed him. I came

back out with water dripping down my face and the back of my neck, my mouth rinsed out.

As I approached, I studied Oort. Short and stocky, he looked almost more grown up than his tall, lanky brother did. But there was something so young about Oort. He was practically vibrating with expectation and excitement as I approached him.

As soon as I was close enough, he started speed-walking down the hall. A few moments later, he pulled up short in front of the room with the great window. Then he turned and faced me with a look of chagrin on his face. "You probably don't want to watch it with the rest of the Ferrymen, do you."

"Watch what?"

"Never mind." He shook his head once, fiercely, and doubled back. "There's one other room you could watch it from."

I followed him back and through a small door I'd noticed before but never been allowed through. It led to the second level. I'd seen Ferrymen coming down from there, but I wasn't sure what it held.

"Our living quarters," Oort answered, like he'd guessed my unspoken question from my expression.

The doors to each chamber were slender and short. Both Oort and I could stand straight in the hallway, but Kupier or Aine would have had to slouch down in the short second floor. Oort led us through a door and into one of the rooms. It had an unmade bed, a familiar blue cap hanging on a hook, and a little cabinet with a few sets of clothes folded at the bottom. There was a sink with a cracked mirror that had a toothbrush in a cup soldered to the edge. Next to the bed was a crate of old, yellowed books. Wow. I hadn't seen that many books in one place outside of a museum. They must have been ancient. Passed down from a relative?

"Here," Oort said to me, his voice no longer in a whisper. The room we were in had two port windows, the same size as in my room, and Oort nudged me over to one of them.

I slouched over and peered out. The sun was a distant, glowing orb, looking almost icy through all that black of space. From this distance, it wasn't much bigger than any star in the sky. Maybe four times as big. But it sure was bright. I'd heard that, when you're close enough to it, the sun is actually warm. But I'd never actually experienced that. It sounded nice.

"You brought me all the way up here just to see the sun?"

"Just watch!"

"You're not supposed to look directly at the sun. You brought me all the way up here to blind me?"

"We're 19 astronomical units from the sun, Glade. I think your poor little eyes are gonna be fine. Unless Datapoints have weak eyes or something."

I couldn't tell if he was teasing me or genuinely asking, so I didn't respond.

"What is it I'm looking for?"

"Just wait."

So I did. Nearly ten whole minutes. The ship was moving steadily in one direction and then the next. We were toggling through the air first backwards and forwards, then up and down. "Who the hell is piloting this thing?"

"Kupier."

"Your captain can't drive worth sh—" I broke off immediately when I realized what was happening.

He wasn't driving terribly on purpose. He was fishing for a

certain angle. The *perfect* angle. And as I watched, the ship shifted, and a distant Saturn with its crown of rings came into view. From our angle, it was on a perfect plane with the sun. It was about the size of an orange as it crossed my port window. One side was lit up by the sun's rays, all pale yellow and orange, with just a hint of green in places. The unlit side was so dark it melted in with the black space around it. I'd never seen Saturn this close before – only as a distant pinprick in the sky from Io.

And never like this. Usually, Saturn was pictured wearing her rings like a skirt, around the middle. But the planet was tipped, the way it occasionally was during its cycle around the sun. The rings of Saturn, from our angle, were in a perfect circle around the edges of the planet, making it seem like Saturn had many haloes.

Still, the ship moved and shifted. I'd thought the shifts the ship was making were small, but I realized soon, from the speed with which Saturn's position shifted in our view, that the Ray must be moving at an incredible rate. Damn near lightspeed.

Saturn shifted an inch. Then two. Then three. And there… The edge of Saturn's halo kissed the edge of the sun from our view. And oh, what a view. The sun set the halo on fire, turning Saturn's rings into a golden, burning half-smile. And still our ship kept moving. The planet crept in front of the sun, taking bigger and bigger bites out of the most powerful thing in our solar system.

I held my breath, gripped the steely edge of the port mirror so hard my knuckles turned white. It was gonna… it was gonna…

Bingo.

"Oh my God," I muttered as the ship shifted Saturn into a perfect eclipse over the sun. We were plunged into blackness except for the thin ring of light that surrounded the planet, that absolutely set Saturn's rings on fire. Saturn wore a burning crown, a shade of gold I'd never seen before and would never see again. It was perfect. Gloriously gorgeous.

"Oh my God," I whispered again, and a tear traced its way down my cheek as I watched the sight. I brushed the tear off myself brusquely, unwilling to look away from the sight before me, but I pressed that tear between my thumb and finger in amazement. When was the last time I'd cried? When I'd left for Datapoint training? When Daw and Treb had gripped the pockets of my pants with their grubby hands and begged me not to leave?

I squeezed the tear once more and hoped my sisters could feel my love for them. How I would do anything for them. I'd long ago lost track of Jupiter's orbit around the sun.

The ship shifted then, seeming to resume its normal course, and Saturn dipped upwards in the window, out of our view. The sun was just the sun again.

I took a deep breath and realized that I'd basically been frozen for the last half hour. The incredible sight had held me captive completely.

"Wow," was all I could manage as Oort and I turned toward one another.

"Yeah," he agreed. "That was definitely the best one I've ever seen."

"You've seen other eclipses?"

"Yeah," he said, shrugging. "They're like a gift from Kupier. When we've done something particularly hard or grueling, or if we lose someone, he tries to find something like that that he can give us."

My brain blanked, unable to comprehend what Oort was saying to me. "A gift."

He nodded.

"From your leader."

Oort nodded again.

"Because…"

Now Oort looked at me like I was stupid. "Because he's a good person. Who wants us to know he appreciates what we do."

My mouth dropped open, either in shock or because the eclipse had short wired my brain.

"Why are you in my bedroom with a Datapoint?"

Oort and I whirled around at Kupier's voice in the doorway. He leaned there, his plain face quirked into that smile of his, one of his shoulders against the door jamb. It hit me all at once just how tall he actually was. He had to slouch considerably to stand in that short doorway, but it didn't look awkward. It looked easy. And comfortable. He always looked comfortable, I realized.

My eyes skated over that face of his, his overlarge nose and the hair that had grown in even more since I'd first met him. And a feeling I'd never felt before took me by surprise.

My stomach tightened. Just once. Like a fist had reached inside me and given it a squeeze. I didn't like the feeling, but just like that it was gone. It left me with a heart that beat just a little too fast and palms that were just a touch too warm.

"I wanted her to see it," Oort replied, a bit of defiance in his voice.

Kupier ducked his head. "Alright." His eyes shot to mine. "What did you think?"

I cleared my throat and flattened myself back against the wall as he stepped into the room. It was really small with the three of us. "It was pretty."

Was that my voice? Sounding all... girly? Couldn't be.

Kupier nodded and sat down on his messy bed; the springs squeaked and I watched in detached interest as he toed off one of his boots and then the next. "Yeah. We were lucky that Saturn was in Taurus."

I furrowed my brow. What the hell did that mean?

He looked up at my befuddled expression and chuckled to himself.

"That Saturn was tipped like that," he clarified.

I just continued to stare at him with my brow drawn down. Because he'd gone out of his way, literally, to give his crew the gift of an eclipse. Because he'd asked them to give up their weapons. To show me and Sullia that they meant us no physical harm.

My eyes can see nothing but the burning blue light. I can't move my hands or feet anymore. It's been days. I know it. My stomach is beyond hunger. The integrated tech is a constant, screaming whisper in my brain. It tells me what to do. I say no. It tells me what to do. I say no. It tells me what to do. I say no, but... I don't slam the door on the tech. I let it in just a little bit. Instead of letting it take me over, I let it twist with me. With my brain patterns. Suddenly, the tech stops hurting me. It doesn't feel good. But it's not hurting me. I'm syncing. I'm syncing.

I expect the light to shut off. I expect to be told I'm good for what

I've done. I've finally synced. But the light stays on for eight more hours. No one comes for me.

This gift from a captain to his underlings made no sense to me at all. What a waste. He'd wasted fuel and time and energy. All for what?

The fiery gorgeousness of what I'd just witnessed burned through me, though. I thought of the tear that was just now drying on my finger. I studied Kupier's plain face as he said something to Oort that I didn't listen to. What an idiot. What an... unusual man. His eyes shot over to mine just once. With that perfect, glowing blue that made his face anything but ordinary.

It was official. I didn't understand him at all. I'd been living with Datapoints for so long, in a way, that I was spoiled. I always knew what they were going to do. Their actions were logical. Once you figured out a Datapoint's main goal, you knew exactly what to expect from them. Sullia looked out for number one. Dahn wanted to be the best, to excel. But Kupier? I had no idea what to expect from Kupier.

"Well, I'm glad you liked it." His voice was gruff and tired. I wondered if he'd slept at all yet.

Toeing out of his socks, he reached back and pulled his shirt off in one smooth motion and draped it over the iron post of one bed. My stomach did that tightening thing again. I didn't like it at all. He had a tattoo on his chest that was dark and blurry as my eyes skated across it. I desperately wanted to see what it was, but for some reason, my eyes wouldn't let me focus.

I found myself looking at the ceiling as Kupier stuffed his socks into his boots. "Alright, kids," he said, stretching out on his squeaky cot. "You're welcome to stay, but I've gotta get some shut-eye."

And just like that, with the blanket half over his torso and one arm tossed casually over his head, his eyes fluttered closed.

I inched toward the door and Oort followed me. I swear Kupier's breaths were already even by the time Oort shut the door behind us.

"He would really sleep with us in the room?" I asked.

Oort snorted. "Oh yeah. He can sleep anywhere, anytime." He snapped his fingers. "Once he fell asleep at the dinner table, spaghetti on his fork still. My older brother tore up a napkin into little pieces and stuffed them one by one into Kup's nose."

The memory lit Oort with joy for just a second, but it faded into sadness. A sadness I recognized. It was pain that came from remembering someone you loved. Someone who was gone, but when your love for them still burned.

It was such a strange pain. When your heart kept growing love for someone, but had nowhere to put it.

———

For the next ten days, I avoided Kupier. I didn't like the strange feeling in my stomach he'd given me. And I didn't like being in such close proximity with someone I couldn't predict in the least.

But even though I was trying to avoid him, it also seemed I couldn't go anywhere without accidentally running into him. In the small galley kitchen, he was suddenly there behind me, his rough palms on my shoulders, moving me to the side so he could grab the peanut butter. In the main room, where I'd come for a moment of quiet, there he was, scribbling notes in a note-book. In the hallway outside of my quarters, he was rushing past, whispering directives to a Ferryman and flashing a quick grin at me as he went by.

The ship was small, sure. But it seemed that if I left my room, there he was. It was annoying. And confusing.

Other things that were confusing? The towel and soap I'd found sitting on my bed one night. I didn't have to take miserable cold showers with nothing to wash or dry myself anymore. The next day it was a toothbrush that I found, and a tiny tin of powdered toothpaste. And the next day it was a few sets of clean, oversized clothes.

Sullia appeared at breakfast one morning with clean hair and a new shirt on. So I knew they'd done the same for her. And it confused me even further. On one hand, I understood. They were buttering us up to do what they wanted. On the other hand, it seemed desperately important to me that I understand if these were actual signs of friendship or not. My logical Data-point brain couldn't make sense of the information I'd received. I hated it.

It was a week and a half after the eclipse when the sounds of fighting attracted me to the main room with the big window. I leaned in the doorway of the room, unnoticed, as Kupier and a Ferryman whose name I didn't know engaged in hand-to-hand combat.

The wiry Ferryman moved fast and erratically while Kupier moved with smooth surety, blocking and parrying each blow. They must have been at it for a bit because the wiry Ferryman was wheezing, out of breath, and Kupier's t-shirt stuck to his sweaty back. I noticed for the first time that he wasn't quite as thin as I'd thought. He was just so tall that it looked that way.

Kupier ducked a kick, rolled, and popped up, jabbing the other man in a clean rib shot. The man growled with frustration and tried again.

I watched for a few minutes more. It was good to see training like this. I hadn't realized how much I'd missed the daily rhythm and schedule of the Station. Back there, I would have spent time sparring or coaching every single day. I wanted to stay and watch for longer. Actually, I wanted to stay and coach, but then I remembered that I had no business coaching two Ferrymen on their fighting skills. They could stay subpar for all I cared. The more subpar the better, actually.

I was just stepping back into the hallway when the wiry Ferryman spoke. "Damn it, Kupier! You're too fast. I can barely remember the moves you taught me when you're already striking from the other side!"

"Wait a second." I stepped back into the room. Apparently, I couldn't hold my tongue a second longer. "You're trying to remember moves *while* you're fighting?"

The wiry Ferryman looked up at me, distrust and surprise on his face.

Kupier looked up, too, from where he was crouched on the ground, although he didn't look surprised to see me in the least. No. He looked… pleased. "Glade Io, this is Roost. He's one of our reserve pilots. And a communications man. He could get a message clear across the galaxy if you needed him to. Roost, this is DP-1."

I didn't miss the teasing smile on Kupier's face. Just as I didn't miss the brief glow of pride on Roost's face as his captain had complimented him. Still so strange to me. To see a leader do things like that.

I nodded briefly at the introduction and took a step further into the room.

"You don't concentrate on moves when you're fighting?" the wiry man asked me. One of his hands nervously traced the Ferryman's tattoos at his wrists. Three concentric rings. They all had them.

I narrowed my eyes, thinking of a way to explain it. "No. Of course not. Kupier, what's in your mind when you fight?"

He tilted his head to one side. "I don't know. Nothing." He laughed at himself. "Well, not *nothing*. That sounds dumb. But nothing in particular, I guess. Scents, sounds, stuff like that. But things just kind of go in and out. Like a wave in a lake."

"Sure. That's how my friend Dahn fights, too. And that could work for you." I tossed my head toward this Roost guy.

"I don't think so." He scraped his hand over his tattoos. "I've never been very good at that kind of thing. That Zen thing."

"Yeah. Me neither. So do what I do then." I took another step toward them. "Picture *one* thing instead of nothing."

"Like what?"

I shrugged. "Whatever you want. But something with a... spirit. Something that does what it's naturally supposed to do. Something that understands its instinctual side."

Roost stared at me blankly. "Like what?" he repeated blankly.

My eyebrows went up forcefully and irritation laced my tone. "I don't know. Whatever you want. An animal of some kind. Something you've seen or heard of that inspires you. Or a

116

force of nature. A sandstorm. A blackhole. The sun. Ever been to Io? There's some killer volcanoes—"

"What do you picture?" Kupier asked me. He was still in a crouch, balancing on the balls of his feet like the energy of sparring had him by the throat.

I hesitated. It seemed personal somehow. "A certain animal. That used to live on Earth."

"Which one?"

I paused, but then went ahead. "Have you ever seen a video of a horse?"

"That's it!" Kupier snapped his fingers and pointed at me, delight sharpening his features, making his blue eyes even bluer. "That's what you remind me of when you do that hair-tossy thing. A horse tossing its mane."

I pursed my lips, refusing to smile. "That's what Dahn says, too."

Kupier's eyes narrowed, just for a second, before they resumed that squinty playfulness. "Wanna fight?"

I was already striding across the floor as if I'd anticipated his question. I yanked off the oversized sweatshirt I'd worn so I was just in a t-shirt and my black cargoes from the Station. "Hell yeah."

————

If the eclipse had been a gift for his crew, then publicly sparring with Glade was like Christmas, Hanukah, and a lifetime of birthdays all rolled into one. And Kupier knew it. That's why he was doing it.

Well. That and the fact that he wanted to see if he could beat

117

a Datapoint in hand-to-hand combat. And the fact that he pretty much liked doing anything that included Glade.

He struck that last part from his thoughts.

Kupier eyed her as he jumped from side to side, swinging his arms to loosen them up. She, on the other hand, was doing nothing to prepare besides watching him. She wasn't even stretching. He couldn't wait to wipe that smug look off her face. Kupier ignored the crowd of Ferrymen that started piling up at the doorway. "Nothing that'll leave a scar or take more than two weeks to heal."

Those were his standard rules with his Ferrymen when he sparred with them.

But she scoffed. "Whatever you say. I didn't think you were so concerned with looks, pretty boy."

He laughed outright at that one. He'd never been called pretty a day in his life. He liked this trash talking side of her. The bright excitement in her eyes. For days, she'd been prowling around the Ray, on edge for some reason. She'd been like a panther in a cage. *No,* he corrected himself, *like a wild horse behind a fence.*

She'd been spoiling for some exercise, and this was the big moment for it.

He clapped his hands together. "I'm confused. You want to talk about fighting or actually fight?"

She tossed her hair back and it caught the light. She said nothing and barely moved, but Kupier's experienced eye saw the way her body realigned. The way she readied herself for battle.

The two of them circled one another. Kupier couldn't stop the grin from spreading over his face. Glade, on the other hand, glared at him like she could tear his throat out with her eyes.

He recognized patience when he saw it. He knew how much of a tool it was in combat. Too bad he'd never had any.

Kupier sprang across the five-foot distance between them. He held one hand up as if to strike and sneakily hooked his opposite leg behind her knee, sending her tumbling forward.

She took the fall into a graceful tumble, basically front-flipping through the air as she took him down with her. Kupier laughed in pain as she slammed her shoulder into his then, pinning a pressure point and making him see spots.

She was fast. And smart. And trained. But Kupier was bigger. He firmly gripped Glade around the waist and tossed her off of him. She landed on her feet and wasted no time in charging him.

Kupier laughed again as he barrel rolled across the floor to avoid the booted foot that attempted to stomp into his stomach, but not before he grabbed her ankle and took her tumbling with him. He got an elbow to the jaw and a knee right into the side of his thigh. He gasped for breath. And still came up laughing.

They sprang apart from one another, both of them regaining their footing. He flashed those white teeth of his in her direction and he could have sworn she growled. He was surprised and weirdly pleased when she charged him again, her fists raised in a fighter's stance. He had just enough time to notice, again, the hitch in her step. He wondered what had happened to her leg.

He ducked her first swing, but found that she'd anticipated the move, sending him pinwheeling back with a jab to the mouth.

Kupier tasted blood as he spun backwards and used the

simple physics of his height and weight to overpower her into a headlock. She screamed in frustration. That was the only warning he got before she twisted right out of his grasp and somehow ended up on his back, panting into his ear and gripping his neck in a way that made his reality swim.

"That's right," she muttered as he staggered them across the concrete floor, his arms making half-circles.

He could have sworn she chuckled when he fell to his knees, most of his vision black. But that chuckle dissolved when he shocked the hell out of her by flopping onto his back. Full stop, full weight. He grinned again when he clearly heard an 'oof' in his ear.

He knew he probably should have scrambled away from her the first chance he got, but when her hands fell away from him, he found that it was actually kind of nice, lying on top of a warm, wriggling Glade.

He cackled in surprised pain when she jammed one finger in his ear and one in his eye. Kupier contracted like a snail and rolled right off of her. Only to have her stand over him, one booted foot at his neck.

He didn't think twice before he used one of his long arms and grabbed her by the belt, sending her into a tumbling pile on top of him. So, she was faster, more ruthless, had better technique, and was determined to win. Kupier figured he only had one more tactic that might get him out of this scuffle as the winner. He gripped Glade tight around the ribs and smashed her to him, knee to knee, hip to hip, in an inextricable bear hug.

He laughed again as she struggled against him, the rage apparent in her voice.

"Stop. Laughing," she growled, each word punctuated with

a vicious punch to his ribs. It was just enough to have his arms loosen, and she pushed up and away from him, one hand closing over his throat.

A voice rang out and cut through the sound of their harsh breathing. "Kupier!" Both Kupier and Glade's heads snapped to the side.

It was Aine who had spoken from the doorway of the room. She was out of breath, as if she'd been running, and she frowned at the way Glade was crouched over Kupier, the Datapoint's hand on Kupier's throat.

But Aine's eyes only sought Kupier's. "We're here."

Kupier nodded and sat up. He was vaguely surprised when Glade immediately released him, sitting back on her haunches. Their faces were just a foot apart as they both panted, facing each other. Kupier's elbows rested on his pulled-up knees.

"Where are we?" Glade asked. And it was almost like it was the very first time they'd ever *actually* spoken to one another. This wasn't a test. This wasn't her desperately trying to size him up or grab whatever information she could. She wasn't looking for a way to get her way or win. She was just asking him. Genuinely asking a question. And, more than that, she was expecting a genuine answer. She trusted him to tell her the truth, without subterfuge, or scorn, or rebuke. And that, Kupier knew, was a huge step in the right direction.

He rose up and extended a hand to her, hauling her up from the ground.

"Charon," he answered, holding those dark brown eyes of hers with his own blue ones. "Home."

CHAPTER NINE_

I don't know what I was expecting Charon to be like. But this wasn't it. It was a wasteland. Everyone knew that Charon was a colony that had barely survived. Since its exile from the solar system all those years ago, it had just barely limped along. But looking down at it from the ship, I saw how bleak it really was. They hadn't survived; they'd nearly destroyed themselves. There were no signs of life on the surface. There were only burn marks and pitted craters indicating warfare.

Sullia and I had watched it coming closer and closer in the small port windows of our bedrooms. With its red splotches and gray, pockmarked surface, it looked supremely desolate.

"Where's the colony?" Sullia had called to me from her room.

"Must be underground," I'd called back.

It wasn't the only one of our solar system's cols that were underground, but it was the first one I'd ever been to. Io's colony was above ground. Heated by the volcanic activity all around us, we lived inside of a giant dome of synthetic gases that protected us. The same as the Enceladus colony and the Europa colony. The Moon colony was mostly underground, with just a few outposts on the surface.

"Christ," Sullia griped. Underground colonies were not highly thought of. With their being characterized by dark and dirt, the only people who ever saw them were usually the people who were born there.

Now, three hours after I'd been told we were arriving on Charon, we landed. Docked well underneath the great mountain on the surface, Sullia and I were side by side as we stepped off the Ray and into Moat, the main city of Charon.

Well, actually we stepped onto a dingy, dark landing pad. But it was located within the city limits.

I had no idea what to expect. No one had told me what we were doing here, what was expected of me, or how long we'd be here.

"Don't look so worried, DP-1," a familiar voice said in my ear as he brushed past me on the landing pad. "We've got oxygen on Charon."

I scowled at Kupier as he bounded toward a group of people waiting on the far side of the cavernous room.

"Kup!" A little girl's voice shouted, and then I spotted her. Dark haired and slight, she practically flew across the room and into his arms. Kupier immediately tossed her into the air before squeezing her tight.

He said something low that had her laughing in delight.

A minute later, a tall, thin woman came over and reached for him. She had dark hair, too, down her back, and they embraced with the little girl held between them.

"Mom! Misha!" Oort hollered practically in my ear moments before he raced across the landing pad to join his family.

A strange tug inside of my chest had me practically wincing. I had no idea how my sisters would greet me if they saw me now. Would they shout my name and sprint toward me? Would they be shy? Or worse, would they be scared?

"Glade! Sullia!" Kupier called across the landing pad, motioning us over.

Aine pushed past me, making me stumble forward as she sent one scathing look over her shoulder at me before she headed off in another direction, alone. I watched as the Ferrymen we'd been riding with over the last weeks dispersed, calling things to one another. Some of them greeted family; others didn't.

A group of men in gray clothing were opening up the belly of the ship, hauling out goods I hadn't even realized we were carrying.

Sullia tugged on me. "Come on," she muttered.

But by the time we'd made it over to Kupier's family, she had a bright smile pasted to her face.

"Glade, Sullia, this is my mother, Owa, and my little sister, Misha." The two of them nodded at us, Misha looking intrigued and Owa looking suspicious. "You'll be staying with us."

He must have cleared it with his family, because none of them looked surprised at this latest bit of news. I, however, felt like I'd been hit with a sock full of volcanic rocks. He was bringing us to his home? What the heck was that about? My head hurt as I tried to analyze this new piece of information. What kind of game was he playing?

Sullia was already smiling that sickly-sweet smile of hers and demurely clasping her hands in front of her chest. In comparison, I must have looked like he'd just told us we were going to be attempting to colonize the sun.

Kupier caught my eye and leaned around Sullia to clap my mouth closed with one hand. He winked and shrugged at the same time. *Just go with it*, he was saying. I shrugged back, still completely off kilter.

Two hours later, I still hadn't regained my balance. Even as I sat quietly on a small mattress that Kupier's mom had made up for me. Sullia was reclined on the one next to mine. I was extremely confused about a few different things. I still couldn't believe that Kupier was letting Datapoints stay with his family, first of all.

But the other and almost more confusing point was all that we'd seen on the way to Kupier's home. The underground city of Moat *wasn't* decrepit and barely hanging on to life, the way I'd always heard. It was teeming with activity. Yes, it was as dark and dingy as all underground colonies were, but there were people laughing and chatting on every corner. Children raced around on small wheeled crafts. There were house cats flirting in the windows of the crammed-in housing. And more than that, the people looked pretty well fed. Maybe not as well fed as we were on the Station, but this was not a city on the brink of desolation. I didn't understand. It didn't jibe with anything that we'd been told about the lost colony of Charon.

"I can't believe they're making us sleep in the pantry," Sullia griped from where she lay beside me.

I looked around us. It wasn't exactly the pantry. But it was definitely a small room located off of the kitchen. There were packed dirt floors, just like everywhere else in the house, but our mattresses rested on a colorful woven rug.

I shrugged. "Who cares? The blankets are warm."

I traced one hand over the heavy green blanket that sat on my bed. It was lumpy and irregular, looking like it had been washed a thousand times. A mom had made this bed. Kupier's mom with her pretty, tired eyes and slender hands had come in here and made this bed. For me. The thought stunned me for some reason.

I couldn't remember the last time a mom had done anything for me.

And there it was. A memory of my mother. I was maybe eight years old. It was three years after the Culling. We'd been on our own for that long. I'd come in from playing outside and I was dirty – my hands and my pants, both. My mother was making dinner in the kitchen and I started to wash up without her having to ask. My mother had come up behind me and kissed the top of my head. She braided my hair back, the way she often did, while I finished getting the black volcanic ash out from under my fingernails. When I was done washing up, I liked the feel of her playing with my hair so much that I started in on the small pile of dishes that sat in the sink. I washed each one and set them aside to dry.

"You help me so much, Gladey," my mother had whispered then, squeezing my shoulders. "What would I do without you?"

I'd shrugged, already practical – even at eight years old. "I'm not going to leave you, Mama. You won't have to find out what you'd do without me."

I'd turned and looked at her over my shoulder, and she'd looked so much older than I'd ever seen her look. She looked exactly like that one photo of her mother that she kept in a drawer in her bedroom.

"You're so strong," she'd whispered to me. "So strong it scares me."

I'd never understood what she meant by that until after we'd gotten back my results for the Datapoint testing. She'd known, even after all of her warnings, that I wasn't going to be able to blend in forever. I was destined to be a Datapoint. And there was nothing she could do to hide it.

"You alright?"

I jumped a little and turned to face Kupier in the stooped doorway. Tracing a hand through my hair, I nodded. It had felt strange to think about my mother, as I almost never let myself do it. But I was alright. I nodded again.

"Okay," he said slowly, like he didn't believe me. His bright blue eyes bounced between my brown ones for a moment. And then he reached into the room, gripping the doorway with one hand and grabbing for my hand with the other. "Come on out here a second."

He hauled me right off the mattress so fast that an involuntary breath of happy noise puffed out of me.

"You too, Sullia." But I noticed that he didn't reach for her.

I wondered for half a second if Kupier could see through Sullia the same way that I could. I wasn't sure why, but I hoped he could.

We followed Kupier out of our room and through the kitchen where we'd heard someone clanking around a while ago. Some unfamiliar but savory scent curled through the air and my stomach growled in response.

He ducked through another low doorway and I followed

him. The whole house was low to the ground and dim, the way any underground colony's homes would be. But somehow, it was still homey. It was scrupulously clean, despite the packed dirt floors, and there were bursts of color in every room.

The room we stepped into was a dining room of sorts with a low metal table that was maybe a foot off the ground. His family sat around the table, directly on a colorful rug. I couldn't help but inhale hard at the scents wafting off the dishes that sat before us.

"Join us," Owa said from where she sat at the head of the table. Her voice was friendly, though her eyes were still a touch distrustful as they batted back and forth between Sullia and I. I didn't blame her.

We were eating with Kupier's family. In his childhood home. I still couldn't believe it.

We don't have to be enemies.

Sullia was already folding herself down next to Oort, that same silky smile pasted on her face. I only sat once I felt rough palms at my shoulders. Kupier practically forced me to take a seat at the table, and when I looked back he was shaking his head at me, a playful smile at his lips.

He strode around and sat across from me, his mother on one side and Misha on the other.

"So," Owa said from my left. "Kupier tells me you're from Io?"

She served food onto my plate. I forced myself to look up at her kind face. For some reason, looking at her was like looking into a bright light. With her dark hair and dark eyes, she didn't look a thing like my mother. But this wasn't the Station. It wasn't the Ray. This was a home. The first home I'd been in since my own. And it made words stick in my throat.

I nodded instead of speaking.

"And you're from…" Owa prompted Sullia.

Sullia's eyes narrowed for just a second, with that suspicion that ran so naturally through her veins. "Enceladus."

"I've been there," Owa said quietly. "It's lovely. Especially the view of Saturn."

"We saw a Saturnian eclipse, Mana," Oort said, his mouth full of food. I knew that *Mana* was a term for mother that was often used in the outer cols, so at least that was as I might have expected. "Saturn was in Taurus!"

I knew that Oort was young, but right then, with his eyes bright and his mouth full of food, I wondered how Owa had ever let him board the Ray.

"Is that right?" Owa smiled, her eyes darting straight to Kupier.

Kupier merely grunted; he was bent over his plate, cramming a bite into his already full mouth.

"I'd never seen anything like it." The words were out of my mouth before I could think twice. Every head at the table turned to look at me, and instead of saying anything else, I jammed my first bite of food into my mouth. I couldn't stop my eyes from widening as the flavors uncurled over my tongue. "Oh my God."

I clapped a hand over my mouth as I savored the bite. Good Lord. It was literally the best thing I'd ever tasted. I hadn't expected much when I'd seen the brown stew and the equally brown bread. But the flavor was complicated and warm and… Kupier was grinning at me.

129

"Nobody can resist Mana's cooking." That smile of his lit his blue eyes. I swallowed hard as I watched him whisper something to his mother. She smiled back at him, small but true. And as I studied her sophisticated face, I saw Kupier there. The line of her nose, the height of her cheekbones. Kupier looked like his mother. The realization surprised me, because he was so plain and she was so... but the thought trailed off as I studied him, too.

Because, sitting there in the dim but colorful light of his childhood home? He suddenly didn't look plain to me at all. His hair had grown out since I'd first seen him. He wore a soft blue shirt with a hood bunched at the back. Something that had been washed a hundred times, just like my blanket in the other room. He looked comfortable, but Kupier always looked comfortable. This was somehow different. The lines at the sides of his mouth were deep while he tore a piece of bread for his sister, like he was holding in a smile.

My stomach did that thing again. That clenching, tugging thing. I instantly dropped my gaze away from him. I felt the tickle of someone's eyes on me and, when I looked up, it was to see Owa studying me. She didn't drop her eyes immediately, and I was confused by the look on her face. Knowing and surprised all at once. I wondered, briefly, what she saw when she looked at me.

———

When Kupier crept across the kitchen in the dead of night, he was fully prepared to get punched in the face for waking a sleeping Datapoint. He just hoped Glade would do it quietly. He didn't want to wake Sullia.

After three days at home, he was positive now that he didn't trust Sullia. He didn't trust that smile of hers. The one that said she was happy to be here. He didn't trust her when she spoke and he didn't trust her when she was silent. If he hadn't seen firsthand just how well Glade could handle herself in a fight, he wouldn't have wanted the two of them to sleep in one room. Not that there was any room to spare in his mother's tiny house. He and Oort were already sleeping on the floor in Misha's tiny bedroom.

Kupier sighed. He had to remind himself that Misha and Mana didn't need more room than they had. It was just the two of them most of the time.

Kupier pushed his thoughts away as he came to stand in the doorway of the Datapoints' room. He frowned. He didn't like thinking of them this way. As the Datapoints. It lumped Glade in with Sullia, and to Kupier, they couldn't have been more different.

Kupier held still for a minute and let his eyes adjust to the darkness of their room. Sullia slept on her back, her face resting but not relaxed. She looked like she could open her eyes and be perfectly awake at any given second.

Glade, on the other hand, was curled on her side like a toddler. She was just a lump under her blanket, only that river of shiny hair visible. Kupier wasn't sure why that made him want to laugh out loud, but he swallowed it down and quietly leaned forward, nudging her foot with his.

He'd expected to slowly rouse her from sleep, but the second they touched, she whipped back the covers, her eyes clear and scanning the room. If it hadn't been for the way she blinked, fast and then faster, he would have thought she hadn't been sleeping at all.

She caught sight of him in the doorway and he instantly held a finger over his mouth and looked pointedly at Sullia.

Glade sat up, the covers falling away and her hair tumbling everywhere. Kupier looked at her because it felt good to look at her. She was all soft from sleep, her dark hair and eyes inky in the shadowy room. She reached for a sweatshirt on the floor next to her and tugged it on as she followed him out into the kitchen.

"What?" she asked him, rubbing the heel of her hand into one eye.

"I want you to come somewhere with me."

She froze and looked back at the room. "But you don't want Sullia to come."

Kupier raised an eyebrow halfway up his forehead. "Do *you* want Sullia to come?"

To his utter delight, Glade burst out laughing. It was muffled by the hand that she'd clapped over her mouth, but it bubbled right out of her. It was the first time he'd made her laugh, and in that second, he resolved that it definitely wasn't going to be the last.

He tossed his head in the direction of the front door and led Glade through the house. He stepped out into the narrow, dim alleyway in front of his house immediately, but paused when he saw that Glade hadn't followed him. She stood in the doorway, shadows throwing a pattern over that serious face of hers.

"Come on." He gestured for her to follow him.

"You want me to follow you out there. Alone."

He narrowed his eyes. "You won't be alone. You'll be with me."

"Right." She didn't move at all.

Kupier let out a rough breath as he took a quick step forward. He wasn't frustrated. He was sad. She didn't flinch away from him, but she did stiffen when his hands landed on her shoulders.

"In case my actions haven't made this clear, I'm just gonna come out and say it." His eyes searched hers and she held perfectly still, looking up at him. "I'm never going to hurt you." He squeezed her shoulders and his fingers slid just a little bit down her arms. "And I'm never going to let someone else hurt you, either."

She frowned at him. He frowned right back.

"What?" she asked dryly. "You want a hug or something?"

Kupier let out a huffing laugh. "I'd try, but I don't feel like getting chopped in the throat right now."

He could have sworn that her frown softened at the corners of her mouth, but other than that, she said nothing.

Kupier dropped his hands and stepped back from her. If she didn't trust him, she didn't trust him. He wasn't going to punish her for it.

"Alright," she sighed, tipping her head to one side. "Where are we going, then?"

He tried to fight back his grin, and didn't wholly succeed.

CHAPTER TEN_

I would never get used to living in an underground colony. Every windy corner we turned, I kept looking up, expecting to see the sky. And all I ever saw was a packed dirt roof. Sometimes it was a good fifty feet up and sometimes the ceiling was low enough that Kupier stooped as he led me through the back alleys of Moat.

There was the scent of rich soil, not unpleasant, and after a while I realized that it was getting stronger.

"Are we going down?" I asked.

He nodded. "The city has a bunch of levels. We're on the fourth one right now, mostly residential. We'll cut through the fifth level and head to the sixth."

Sure enough, a few minutes later, after we'd skirted past more darkened, sleeping windows, it became clear that we were descending even further. The ground under my feet slanted and the walls of the alley had started sweating.

"Is there water under the surface here?"

"Yeah. An underwater ocean. We have cryovolcanism here. It's like your volcanoes on Io, except they're ice instead of lava."

"Hmmm." Being someone who'd grown up on a highly volcanic planet, that didn't sound like a volcano at all to me.

We got to the bottom of the dirt ramp and Kupier paused, his ear cocked like he was listening for something.

He took a few steps and I followed, though I noticed that he was shielding me from view, pressing me closer to the wall than he had before.

I started to hear more noises, the farther down we wound. Voices in the distance, metal clinking. I smelled soot and smoke, and heard a shout of laughter. "Is this the fifth level?"

He nodded.

"What happens here?"

"Ah. Manufacturing. Sort of?"

I raised my eyebrow, about to ask him exactly what 'sort of manufacturing' could possibly be when a group of men came into view in front of us.

They were mostly shadowed, lit only by the orangey glow of the service lights lining the exterior wall. I saw tools slung over their shoulders, and a few of them were laughing and jostling one another.

Kupier grabbed my elbow and pushed my back against the wall, tossing the hood of my sweatshirt over my hair. I stiffened, pushing back at him, but one of his elbows went onto the wall over my head as he leaned into me.

"Be still," he hissed, dropping his head down to my ear.

I realized then that he was hiding me, his back to the men. Apparently, he wasn't wanting to draw attention to us.

I held perfectly still, my eyes glued to his chest as he leaned over me. The men passed by, and if they noticed the couple wrapped up in shadow, none of them said anything. The second they were past us, Kupier grabbed my hand and tugged me along.

"I take it we're not supposed to be here?" I asked.

He smirked at me. "It's better if I don't get caught bringing a Datapoint down to the sixth level. I happen to like my head attached to my shoulders."

"You could get executed for this? What the hell is the sixth level?"

He tugged me into a jog as we made our way along the exterior wall of the alley. He veered down a small entrance on our right and we took the darkened stairs two by two. I guessed we were skipping the rest of the fifth floor entirely.

"What exactly do you know about people from Charon, Glade?" he asked instead of answering my question.

"Ah," I wracked my brain. "That they're rebels. And that they – you – were making dangerous weapons and had to be separated from the rest of the cols. Cut off, I guess, is a better way of putting it. And that's how the Ferrymen came to be. A terrorist organization that started when the Authority cut you off."

Kupier laughed humorlessly. "Wow. Once again, what a convenient bit of information for the Authority to have given you."

"Well," I snapped. "What do *you* say happened, then?"

Kupier looked back at me for a second, pausing, with shadows like crow feathers over his face. His eyes were somehow still light, even in the suffocating underground dark of Moat. When he started walking again, this time his warm palm was pressing against mine, his fingers closing around my hand.

I opened my mouth to say something about it, but he spoke first. And when I tugged at my hand, he just firmly held on.

"We weren't cut off. We separated."

I raised a skeptical eyebrow. No colony would ever willingly separate. Each col had its own specialty, something that it made or produced that the rest of the solar system needed. And likewise, each colony needed something from all the other cols. To separate would be to live without essentials. It would be to cut yourself off from products and supplies that were necessary for survival.

Kupier read my facial expression. "It's true. Charon separated because we became self-sufficient. We didn't need the other cols and we certainly didn't need the Authority, stealing our tech and trying to impose a brutal rule of law."

"You became self-sufficient," I repeated blankly.

Kupier nodded. "About 30 years ago. You see, Charon is made of all the outlaws, or it was originally, at least. A long time ago, before the Culling even began, the Authority used to send 'troublemakers' out here to live on this col."

"Why the air quotes?"

"Because who they called troublemakers were really just free thinkers. Innovators. Inventors. Artists. All people with ideas that scared the Authority."

I frowned. "The Authority isn't scared of innovators or inventors. They're always on the lookout for new tech that we can use. They foster people with good ideas and good minds."

Kupier shook his head. "No. They foster people with good ideas and good minds who are also willing to do what they're told. The Authority has no use for people who aren't… malleable. Thus, the exile to Charon."

I could see from the look on Kupier's face that he not only believed what he was saying, he knew it. But honestly, this didn't make sense to me at all. The Authority wanted people who listened, of course, but they weren't in the business of exiling brilliant minds. I had never heard anything like that before.

"That was about a generation ago. Most of our grandparents were from the original exiling. The good part about it is that almost all of the children who have been born here on Charon have been incredibly brilliant. Free thinkers."

I could see where he was going with this. "You're telling me that, in just two generations, people on Charon invented ways to be completely self-sufficient, on their own in the solar system?"

He nodded, his eyes solemn. I tilted my head to one side and the tech on my cheek must have caught the light because his eyes fell there instantly. His hand flexed in mine.

"That's what I'm telling you."

"So why would the Authority tell us that you'd been cut out?"

"Because they didn't want other cols to get any ideas." He shrugged. "Because being self-sufficient means that we don't need the Authority. And the big secret is that the Authority needs the cols more than the cols need the Authority."

I blinked my eyes for a second before tipping my head back and groaning. "Good Lord. You sound exactly the way I thought a Ferryman would. All this conspiracy and revolution crap." When we'd been cautioned about Ferrymen, we'd always been warned about the kinds of things they believed. The kinds of things they would try to get *us* to believe.

Kupier nodded, though there was a flare of something in his eyes. "Of course I sound like a Ferryman. I am one. And proud of it. I'm proud to see things clearly."

I scoffed.

"You want to know the truth?" he asked me.

I shrugged. This would be the truth according to Kupier.

Instead of speaking, though, he tugged me down the ramp even further. The level that he led me through next was definitely different than the residential area. Where the fourth level had been, there'd been hut after hut, one sandwiched in after the next. There'd been narrow alleyways, some of them only big enough for a child to sneak through. There'd been people leaning out of their windows to talk to one another, laundry hanging on lines between houses. The residential quarter had been filled with noise, bustling with people.

The sixth level was deserted. And as my eyes adjusted, I realized that it wasn't made up of many rooms or huts jammed together. No. It was a humongous cavern. Natural, from the looks of the irregular and vaulted ceiling, the geodes sparkling in the walls. The sixth level stretched on, as far as the eye could see. I knew without asking that it spanned the entire city.

"What is this place?" My voice was hushed, and still I felt I could hear it echo.

"This is the real Moat." Again, with that humorless laugh. "This is where we came when the bombs dropped."

"Bombs?"

We scuttled through the sixth level, and I was immensely relieved when he didn't cut across the middle of the huge cavern, but rather continued around the exterior wall. I was still craning my head, trying to see all the way to the glittering stalactites on the ceiling, when he tugged me sideways and through a door I never would have seen on my own.

Kupier flipped on a small service light to our left and I blinked my eyes in pain even though the light was dim. But even when my eyes had begun to adjust, I kept blinking. Because what I saw didn't make sense in the least.

It was the last thing I'd ever expected to see juxtaposed against the great, geological cavern. This small room with dirt-packed floors was filled to the brim with... computers.

"An archive?" I asked him. It was the only place I'd ever seen so many computers in one place. The most interesting part was that all of them were from different eras. They were of all shapes and sizes, denoting different generations of use. Most of them, I'd only ever seen in photos. My tongue went dry at the exact same second that my fingers started to itch. What I wouldn't give to mess around on some of these. I hadn't been allowed to touch a single piece of tech the entire time I'd been with the Ferrymen, and I was parched for it. There hadn't been a longer stretch in my waking life that I'd gone without solving some computer puzzle. Without coding or fixing something in the Station. Even at home on Io, there'd always been some old desktop to screw around on.

Kupier nodded. "A complete historical archive of our solar system."

I took a step into the room and froze at his next words.

"It's the other half of the reason that the Authority bombed Charon."

"What?" She only turned her chin, keeping her back to Kupier.

"Twenty years ago." His voice was so quiet and clear that it almost, almost, sounded like his older brother's. The real leader of the Ferrymen. The man who really should have been the one here and explaining all this to Glade. But he wasn't. Luce was just one more thing that the Authority had taken from Charon. From its people. From Kupier. "We weren't always an underground colony. We had a great city above ground. Didn't you see the wreckage when you flew in? That sure isn't naturally occurring. After we separated from the solar system, proclaimed our sovereignty, they knew that they couldn't have word getting out that separation was possible. So, they announced that they'd cut us off for being rebels. And then they bombed the hell out of us. They wanted it to seem like no colony could possibly survive without them. They wanted us to be a broken shell of a colony. That anyone who survived, which they deemed unlikely, would suffer until they eventually met their death."

He was sure that she wasn't believing him. He could see it in the stiff set of her shoulders, the stubborn rise of her chin. So, he stepped around her, shifting her to one side with his palms on her shoulders. He strode to one of the computers, powering it on and navigating to the files he wanted to show her.

Images.

First there were shots of the radar that had sensed the bombs coming. Had tracked them. Then there were the Charon-wide alerts to all citizens to evacuate their housing and make their way toward level six. There were photos then, of the bombs as they entered the atmosphere.

His eyes on the side of Glade's stubborn expression, he clicked on a video. Dark, glittery images of the cavern right outside their door. In the video, it was packed with people. Thousands of people. Families were huddled together, babies crying, blankets over shoulders. And then the entire thing shook with a tremendous, eardrum-shattering bang. Everyone screamed, stalactites falling from the ceiling of the cavern. The camera fell and the video went black.

He knew it was brutal, but he clicked into another video, and this one showed the same thing from a different angle. And then there was another. Her frown deepened, but her face showed no sympathy for the people in the video. She merely watched.

And then he showed her the pictures. First there were the before pictures of Moat. Parts of it had been above ground. The atmosphere had been modified by great machines. People had walked freely. Seen the stars at almost all hours of the day. Made wishes on Pluto. Squinted one eye at the sky and pinched the sun between two fingers.

And then, after the bomb. The landscape was a wasteland. There weren't even remnants of the structures that had existed. The atmosphere was forever altered. The people of Charon were condemned to the underground.

Kupier watched Glade so carefully that he could see the images reflected in the glitter of her eyes. She barely blinked.

But when she did blink, she shook her head at the same time, as if she could shake this new information right back out of her mind.

"You really think they bombed you because you tried for sovereignty? Because you have a room filled with old desktops?

Kupier. This is insane. This is propaganda that someone has fed you."

He laughed then, a hearty one, because the irony was too real. "No, Glade! You're the one who's been fed the propaganda. Don't you understand what you're looking at here?" He swept his hand over the entire room, thirty feet by thirty feet, filled with computers. "This bunker is filled with actual historical records! Compiled by hackers and computer geniuses so good that the Authority quarantined them on Charon!"

Glade shook her head. "Yeah. Kupier, I just really don't believe you."

It was then that he knew he was going to have to go in for the kill shot. He really didn't want to do it. If there had been any other way to convince her of the truth, he would have gone for it. But he could see the skepticism on her face. And worse? He was starting to sense her loyalty to the Authority. It had been hypothetical before. But now, faced with this incendiary information, she was doing exactly what he'd feared she would. She was siding with what she'd always thought she'd known.

"I'm not saying this is some alternative history book, Glade. This isn't a room that's filled with opinions and perspectives on moments of history in our solar system. This is a room filled with *evidence*."

"Evidence of what?" she asked, throwing her hands up in the air in frustration.

"Just sit." Hands on her shoulders, he guided her to a chair.

He flicked on one of the bigger monitors next, and navigated his way toward the program he wanted to run for her. She clucked at his clumsy attempts through the network. Computers weren't really his thing.

When he turned back to face her, she had her arms crossed over her chest and her hair spilled to one side. "A forty-five minute video? You're really going to make me sit through the entire thing? You know, this would really be a lot simpler if you'd just let me plug in my tech."

She gave him a toothy smile that she'd never showed him before and Kupier stared at her for a second, his heart strangely noisy in his chest. And then he shook his head. "Yeah, right. I'd rather we kept your tech off for the time being. I kind of like having a functioning brain, thank you very much."

Her frown returned instantly. "Are you saying that, if my tech could read you, I'd cull you?"

He nodded, halfway shrugging, like, *Whaddaya gonna do?*

She frowned further. That smile she'd just shot his way might have jumped his heart a little bit. But he had to admit, there was definitely something about that frown.

"Are you saying that you're murderous and violent?" she asked slowly.

Her knuckles whitened where they clasped together and it was that that kept him from making a joke.

"No, I'm not either of those things. And I'm saying that you would still cull me." He sighed and scraped a hand over the top of his head. His hair was getting too long. He dragged his hand over his chin. His beard was, too. He sighed again. "Just watch."

With a few keystrokes, Kupier activated the program. He considered going to the back of the room, where he wouldn't have to watch this entire, monstrous thing again. But he thought of those white knuckles of hers, and went to sit on the floor at her feet, leaning back on one leg of her chair.

This wasn't going to be easy for her to see.

CHAPTER ELEVEN_

I was sitting like Haven again. The casual cross of one leg over the other, the slight lean to my shoulders, the skeptical eyebrow. I could feel the tension in Kupier's body where he pressed up against my leg. He was leaning forward, his hands steepled under his chin like a man in a house of worship. I shifted slightly away from the heat of his back.

The video was a journey through time. It started with memos and documents, correspondence between members of the Authority from almost a hundred years ago.

'Din Io,

I recognize now the wisdom of your words. There has been trouble here on Enceladus. I have yet to figure out what the leader's demands are. But you're right. It would be easier to get rid of him than it has been to work with him.'

And another.

'The remaining members of the rogue group have been dispatched, in the way that you suggested. They should be reaching Charon in the next month.'

There was letter after letter between Authority members, confirming exactly what Kupier had told me. That all of these 'rogue' members of the cols had been getting shipped off to Charon almost a century ago.

I frowned as I continued watching. I wasn't sure what I'd been expecting, but it wasn't this. I felt the way I did when I was in class on the Station. Mildly interested, slightly bored. Kupier, on the other hand, was reminding me of Dahn. Devouring every bit of information on the screen, immediately clicking it into place amongst everything else he'd ever learned about our world. The only difference was that Dahn believed in the complete righteousness of the Authority, and if this video was any indication, Kupier believed in its complete corruption.

My heart sped up just a touch when I saw what came next. Letters between these same Authority members, congratulating one another on the success of the extraction program. Admitting to each other that some supplies were going to have to be regularly sent out to Charon. It wasn't a death sentence for those citizens after all, ha ha ha.

Interesting.

And then.

Letters and emails and personal journals of Authority

members all flashed over the screen. They discussed 'the Extraction' in great detail. They compared the peacefulness of all of their cols. They realized how much better things were with the rogue citizens removed, not causing dismay and dissension among the other citizens spread over other cols.

Whoever had fabricated this video had gone to great lengths. None of what I was seeing was difficult to fake, in theory, but everything did look pretty authentic. All the different handwriting... and it must have been a pain in the ass to acquire all these different types of paper that the alleged Authority members had written on. I could almost understand why Kupier was holding all of this in such high esteem. As if it were real.

And then there was a historical record that I was very familiar with. They hadn't had to fake this one. Every citizen in the solar system knew this one. It was the first draft of a piece of legislation written by Din Io. It was framed and on the wall of most rooms in the Station. I'd studied it in school.

'We cannot, as a good and just government, sit by and condemn our citizens to a life penned in with lesser individuals. We are an orphan species as humans. Earth is no longer our home. We live scattered and confined. And I find, on this day, that it is the government's duty to protect the common citizen from the dangerous one. We cannot run free on our inhospitable planets, penned in as we are to our small colonies. It is the government's job to cull dangerous individuals for the good of our futures, our species, our precious world.'

There, right in front of me, was the birth of the Culling. The godfather of the idea and the document that had started the legalization of the process. The process that an entire solar system trusted as the best way. More than that, as a way to define our people.

I cocked my head as I read the familiar words. We'd always been taught that the idea for Culling had been something that had occurred to Din Io like a lightning bolt. That he'd just naturally had the insight into human psychology that was necessary for him to understand what had to be done to keep us all safe.

But according to these 'original' documents from the Ferrymen, it seemed very clear that this Extraction program they'd run to Charon was the thing that had started it all. It had made it very clear that subtracting certain citizens from the population was much better for the society as a whole.

And then Din Io had come up with the idea of Culling the violent.

Could it be true? I shifted in my chair, shaking my head to one side as if I could erase the question from my mind. But, of course it wasn't true. This was a bunch of crap that the people of Charon had scraped together in order to radicalize the Ferrymen. Right. They were an estranged, unhappy people who were trying to blame their problems on the Authority. Every document that I was seeing must have been faked. There was no way to prove that they were real. *So there.*

I crossed my arms over my chest and planted my feet flat on the ground. I had the strange desire to bounce one foot and I didn't like it. I just wanted this to be over.

The video went on. I saw draft after draft of the legislation until it was perfect. Until there wasn't a chance that Culling could be considered murder. But there wouldn't be a Culling for thirty more years. Din Io would never get to see an actual Culling.

No, the technology wouldn't be effective enough for a long time after he died. No one was comfortable with executing a Culling until the tech could be trusted completely. And that's where the video took me next.

Against my will, I found myself leaning forward just a little bit. There was surprisingly little information available about the development of the integrated tech – it made sense to keep such a powerful tool as secret as possible — and here was a whole history lesson on the subject.

Schematics and blueprints scrolled across the screen and my brain did everything it could to interpret the documents as fast as they came across the screen. I could imagine the upside down image of them reflecting against the dark of my eye. Uploading. The second a Datapoint gets their integrated tech, listening becomes more like uploading. But my tech was off, dead silent, and all I could do was try to drink in all the information in front of me.

Unlike with the first part of the video, I no longer had my own version of the facts to rely on. And, unlike with the first part of the video, this wasn't, on its own, damning for the Authority. This was just the slow and methodical advancement of scientists and engineers. Maybe that was why this portion of the presentation seemed a bit more believable than the rest. The progression of the integrated tech from prototype to prototype looked real to me.

I shifted in my seat. *If this is real, then could the rest be real?*

Ridiculous. I shook my head. If my tech were activated right now, it would be informing me of all the ways this video had

149

been hacked and doctored. There would be no question of whether or not the Ferrymen had altered this information. So, I just needed to keep my head on straight here. This was all manufactured, fake.

The video took me through all the supposed pilot programs for Datapoints. I winced, but didn't look away as I watched videos of the first integration processes. I'd seen a few stills in the one lesson we'd had on the topic, but never videos before. And those photos were on the wall of the Station, a way of honoring the first Datapoints to attempt to integrate more than a piece of the history.

I say *attempt* because they didn't successfully integrate right away. None of the original four Datapoints to attempt the pilot program survived the integration process.

They started from scratch. Redeveloped the tech. With the next group, it worked. And with the next group, it worked even more smoothly.

All this I already knew. I glanced down at Kupier, his face next to my knee, lit blue by the screen.

And when I looked back up, my stomach tightened reflexively.

Because there was a face I recognized, but perhaps thirty years younger. Jan Ernst Haven. But with black hair. The color difference was startling. It had never once occurred to me that he hadn't always been silver.

Then came letter after letter. His first correspondences with other members of the Authority. It was his first few years, and he was considered an upstart.

I leaned forward in my chair. It looked like...

He was attempting to convince the other Authority members that the parameters of who got culled should be expanded.

'I find myself wondering about this word, *violence*. It's one that we hold almost sacred, as it is who we have deemed necessary to cull. But unrest, dissatisfaction, resistance, aren't these a certain kind of violence, as well? We are here to bring peace to our citizens. Their quality of life is in our hands. Are we not abandoning them at the eleventh hour? Are we not condemning our people to live alongside those who, though perhaps not physically, may end the lives of those around them through rogue leadership and unrest?'

I squinted at the words. That didn't make sense at all. He was suggesting that those who didn't agree with the Authority should be culled? I wracked my brain. I'd never heard him say a single thing like that. I glanced down at Kupier again. He was staring rigidly at the screen.

My heart galloped in the cave of my chest. Ridiculous, I told myself. I knew Haven personally, and he'd never suggested anything even remotely like this. *So why do you believe it?* That small, terrible voice asked me. I didn't believe it. All of this was doctored to look a certain way. There was no reason to believe that Haven had wanted to engineer the program in order to cull whoever the hell he wanted to cull.

I slipped down an inch in my chair, my knee pressing Kupier's back, and I realized it was because I was sweating. I wiped my palms on the legs of my pants.

Next was letter after letter from Authority members, all of them rejecting the ideas that Haven had brought up. There was outright condemnation of the ideas. In fact, there was outright condemnation of the original Extraction at all.

One Authority member wrote:

'Though the idea itself gave birth to our greatest societal achieve-ment, the Culling, we must move on from the idea of Extraction, as it was a cruel and expensive practice. A stain on our history.'

So, if it were true, that they'd really extracted people to send to Charon, they didn't want the citizens to know. And they didn't want to make the same mistake of doing it again.

I watched as more very familiar images came to the screen. Brain scan after brain scan. Brains to be culled and brains to be left alone. I could recognize them with no trouble. And the sight of them was strangely soothing to me. I'd spent years studying them, after all. Culling was my life's work. My entire world.

And then. There were images of code. Some of it written in a hand that looked strangely familiar to me. Other parts of the code were inputted into a dummy computer, in an attempt to see what they would turn out. I was shown draft after draft of one program, attempting to be written from scratch.

No. I leaned forward in my chair. This wasn't a program that was being written. This was a virus.

I frowned. I recognized that handwriting.

I watched as, little by little, I could follow the arc of the evidence being presented to me. This virus was apparently being inserted into the Authority database. The very thing that synced with all of our integrated tech.

But what did the virus do? I watched in sickened fascination as my question was almost immediately answered.

We were back to the brain scans. I recognized them as coming from people needing to be culled. They were violent and prone to murder. But then there were different brain scans in the screen next to the first. These ones I didn't recognize. I'd never seen ones like these.

The red on these brain scans were in strange places, suggesting activity in different parts of the brain. I didn't know what to make of them. What did they mean? And almost as if I'd asked the question out loud, words appeared in that same handwriting, below the many images of the scans. *Rebellious. Stubborn. Defiant. Artistic. Rogue.* And then there was one word underlined five times. *Rebel.*

I leaned forward. So these were brain scans for someone with these traits? How was it that I'd never seen one before? I knew that people like that had to exist. And if they existed, then I would have come across their brain scans at some point in the hundreds of simulations I'd undergone.

But then I sat straight back in my chair as I realized that the virus had initiated on the screen. The two brain scans were over-laid, the violent and the rebel, one over the other. The rogue brain scan disappeared, absolutely dissolved into the violent brain scan.

I made a noise as if I'd been slapped.

This virus made rogue brain scans appear to be violent? Murderous?

My father.

The thought choked me. *Murderous.*

No. Rogue.

I felt a rising tightness in my throat, in my head. I wasn't getting enough air. And then it hit me whose handwriting that was. I knew exactly whose it was. I'd seen it a hundred times on the desk in his office. Jan Ernst Haven's.

I glanced down at Kupier. His face still blue and his eyes still forward. Kupier believed this. Wholeheartedly. Enough to lead people into battle over it. Enough to risk his life. To fight the Authority. And he was sharing all this with me because he wanted me to believe it, too.

Murderous.

Rogue.

I slammed my eyes shut for a second as my brain rearranged all the books on the shelf. As a Datapoint, I had to ask myself one question. Does this make sense?

And the truth? The truth was that part of me, some small, defiant part of me, wanted it to make sense. I wanted a world where my father wasn't secretly violent and murderous. I wanted a world where Kupier wasn't on the side of truth, or morality.

But this video? It was asking way too much of me. There were so many ways this information could have been altered.

I felt a horrible relief leak through me. Relief because I realized that I didn't believe the things I'd just seen. This *didn't* make sense. I'd never seen a single shred of evidence that there was a virus in the culling program. I'd never heard Haven say a single thing about culling anyone who wasn't violent.

The Ferrymen were wrong. I didn't believe this. Especially not the part about culling was coldblooded murder. No. Culling was good for society. Necessary. And no one was culled unless they were murderous.

I'd been freaked out there for a second. Of course, it was a lot of information to digest all at once, but ultimately, it was a tremendous relief to know that I didn't have to turn my world upside down completely. That I didn't have to reorder every belief I'd held since birth.

I looked down at Kupier, at the tilt of his neck as he scraped a hand over his face, and I was big enough to admit that for one second, just one second, it had all made sense to me. His side of things. Because my father had been culled. *Murderous*, they'd called him. My father the murderer. That had never once seemed real to me.

My father, the rogue? That I could believe. And part of me wanted to.

But it wasn't true. And it was time I got used to it. My father had been murderous. I just didn't know it. The Ferrymen were wrong. Kupier was wrong.

————

If he'd been expecting tears, or for Glade to stumble from her chair, for her to yell or rage or despair, well, he would have been sorely disappointed.

But he hadn't been expecting any of those things. Because he knew Glade.

So when Kupier flicked off the screen and turned to face her, he wasn't surprised when she just raised her eyebrows at him, looking at him dully.

"Very interesting stuff you've got there."

Kupier nodded, eyeing her. He wished for x-ray vision. He wanted to see the tremble of her heart in her chest, the whirring blood in her veins. She looked bored, unamused, and skeptical. But he would have bet the Ray that, on the inside, she was scrambling to keep her world in order. He said nothing and she watched him carefully.

"Is there more?" she asked. "Or can we head home now?"

Again, he said nothing. He merely reached out to take her hand, pressing his palm against hers.

He didn't want to push her. Not tonight. But time was running out. They were practically counting down until the next Culling. And he could see that he needed to test her trust for him. He'd worked so hard to build the bridge between them. But what good was it unless he walked out onto it?

"Yes." He spoke quietly and reminded himself of Luce again. "There is more. Do you remember the first question you ever asked me?"

Glade shifted. Her face serious, but her hand still clutched in his. "I asked you why you'd brought me to the Ray."

He slid his hand up to her wrist and slowly, gently, traced his fingers up the tech that was embedded there. "Because of this."

"My tech?"

He nodded. "Well, because of what you can do with your tech."

Her eyebrows furrowed. "Culling?"

Kupier barked out a surprised laugh. "God, no. Didn't you see the video? Yeah, I'm very firmly against culling." He jabbed a thumb behind him and flashed a smile her way.

"What for, then?"

"For your ability to access the Authority Database."

"You want me to take out the virus you *think* Haven implanted in the database?" Her tone was dripping with skepticism, but he didn't let it bother him.

"No. I want you to destroy the entire thing."

156

This time, it was Glade who laughed. She tugged her hand from Kupier's and dug the heel of it into her eye again. "Kupier. That's insane. Even if I would do that, which you couldn't force me to do, there's no telling if I even could. Not without direct access to the Database. Any attack done remotely would immediately be shut down by our defense team on the Station."

"I know."

"Then what the heck was the plan?" Her voice was frustrated and exhausted, and just a little bit fascinated. She was looking at him like she'd never seen him before, and maybe, in a way, she hadn't. He'd let her see his goofy side, his light-hearted side, his loving side. Yes, he'd shown her his stern side, his leader side, and even his warrior side. But he'd never shown her this, his stone-cold determined side.

The Authority had alienated his planet. They were attempting to weed out any person they wanted, with no powers of checks and balances at all. They'd murdered Luce. And now Kupier was two steps away from pulling the plug on their asses. She could see it in his eyes, he was sure of it.

"I know where the mainframe is."

She took a step back from him and blinked. "No one does."

He shrugged. "I do."

Glade cocked her hip out to one side and lifted an eyebrow. "Fine. Where is it?"

He was tempted to mimic her stance, but he knew how insane his answer was going to sound to her, and he didn't want her to have any more reason to doubt him. "Earth."

Now Glade tossed her hands into the air and really did laugh. She dragged her hair away from her face as she paced a few steps away and back. "Oh my God, Kupier, you've got to be kidding me. Who's been telling you spooky bedtime stories? Earth? For the love of— Earth?!"

He shrugged. "If you think about it tactically, it's the perfect place to hide it."

"Yeah," she said, and popped that hip out again. "Except for the fact that it's an uninhabitable wasteland. Toxic, destroyed, poisonous, and barren. But sure, if you say so, yeah! Perfect hiding spot."

Kupier sighed. "Parts of it are. But most of it is completely fine. Perfect, actually. The Authority live there, as well as about 400 others. Elite and rich people who've bought their way into paradise. And that's where they keep the Database mainframe."

She stared at him now. Just stood still and stared. Her voice was deflated and slightly sad when she spoke again. "You're insane, Kupier. Brainwashed. I – God, I didn't realize how crazy this all was until just now."

Kupier gripped her shoulders like he had so often in the past and moved her aside to get to the monitor.

"Just give me a second."

He fumbled around on the server, looking for the next thing he wanted to show her. He cursed when he found that the file was locked. He should have had someone unlock it. He should have known that she'd have to see it to believe him.

Glade sighed deeply and leaned over him, her hair sweeping down over one of his shoulders. He watched, equally impressed and intimidated by her skills on the computer as she hacked into the video in a matter of seconds.

This one was just a series of images with authentic time-stamps at the bottom.

"Our ships aren't traceable. So we've been able to get pretty damn close to the Earth," he told her as her brow pulled low over her eyes.

He didn't watch the screen. He knew what he would see there. Instead, he watched her. The upside-down reflections of Earth in her eyes. She frowned hard. And then harder. She'd been expecting to see Earth as a burned-out hull. A sunbaked desert, destroyed from nuclear bombs and climate change, these being the only signs left from the humans who'd once inhabited it.

But that's not what she was seeing, he knew. She was seeing images taken less than a year ago. Green and lush landscape. An entire hemisphere of Earth had weathered the human storm, and was fast recovering. There were rivers and lakes of freshwater. There was even an ice cap in one of the pictures. Autumn colors in another.

Glade clicked out of the video and turned to face Kupier. "You're telling me that you want me to – willingly – go with you to Earth. Land there, no less. Hope I don't grow a third eye from the poisonous atmosphere. Manually hack into the Authority Database. Destroy it. Thus destroying all integrated tech and bringing down our entire system of government?"

He shrugged. "More or less."

Glade blinked at him exactly the same way that she had when she'd called him crazy. Kupier knew when to fold. She needed rest. And time. She trusted him, but she didn't believe him. That much was clear. And there was no way to force her to believe. Just like there was no way to force her to do what he asked. If he tossed her on a ship, brought her to Earth, and plugged her in to the mainframe, with one line of code she could have the entire solar system's weapons pointed straight at his heart. She needed to believe in what they were doing for it to work. He needed her to believe.

And right now, she didn't look like she was going to believe him. She looked like she needed to rest. Kupier sighed, rose up from where he'd been crouching, and took her hand again, leading her out of the bunker. He considered their path back to his mother's house and didn't go the way they'd come. He'd wanted simply to get her here as fast as they could, but now he wanted a less risky path.

He led them back through the sixth level, through the cavern. And even twenty years later, there was still evidence of the bombs that Haven had dropped on Charon. Fallen stalactites, semi-cave-ins. There were huge crystals that had fallen from the wall and smashed. There'd been no reason to waste time or energy on clean-up of this room. Not when so much else had to be righted.

He led Glade through to a back staircase that led directly to the third floor. The market floor. It wasn't the fastest way back to his house, but it was the safest. Her hand clasped in his, she followed behind him as he wove through the darkened and quiet booths. Somewhere across the humongous level, he could hear some vendor opening up their booth. He could smell a savory sweet baked good rising in an oven somewhere. That brought a small smile to his face. It had been three days since they'd returned to Charon with a shipment of supplies. None of which Charon desperately needed, but all of which they'd use. The next few weeks at the market were going to be filled with treasures and treats like whatever baked good he could smell at that very moment.

They made it to another small alley that led down to the

160

fourth level, and they were almost home. In fact, he could see his front door when Glade tugged at his hand.

He came to a stop and faced her. He'd never seen her eyes look so black before. Like if he leaned forward just a touch, he'd fall in and never stop falling. Her hair swam around her shoulders as she looked up at him. And that frown. He opened his mouth to say something, but she beat him to it.

"Do you believe all of that?"

"Yes." He'd answered her without a second's hesitation.

She frowned even further. "You don't have any questions about any of it. There's nothing that you think might have been skewed in a certain direction? You think that all of it is undeniable fact?"

He paused, gathering his thoughts. He didn't see the look she gave him while he considered her question. He didn't see that the care with which he answered her showed her far more than that video had. "I suppose no fact is 'undeniable.' People get all mixed up between truth and fact and belief. But yes, I believe that that evidence incriminates Haven. I believe that he has motives for altering the Culling program. And though I don't understand what those motives are, exactly, I believe that he's been successful at getting what he wants."

His eyes flicked up to hers, blue into black, and he pulled the marble out of his pocket, clutching it as if he could squeeze the truth right out of it. "And I believe that the entire system is faulty. Not just because of Haven's lie, but because you can't create a computer program that simplifies who gets to live and who gets to die. It doesn't work that way. Trial by jury—"

She pursed her lips and rolled her eyes, but he continued speaking anyway.

"Trial by jury, though rife with faults, is the best answer we have for protecting the people of this solar system, and holding the violent accountable for their actions. It's not perfect, but it's infinitely better than government sanctioned mass murder of the innocent." His voice was getting calmer and calmer, and for one butterfly of a moment, Kupier could hear Luce's voice overlap with his own. He sounded like his brother. "I don't care which geniuses created the Culling program. I don't care how airtight the Authority says it is, or you say it is. In the end, we've created an algorithm that takes human life. That plays God. And not only do I reject that… I fight against that."

Her eyes flattened as they looked off over his shoulder, into the distance. Kupier could practically see her thoughts racing. He knew how a Datapoint's mind worked. He'd studied it. She was picking up each piece of new information, turning it over in her brain. He knew that she'd put the pieces together in a million different arrangements before she decided what made sense to her. She was logical, analytical.

But, he realized – as he looked down at her in an old green hoodie of his, with her hair an inky slide all around her, her eyes ever so slightly squinted in concentration – she was also emotional. He'd been told that Datapoints were like computers. They were as devoid of emotions as a machine. But not once had he experienced that in Glade.

She could be cold, sure, but that was just on the surface. Below that, she was teeming with feeling. He knew it just from looking at her. But now that he knew her so much better, he could practically *feel* it coming off her in waves. The very first thing he'd known about her was that she'd helped her younger friend escape the Ferrymen ship. The second thing he'd known about her was her loyalty to the way she was raised. He'd even seen her exhibit loyalty to Sullia.

He'd seen her rage. He'd seen her be brave. He'd seen her be sweet. God, he'd seen her laugh. She wasn't a robot, or a computer, or a machine. She was a human.

But looking down at her, he watched her eyes tighten more, her hand scraping over the dead tech on her arm. She was forcing down her humanity. She was making herself be a Datapoint before his very eyes.

"Kupier..." she started.

"No," he cut her off immediately, closing the distance between them with one step. She was a human, he was a human, and emotions were real. There was more in this world than just information. She needed to know everything.

Kupier could feel the heat kicking off of her as his chest bumped against her, crowding her against the alley wall. First her brow furrowed as she glared up at him, but seeing the expression on his face, her eyebrows smoothed even as her breath became choppy.

"No," he said again as he brought his hands to her shoulders, then down all the way to her wrists. "Don't decide how you feel right this second." His hands went up her arms to her shoulders. He dropped his head so that there wasn't room for even a breath between them. Kupier blinked and realized that he'd tangled one of his hands into the silky hair at the back of her head. He was tipping her face up. "Promise me you'll wait to decide how you feel. Promise me you'll take your time."

His face was so close to hers that their noses could have touched if either of them had moved. Neither of them did. Except for his eyes, which searched hers. He thought again of

163

blackholes, of being sucked in to a different world. And then, as one of his hands slid to her waist, he thought of jumping in headfirst.

"Okay," she said. "I promise."

And then she jerked her head out of his grasp and shoved him back a stumbling inch. He could have sworn that he'd felt an intentional elbow to his ribs as she strode through the alley and into the door of his house.

Kupier watched her go. He dragged a hand over his face and let out a long, slow breath that ended on a chuckle. He had to laugh at himself.

Leader of the Ferrymen. Tying himself in knots over a Datapoint.

But, as soon as he had the thought, he dismissed it as wrong. She wasn't just a Datapoint. Just like he wasn't a just a Ferryman.

She was Glade, and he was Kupier.

CHAPTER TWELVE_

I didn't believe it. Not any of it.

I lay in my bed until I heard Sullia stirring and then got up to have breakfast with Kupier's family. I sat across the breakfast table from Kupier, felt his eyes on my downturned face, and still, I didn't believe it.

I, of all people in this solar system, knew exactly how easy it was to alter and edit any piece of information to look a certain way. I was a computer genius. And it wouldn't have even taken someone of my level to have altered what I'd seen last night.

The bottom line was that it didn't make sense to me. I knew Jan Ernst Haven. He'd never once said anything about Culling 'rogue thinkers.' He believed in the system. The true Culling system. The one that Din Io had conceived.

Murderous or rogue?

Memories of my father tugged at me. He'd never seemed murderous.

Rogue.

No. I didn't believe it. The Authority wasn't that compromised. Jan Ernst Haven wasn't that backwards. That evil. I didn't believe it. I *was* surprised, though, at how torn my disbelief made me feel. I swallowed down Owa's delicious food and acknowledged, with a lurch in my stomach, the part of me that wanted to believe it. I wanted to help Kupier – because he was Kupier. Not because I cared at all about the Ferrymen's cause.

Or their stupid alternative history that didn't make sense at all. The same one that would mean that Culling, what I was trained to do, was murder.

No. I wanted to help because Kupier had given an eclipse as a 'thank you' to his crew. Because he'd laid down weapons. Because he was currently letting his little sister shove half of a frosted roll into his mouth while she cackled with laughter.

My stomach tightened.

Kupier turned, laughing and wiping his mouth with a napkin, and caught my eye. Those half slices of blue had me swallowing hard. For a half second, I was transported back to the alley last night. To the fan of his breath on my face, the electric blue of his eyes at that distance. God. What the hell had *that* been?

Across from me, Kupier winked, as if he knew exactly what I was thinking about, and something pressed against my foot underneath the table. I narrowed my eyes at him. He was flirting with me. Even a trained Datapoint could recognize that.

"Shoot," Owa muttered as she looked across the room at the rudimentary screen they kept in the wall. It was the fourth or fifth time I'd seen the tablet short out since I'd come to stay with them. "Kup, can you take a look at this before you leave? I can barely get this thing to show me the time anymore."

She rose and yanked it out of the wall, banging it against one hand as she did.

Kupier made wide eyes at me and we both tried not to laugh. I was very familiar with the extent of his computer skills.

"Here," I said without thinking, reaching up for the tablet. Yet, it was very clear that I had not been allowed to touch any piece of tech since landing on Charon, and everything besides that tablet had been cleared out of the house.

Owa's eyes searched Kupier's and she hesitated before handing it over. But seconds later, the tablet landed in my hand. I felt Sullia's gaze burning into me.

But I didn't look up at any of them. I fooled around on the tablet for less than a minute, removed about thirty viruses, reloaded the operating system, and cut out a few of the junk programs that had been slowing everything down.

When I handed it back to Owa a few minutes later, it was with a wry smile on my face. "I thought everyone on Charon was supposed to be a tech genius?"

She quirked a quick smile at me. "We all have our strengths. Thanks for this."

She put the tablet back in its place on the wall and, on the way back to her place at the table, piled a little more food on my plate. When I looked up, I could feel both Kupier and Sullia's gazes on me, but I didn't meet either.

———

"Wake up."

I felt a hard press into my shoulder. And then a more vicious jab.

"Now."

"Jesus, Sullia," I growled, rolling up into a sitting position and squinting through the darkness.

She ignored my tone, and tossed my sweatshirt and shoes right onto the bed with me. "We're leaving."

"What?" I scrambled up. "What are you talking about?"

"When you fooled around with their tablet this morning, I realized they didn't have them locked to our fingerprints. I hotwired one of the doors of a rover skip back at the landing pad and we have about thirty minutes before it takes off."

"What good would a rover skip do us?" Rovers were patrol skips. They never left the orbit of their planets. They usually weren't even equipped to.

"There's three other skips in the belly of the rover skip. I checked. One of them is long-range. Equipped with artificial black holes."

My heart leapt and plummeted at the same second. This was real. This was actually a way off of this colony. Back to the Station. We could be back to the Station in a week. Away from the Ferrymen. From the constant danger. My hand grazed over my arm and cheek. I'd have my tech back. The thought was both exhilarating and deflating at the same time.

But I'd be home. In my own world. Where things made sense.

And I'd never see Kupier again.

"Unless," Sullia spoke again, her eyes watching me closely. "You don't want to come?"

I glared up at her and, in that moment, I thought I hated her. She was so sure of what she wanted, who she was. She had been from the very start and it drove me insane. I would never in a million years want to be anything like Sullia. But I envied her knowledge of herself. Of the surety of her decision. And now she was going to watch me struggle.

"Look, Glade, I don't care if you come or not. But I'm walking out of here in two minutes. And I'm going back to the Station."

Images of the Station flashed before my eyes. The gray hallways. The brown blankets on my bed. The door of the simulator. Even Haven's office. I thought of the last conversation I'd had with him.

My stomach roiled when I thought of my sisters. If I stayed here, the Authority would officially be down a Datapoint. The recruitment period for the next group of Datapoints was coming up in eight months. There was no doubt in my mind who they'd select to fill my space. I thought of how Haven had bent the rules and done preliminary testing on Daw and Treb. God, they could be at the Station right now for all I knew. I hadn't let myself think about it when there'd been no chance for escape. But right now? When a rover skip had a ticket for my way back to the Station, I couldn't ignore it. Every second I spent away from the Station was one more second my sisters were in danger.

My decision was made. Quickly, I rose and slipped my shoes and sweatshirt on. Sullia and I were silent as we crept through the house.

We were out the front door in seconds, and sneaking through the fourth level and toward the landing pad which was all the way up on the first level.

I felt myself disappearing into the dark of the alleyways.

169

Away from Kupier. Away from his house. I didn't look back. Not once.

It wasn't until Sullia and I were tucked deep into the belly of the rover skip. Until we'd taken off and were orbiting Charon. Until she was pulling me into the cockpit of the smaller skip that we'd escape in. It wasn't until then that I realized whose sweatshirt I wore.

TWO

CHAPTER THIRTEEN_

Dahn Enceladus' thumbs hurt. That's how long he'd been messing around with the old gaming device he'd shared with Glade. Outwardly, he'd accepted the fact, as had every other Datapoint in the Station. Inwardly... well, he wasn't quite sure what was happening inwardly, but he was certain it wasn't acceptance.

Why else would he be spending all of his free time on the pilot deck, staring out the windows and messing around on the gaming device? Of course, it wasn't his free time exactly. His free time he was still spending by Jan Ernst Haven's side. That was still spent practicing and honing and excelling. But his sleeping time? That was spent on this pilot deck. When the rest of the Station was in their bunks. When only a reserve pilot or two manned the abandoned deck, Dahn sat in the shadows, looking out at the asteroid belt.

The game beeped in his hands and Dahn frowned at it. He was sick of programming these puzzles himself. He missed the way that Glade programmed. She was a wall. And tricky and unexpected. He hadn't had a good puzzle since she'd been gone. He missed how cocky she'd been when she'd solve his faster than he'd solve hers. He missed her frown.

Dahn felt that same annoying tightening in his throat that he'd been feeling ever since she'd been abducted. He swallowed it down. It was annoying and pathetic and he was sick to death of both of those feelings.

He hadn't fallen behind in his work as a Datapoint yet, but he worried that if things went on like this any longer, it would start to show in his performance. He wouldn't disappoint himself in that way. And he wouldn't disappoint Jan Ernst Haven.

Dahn rose, telling himself, the way he did every night, that this was the last night he'd come to the pilot deck when he should be sleeping. This was the last night he'd mess around on the gaming device. This was the last night he'd think of Glade Io with a tight throat. This was the last night he'd wonder if there was more he could have done.

He was halfway across the pilot deck when a bright, glinting flash caught his eye through one of the pilot's windows.

Probably just something metallic shining off one of the neighboring asteroids. But there, in the direction it had come from, was something strange moving through space.

It wasn't an asteroid – it was a craft.

This in itself wasn't that unusual. There were supply skips that came in and out of the Station's orbit all the time, and Dahn cursed himself for the small skip in his heartbeat when he saw it. It wasn't Glade.

He wondered, in what he hoped was a detached way, when

he'd stop hoping. It was an involuntary reaction that he desperately wished he could control.

But he kept his eyes on the craft. It looked too small to be a supply skip. Dahn stepped closer to the window.

"Oren," he called out to the reserve pilot who was currently sitting in the back of the pilot deck – Oren being the only one assigned to the night shift.

"I see it," the pilot called back, frowning at the equipment in front of him as he tracked the craft on the radar.

"Is there a shipment scheduled?" Dahn asked, trying like hell to keep his voice steady.

"Ah..." Oren clicked open the schedule and checked it. "Not until 5 a.m."

"Maybe they're back from the testing early," Dahn said, half to Oren and half to himself. They'd sent out a group of experienced Datapoints to perform testing on new prospects earlier that month. But they weren't scheduled to return for another week.

"No, there isn't any integrated tech in that craft," Oren called back, studying the monitors. "Two life forms, though."

Oren and Dahn exchanged eye contact. They both slowly looked back out toward the window, to where the craft had gotten closer. It was a strange craft; it looked like two different skips had been soldered together to make it. And it moved strangely, too. Clumsy but fast. Dahn blinked. There was no mistaking it. That was a Ferryman's skip.

He looked back at Oren and the two of them made eye contact again for one heavy second.

"No!" Dahn yelled, but he didn't manage to stop the reserve pilot from flipping the emergency switch.

Sirens and light filled the pilot deck, the same as they did every room in the entire station.

"Damn it!" Dahn screamed, realizing that at that very moment Datapoints were jumping out of bed and sprinting to their battle posts. He didn't know who for sure was on that craft, but he had a good idea. And he didn't want a thousand guns pointed in her direction.

The phone sitting at the pilot's left started ringing. He sprinted across the pilot deck and batted Oren's hand away.

"It's Dahn Enceladus," he said into the receiver. "Sir, it's her. I know it's her. Two lifeforms, no integrated tech. Same style of craft that Cast used to get back here. It's her."

He heard Jan Ernst Haven's heavy breath through the phone and Dahn held his tongue, though there was so much more he wanted to say.

"Put on the tractor beam."

Dahn felt something burst in his chest. They were going to reel the craft in. Not shoot it into oblivion. He smacked the phone into the pilot's hand and immediately started engaging the codes for the tractor beam.

Oren silenced the battle sirens and engaged others. The Datapoints weren't needed at their battle posts. But the tactical team was needed on the landing dock.

Dahn didn't let himself think about the number of armed Datapoints who were going to be pointing their weapons at that craft at the very second it landed. Instead, he focused the entirety of his energy on the tractor beam. It was extremely strong and had to be guided perfectly, or else all sorts of space detritus could wind up getting sucked into the landing dock.

Dahn located the craft on the radar and then carefully locked the beam onto it. A bead of sweat rolled down his spine as he engaged the beam. He looked up, out through the windows, and watched as the funky little spacecraft was caught in the beam, visible as only a disturbance in space, a clear line summoning the craft forward.

The second he confirmed the spacecraft was locked in to the tractor beam, he was sprinting away, out of the pilot deck and down toward the landing area. He wasn't supposed to be. He wasn't a member of the tactical team. But there wasn't any stopping him as he barreled from hallway to hallway, jumping an entire flight of stairs at once and then skidding through to the landing pad.

The tactical team was already assembling and he marveled at their readiness. He knew they'd been sleeping just moments before. And now, here they were – dressed, armed and arranged in perfect defensive formation.

Dahn's eyes went immediately to the vacuum doorway that would remain sealed until the outside doors of the Station closed again. The tractor beam seemed to tremble as it dragged the craft in.

Whoever was driving the craft was skilled. The tractor beam could drag you in, but it sure couldn't land you. Dahn watched, his breath in his chest, as the spacecraft touched down.

The second that the vacuum doorway started sliding open, Dahn was sprinting forward.

"Datapoint!" someone from the tactical team screamed at him. But he didn't even pause. He certainly didn't stop.

"Datapoint, stand down!"

He still didn't stop.

The ground exploded near his feet and Dahn fell to his

knees. He stayed down, the blast reverberating in his ears. He knew they were right. He was sprinting toward an enemy spacecraft with nothing more than hope in his chest.

This was insane.

He stayed down, his eyes locked on the craft as a door opened up out of the side.

"Identify yourselves!" The tactical team was creeping forward, and Dahn's tech counted each of them, and their weapons. All armed.

"Sullia Enceladus and Glade Io." That was Sullia's voice.

"Show us your tech!"

Without hesitation, two slender arms came out of the door, revealing the crystal-like technology that only a Datapoint could possibly have.

"Come out, hands up, and slowly!"

Two figures emerged, carefully picking their way down the stairs of the craft. Dahn's heart leapt in his chest – because there she was. And she looked… terrible. There were dark lines under her eyes and her cheeks were sunken. Neither of the exiting Datapoints looked like they'd had anything to eat or drink in days.

Sullia pulled forward and Glade stumbled after her.

It was the stumble in her step that had Dahn rising to his feet again. In all of his years knowing her, he'd never seen Glade Io stumble like that. She didn't walk with her chin down or sadness lining her face. She was proud and serious-faced and steady, always.

He took a step forward.

"Dahn Enceladus! They're not cleared yet!" That was from

the leader of the tactical team, sensing Dahn's need to go closer and stay closer.

But Glade stumbled again and Dahn took off like a shot. He couldn't stand there and watch her like that. Especially after Glade looked up and saw him sprinting across the loading deck. Her eyes lit for just a second and something like relief flashed over her face. She let go of Sullia's shoulder, and in a move that overwhelmed him, lifted her arms to Dahn.

He was just three feet from them when he pulled up short. His integrated tech was going crazy, blinking and beeping about all the armed weapons pointed at his back.

Breathing heavy, his eyes wide, he took a step toward Glade.

"Get away from them! Don't touch them!" It was Jan Ernst Haven's voice that called out from the back of the landing deck now. "Their tech is dead! Don't trust them. Get away!"

Dahn jumped back from Glade as if he'd been burned, heeding Haven's orders and scrambling away from her.

He'd known that their tech was dead, and he felt a blazing humiliation that it hadn't occurred to him that they shouldn't be trusted until they were re-integrated. He should have realized that. But he was too anxious to get to Glade. To make sure she was alright.

Glade frowned at him as she dropped her arms, her eyes going back and forth between Dahn and Haven.

Dahn moved even further back from her, until he was ten feet away. He didn't leave the room, though, and his eyes didn't leave hers. Not even as two tactical technicians rushed forward in front of Jan Ernst Haven. Not even when those technicians raised their neutralizing rays. Not even when he watched the electricity swirl out from the ends of those rays and center onto the tech on both Sullia and Glade's arms.

Dahn stood there silently and he watched as Glade immediately fell to the ground, her body writhing in excruciating pain for a moment and then another. Until she fell limp. Unconscious and inert. It was only after Haven's brisk nod that Dahn went to her side, and scooped her up in his arms and carried her out.

———

I was having the nightmare about integrating. The one that had plagued me for months. It always felt so real. The blue light burning my eyes. My limbs strapped down to an operating table. The tech burning my skin, trying to bore its way into my brain.

But it had never felt quite this real.

I took a deep breath and tasted metal in my mouth, smelled burning flesh. It was my own. I realized, with a horrible lurch in my stomach, that this wasn't a dream. I was on the integration table again. They were activating my tech. I had to sync again. I had to let it back in all over again.

This should have been easy. I'd already done it once. I didn't intend to suffer on the table for days on end again. I stopped struggling against my bonds, letting the blue light sink into my dilated pupils. I breathed through the burning pain on my arm and on my cheek.

"That's right."

I heard the voice in my ear and knew who was with me. I didn't even have to catch sight of his silver hair. He was there. Coaching me through it.

And when I synced this time, it wasn't excruciating. It wasn't even pain. But it *was* uncomfortable. It was like, in my time with the Ferrymen, my mind had become an amorphous cloud. And now I had to smooth out my edges and fit it all into a perfect bowl. But I did it. It was almost like falling asleep.

The last thought I had before I let the tech sync with me was of Kupier. Of his laughing face as we'd fought in the main room of the Ray.

"That's enough," Haven's voice spoke in the first moment after the sync was complete. The blue light switched immediately off, and I was surprised. The first time I'd ever synced, they'd left me on the table for hours afterwards.

I mentally flexed my tech. It was both foreign and familiar, a welcome intrusion as the readouts appeared in my vision. Distances to nearest objects, how many heartbeats in the room. How many weapons. Here was the thing I'd come to rely on. I no longer felt that vulnerable blindness that I'd felt the entire time I'd been on the Ray.

I felt the technicians unstrap my wrists and legs, and I automatically rubbed at the bruised skin.

It was a relief to be back at the Station, I realized. I looked around at the steel walls, the brown carpet. I knew what each day was going to be like on the Station. The only thing I had to concentrate on was becoming the best Datapoint I possibly could. I glanced over at Haven, looking at him fully for the first time since coming back.

"Dramatic entrance," he said in that reedy voice of his.

I shrugged. "Our coms were broken. And we'd been out of food and water for two days. We were pretty desperate to get here."

He paused. "You must have been traveling for some time."

I spoke carefully. My eyes on his. "Charon is a long way away."

"So it is. Sullia said the same thing." His silvery eyes went back and forth between mine and I realized that he was trying to figure out whether or not I was lying. I'd thought I'd return home a hero for surviving a Ferryman ordeal. But, I realized, with a sinking of my heart, that we were not leaving the room right now.

Haven looked down at the small screen attached to his watch. He typed something out in the projected image in the air and exited out. He swiped a hand across his orderly hair.

"You'll understand, I think, that we'll be a bit cautious with you until we understand what happened?"

"Cautious?" I asked slowly, though I already knew exactly what he meant. I just didn't want it to be true.

He cleared his throat. "No stone unturned, Datapoint."

I opened my mouth to say something else, but he was already walking out. Leaving me in the room alone with everyone who'd supervised my syncing. But none of them looked at me as they cleared their things to pack them away.

When the last person left, quietly closing the door behind her and leaving me alone in the empty room, I wondered how long it would be until the tactical team came for me.

It wasn't long at all.

———

Dahn avoided the medical wing of the Station for three days. He knew what they were doing to her. He knew that they were interrogating her. He also knew that almost no one came out of those interrogations the same.

Part of him couldn't help but be relieved that, for the first time in a month, he knew where she was. Even if it was in the medical wing. In hell.

The interrogations, as all of them were taught in training, were as much for information as they were for testing loyalty. They were designed to show who you really were. Through torture and deprivation.

"I heard she's doing well," Cast said as he came into Dahn's room unannounced. He'd been visiting Dahn often since everything had happened with the Ferrymen.

"What's that?" Dahn asked, looking up from the gaming device he was programming.

"Iona, this girl I know on the tactical team, I heard her saying that Glade was surviving. She hasn't cracked yet. In any direction."

Dahn frowned and looked back at the screen of the gaming device. "That doesn't mean much."

"It means that she probably wasn't compromised while she was with the Ferrymen." Cast narrowed his eyes when Dahn didn't agree with him. "Come on, you know they would have figured it out by now if she'd switched loyalties."

Dahn shrugged. "The only thing we can do is wait and see what the tactical team decides."

———

I wondered if this was what being culled felt like. Excruciating pain in my head, so bad that my eyes wouldn't stop watering.

Pain so tight, so pervasive, there was no way to yell, or breathe, or cry. Only, instead of lasting one second, the way a Culling did, this had been going on for at least three days.

The pain released me and I fell flat on the floor, sweaty and weak. And now came the questions.

"Tell me again, Glade Io." The deep voice came from above me. I could smell the leather of his boots. "What is his name?"

"Kupier," I gasped. I'd already given that up hours ago. I was telling them every single thing I could. Besides the one thing I thought might get me executed.

"Good."

I heard the click that often preceded the blinding pain in my head and I knew they were going to press the electrodes again. "His mother's name is Owa. His brother is Oort. His little sister is Misha."

I repeated everything I'd told them before. I'd given up everything that I knew Sullia would have already given up. I desperately wanted my story to match hers exactly. If they found out that Kupier had given me preferential treatment, had spent time alone with me, I was sure I was going to be executed.

There was no way that I could spin that to make it seem like I'd been spying on him. I hadn't been. I also hadn't been considering joining ranks with the Ferrymen, but would the tactical team see that? I wasn't going to bet on it. Any minor allegiances were bound to get me killed. Right here and now. On the floor of the operating room that I hadn't left in days.

I'd already explained about every aspect of Moat that I could remember. The number of ships. The number of Ferrymen with weapons; the number of unarmed civilians. I'd named every member of the Ferrymen that I could. I'd explained about our housing situation on Charon. I'd told the team about helping Cast escape. About my first conversation with Kupier. I'd explained about Sullia. How I'd come to trust her less and less as time went on, and that I'd known she had some sort of plan in the works the whole time.

I'd even explained that I had hesitated to go with her when she'd told me we were leaving that night. Though I hadn't told them why – not the truth of it, anyway. I'd told them it had been because I was scared of getting caught and killed. I hadn't explained that part of me hadn't wanted to leave Kupier.

They were looking for reasons to execute us. Of that much I was sure. They wanted to make a statement to the other Datapoints. That getting captured by Ferrymen was as good as getting killed. *So, don't... get... captured.*

But in the dim, exhausted back of my mind, I worried that they were choosing between me and Sullia. They didn't need both of us to get the information they needed. And if we were both deemed damaged goods, then they wouldn't want the headache and risk of keeping us both there in the Station. I knew that some people might never stop wondering if my loyalty had been compromised.

I knew that, if that was the case, Sullia would throw me to the wolves with no hesitation. She would lie to get me executed before her. She'd do anything.

And, I guessed, as I lay there on the cold floor in my own sweat, I knew that I couldn't guess what her lies would be. So, I'd just try to stick my story as close to hers as I possibly could and hope for the best.

"Good girl."

It was a new voice. One I hadn't heard yet in the course of

my interrogations. Haven was here. How long had he been in the room? I lifted my head to look at him, but found that my neck simply couldn't lift my head more than a few inches.

"She's holding back, sir. There's things she's not telling us." In that moment, if I could have culled the man with the deep voice, I would have. Clearly, he enjoyed violence.

"I'm not," I groaned, my lips dragging against the smooth floor. "I'm not holding anything back."

"Well," Haven said quietly. "I suppose she can withstand more. If you still have doubts after a few more sessions... execute."

My blood felt solid and slow. *Execute*. They were going to execute me either way. If I told them that Kupier and I had become friends. Or if I didn't tell them.

I held my breath as the clicking sound came on. And then the electrodes attached to my head exploded into pain.

I'd known about the interrogations. Both Sullia and I had known that they would be a possibility when we came back to the Station. But I'd never thought they'd go on for so many days. And I'd never thought they'd be this rigorous. There was nothing but the worst pain of my life, threatening to burn me alive from the inside out. There was no way to win. I was going to die. I was going to die. From this pain or from execution. Whether I spoke or not. I'd been kidnapped and I hadn't fought my way out quickly enough. I hadn't killed any Ferrymen. I'd spoken with them. Befriended some of them. And now my own people were going to kill me for it.

I screamed and screamed. Even after the pain stopped. Because it wasn't fair. I hadn't asked to be abducted. I hadn't asked to get along with Kupier. I hadn't even asked to be a Data-point. My father hadn't asked to be culled.

I didn't want any of this. I just wanted to sleep and sleep. Forever. The longest, darkest night known to man. I never wanted to wake up. When I opened my eyes, I saw nothing but darkness.

I didn't wonder if it was because my eyes had stopped working or if I really was in a dark room. I didn't care. All I cared about was sleep.

———

I woke up in a dim room. Strapped to a chair yet again. Home sweet home.

Something smelled terrible. And it took a moment before I realized that it was me. There was water on my lips and I realized that someone must have splashed some over my face to wake me up. I greedily sucked it down. It was the first water I'd tasted since the single glass they'd given me after my operation.

My head lolled to one side and I saw that a port had been stuck into my wrist. On a table to my left was a set of syringes. All of them strangely small and filled with clear liquids. If I'd been a human still, my stomach might have dropped at the sight of the weapons that were going to kill me. But I wasn't a human anymore. I was a ghost. A fossil. Gone was Glade. I was nothing. Just dead.

My eyes fell to my hands and I was shocked by what I saw. I truly looked like a skeleton. The skin was pulled white over my bones and I was so stiff I couldn't even bend my fingers.

I didn't know how long I stayed in that dim room. But the

light never changed, so I knew that I wasn't in an exterior room. I was deep within the Station somewhere.

Sometime later, a long time later, while my eyes were half closed, a door behind me opened. A silver-haired man pulled up a stool next to me and leaned forward on his knees. "You're going to die, Glade Io. And it's such a shame."

Well. I guessed we weren't wasting time on any pleasantries.

"You always had such high potential. Your testing was through the roof. And even before that, when I saw you as a child – did I ever tell you that? That I observed you once, after the last Culling. I knew even then that you had massive potential in this program. And yet. Here we are. You've ceased improving. And now we're questioning the most basic of all requirements? Your loyalty? How could this be?"

"I'm loyal," I heard myself say, and part of me was shocked. How could a ghost speak? How could the dead thing I was even have the strength to say two words? There was no air in my lungs. No space in my brain for thoughts.

Haven studied me for a long time. "Well. You held back from the tactical team. So now we can't trust you."

Calculating what I figured would be the last risk I'd ever get to take in my life, I just plunged in. "I liked the leader. Kupier. I *liked* him. He was charismatic and kind. But I wasn't loyal to him. He tried to get me to help them, but I wouldn't." I dragged my head to one side. "And I figured telling you that I liked the leader of the Ferrymen would get me executed anyways. So, I took a risk and didn't say anything."

Haven's eyes darkened as he narrowed them. He leaned forward, slightly wrinkling his nose at my stench, but he stayed close. I could feel his soft breath on my face. "How shameful, child. To let yourself be taken in by a Ferryman. I thought I would have programmed you better." He laughed softly. "But, like I said. Humans are not computers. Are they, Glade?"

I didn't acknowledge his words.

"Well." He rose and moved around to my wrist. I didn't even have the energy to try and tug my hand away. "Either way, now you'll get to rest."

I felt something get plugged in to the port at my wrist and I squeezed my eyes closed, willing sleep to come to me. Darkness. Quiet.

I heard him walking out of the room. Heard the door close. It was ten minutes later when I gathered the energy to look around, and see the nutrition tube he'd plugged in to my arm.

CHAPTER FOURTEEN_
TWO MONTHS LATER

"Dahn, I swear. If you check on me one more time, I'm gonna sweep your legs." He was like a mother hen. And he had been for the last two months.

In the two months since Sullia and I had been deemed worthy of reentering life as Datapoints, there'd been a myriad of reactions amongst our peers. Some of them like Cast and Dahn had treated me like I might burst into a million pieces at any second. But most had kept a wide berth from either me or Sullia. I thought people were much more suspicious of me than of her. I'd been in interrogations for a full day longer than she had. I figured it had taken me that extra day to end up corroborating the story that Kupier and I had had a special relationship. They'd been able to tell that she'd given up all the truth. Just like they could tell that I'd been withholding. Sullia hadn't initially tried to escape from the Ray. When it was unsafe to return, she didn't. When it was safer, she did. Her loyalty was obviously to herself, not the Station. But she was predictable, reliable, understandable. And for that, she was a valuable Datapoint.

In the end, we'd both returned, knowing that the interrogations were a possibility. They didn't have to know that, if I'd known what they were gonna be like, I might have thought harder about coming back at all. I couldn't speak for Sullia, though. We hadn't so much as made eye contact since the day we'd gotten back to the Station.

He rolled those soft gray eyes at me and had the audacity to look bored by my threat. "You could try."

So I did just that. Striking out of nowhere, I whipped one leg out to the side, catching him around the ankles and attempting to sweep his feet out from under him.

He scoffed, remained standing, and merely cuffed me to the side with one hand to the forehead.

"Pathetic."

I grinned, quick and fierce, and shifted to make another attempt to bring him down, but all good humor fell from his face now. He glanced around like someone might catch us messing around.

"Datapoint," his voice warned me to stand down.

I sighed and fell back into place beside him. I didn't bother to look around and see if anyone was watching me. I knew they were. They always were.

I hadn't hated the Ferrymen when I'd been their captive, not really. But I sure hated them now. Because of them, I was the outcast of the entire Station. My fellow Datapoints either glared at me distrustfully or they stared at me with wide eyes, waiting for me to burst into tears or something.

I'd spent four days in the infirmary after Haven had plugged in my nutrition tube. On the last day, he'd come back and told me a few things. I was officially deemed trustworthy. And as soon as I was healthy enough to go back into training, I was going to have a mentor. The Culling was starting soon. And we needed every Datapoint out in the field.

I hadn't wanted to lay around sipping broth and eating crackers much after that.

The only person who'd treated me semi-normally after I'd left the infirmary was Cast. He'd been almost excited to see me. Well, as excited as any Datapoint could get. He showed me his pilot's training log. Apparently, his stint in the Ferrymen's short-range skip had peaked his interest. We were allowed to pick specialties, and his was flying.

"What was the specialty that you chose, Glade?" he'd asked me.

I'd shrugged, feeling an odd sense of letting everyone down all at once. It must have been my recovery catching up to me. "I never chose one. I liked all the classes equally." Or hated them all equally.

The looks I was getting from all of the other Datapoints, surprisingly, weren't the strangest part about being back at the Station.

It was who had been chosen to be my mentor.

Dahn.

I'd always spent a fair amount of time with Dahn during our free time. And we'd often trained together; he'd always been pushing me to do more simulations. But now that he'd been assigned to me as a mentor? Well, let's just say he was the first face I saw when I woke up in the morning and the last face I saw before bed.

Dahn and I had spent basically the last month and a half joined at the hip, training like maniacs. I'd run hundreds of simulations. And every single time, I'd run scans on my tech for viruses. I'd connected to the Authority Database, like a good little Datapoint. I ran scans for viruses there, as well. Nothing showed up – not so much a blip on my radar. There were no viruses. The Ferrymen were wrong. Dead wrong.

Having that matter put to rest allowed me to throw myself headlong into training. Most of it was simulations. But Dahn made sure to get me back into combat shape, as well. We began every day by beating the crap out of one another. That was the best part of the day as far as I was concerned.

And from there the simulations started. The program uploading. The endless brain scan quizzes. No other Datapoints trained the way we did. Sometimes twenty hours a day. Part of that was Dahn's obsessive personality. I knew he wanted to be the best mentor, who produced the most improvement in any pupil in history. But the other part of why we were training so hard was that we'd been assigned a Culling.

Of all the Datapoints in the entire Station, I had no idea why they'd picked us. It was just a small one. A practice of sorts. On Europa. And I'd been told that a few other Datapoints were doing the same thing on other colonies. Test runs before the big show. The main Culling.

So here we were, on a skip currently bypassing Jupiter and heading straight for Europa.

"Datapoint." A low voice behind me had me nearly jumping out of my skin. Ever since my torture stint with the tactical team, I'd been having trouble with low voices coming from behind me.

But it was just the cook on our travel skip. We'd been traveling for the better part of three days to get to Europa, and we had a fairly large team with us. Pilots, health techs, and a cook.

The cook shoved one bowl of soup into my hand and one into Dahn's. "Something light that won't weigh you down," he murmured before heading back toward the galley.

I looked down at the bowl of green mush in my hands. Apparently, this was Culling food.

Dahn, taking his nutritional needs very seriously, sat down at the table under the small port window and started slowly eating. I followed suit in following him to the table, but didn't eat. Instead, I held onto my bowl and looked out the tiny window.

The skip lurched and I grabbed my soup in both hands. I'd been spoiled on the Ray. As crappy, haphazard, and rundown as that thing had looked, she'd flown like a dream. I knew it was because the Ray was a ship and this was a skip. But I had to admit, it had been a better ride.

And a better view. The tiny port window on our skip was so scratched that I could barely see out of it. I had just the smallest edge of red Jupiter in our view. My mind landed on the big window in the Ray. My mind next tried to land on Kupier, but I skittered quickly away, sending my thoughts elsewhere.

I wasn't letting myself think about him. It was suicide. Becoming friends with him had gotten me tortured for days. It had almost gotten me killed. Thinking about him always made me slower for some reason, too – less on point with my training as a Datapoint. And I couldn't take that risk right now. Not when the entire Station's eyes were on me and Sullia. It was better for me to ignore my time with the Ray and with the Ferry-men, even if my brain made them pop up at all the worst times.

So, I was surprised when it was Dahn who brought them up this time.

"I'll bet this is better than the food you had with the Ferrymen."

I looked up, shocked that he'd bring the subject up. He hadn't so much as acknowledged the fact that I'd been gone. Much less that I'd been abducted. The first time I'd seen him after my recovery, he'd literally shoved me into a simulator. We'd talked about nothing but training since then.

I took an experimental bite of the soup and, yeah, it was pretty good. It didn't hold a candle to Owa's brown stew, but I didn't bother bringing that up.

I nodded to Dahn, avoiding that piercing gaze coming from his soft gray eyes. I'd never understood how his eyes could be both of those things at once, being both piercing and soft. But they were.

He was quiet for a minute, and I got the impression that his brain was working very hard underneath that calm exterior. "What kinds of foods did you eat when you... were with them?"

Now I was just confused. He wanted to small-talk about my time with the Ferrymen? When we were twenty minutes out from landing on Europa for our first Culling? I internally shrugged. Maybe this was normal and I was just being a freak. Nothing had felt the same since I'd returned to the Station. Either the Ferrymen had changed me irrevocably, or the interro-gations had.

"Mostly peanut butter sandwiches. Sometimes soup. Tinned

meat. They made bread fresh on the ship. But mostly everything else was canned."

He nodded. I worked away at my soup and avoided his eyes. "Glade."

Slowly, I gave him my eyes. I'd never seen this look on his face before. He spoke low, as if he didn't want anyone else to hear. "I've got you down there." His eyes flicked to the window, where Europa had just come into view. I heard our skip's landing gears start to engage.

"I've got you," he repeated.

———

Every Culling in every place was different. There were cols that were so primitive that they didn't have power sources for Datapoints to plug into. We had to cull those cols remotely, which was significantly harder on us. That process could zap you of energy for months. Some Datapoints had even died in the last Culling.

I was very relieved that we weren't facing that on Europa. As soon as we'd landed, we'd been brought to the main hall of the small Europian colony. It was a little offshoot of the main city. A village almost, with just a few thousand people.

From the main hall, we'd have a view of the village and of its people. We didn't actually have to have each person in physical sight, but it helped us if we did. We could cull either way. Our integrated tech could see through walls, even distinguishing between two people standing in front of one another. It was very precise.

Dahn was extremely calm as he stood next to me and

plugged his tech into the power source. We could cull without it, but we'd be fools to pass up the extra power. If our tech wasn't getting the power from an external source, it pulled it straight from us.

I looked around the tower where we were setting up. It was a small room with a 360 view of the village around us. Europa had a synthetic atmosphere that turned the sky a pale gray. And parts of the colony had white sand while other parts had swirls of red sand. I looked out at the people standing somberly outside of their homes. They were dressed modestly. In thick, neutral-colored cloth to protect themselves from the cold nights and the hot sun in the day.

We were here to make their lives better.

"Glade." He nodded me back to my place beside him, where I, too, could plug in.

The role of a mentor and his pupil during a Culling was simple. We sorted and culled in waves. Our tech would talk between us and we'd work in tandem, sorting and Culling. When one of us was fatigued, the other would step in. We'd literally done it a hundred times in simulations over the last two months.

I cracked my knuckles before I plugged in and felt that familiar surge of energy race through my tech. Dahn cleared his throat beside me and I felt him there, standing, the heat coming off of his shoulder, almost pressed to mine. But I also felt his tech, as well, reaching out to mine. I could see with my eyes, with my own tech, and with Dahn's.

"Ready?" he asked. And I heard him with my ears and also through my tech.

"Yes."

I felt Dahn cast out his radar, searching for the heartbeats of each citizen. There were a few thousand to find, but between the two of us, it couldn't have been easier. I opened my mind's eye and there they were. Between Dahn and I, we had each pulsing heartbeat tracked in less than a minute.

I felt good. *This* felt good. It felt natural. Like I'd been born to do this. To stand with Dahn and help our society survive. Thrive.

I saw each citizen in my mind. And I arranged them. A long line. Now for the sorting. My tech zoomed in on each and every brain reading that I was getting. Mentally, the ones needing to be culled stepped forward. Not as many as I'd thought there might be. My mind pushed me into a bird's eye view. A thousand little red dots. The brain of each person. And in front, maybe a hundred people – standing forward, waiting to be culled.

"Not at once." He didn't bother with words. Dahn's tech spoke directly to mine. It startled me for a second. We'd never done that before. Spoken exclusively through our tech. His knuckles brushed the backs of mine and I stiffened. This was different from the simulations. *"No hurry."*

My eyes fluttered, but whether they were opened or closed I couldn't tell.

It didn't matter. He was right. I was arranging them to be culled with too many at once. It would fatigue us. We needed to do this in smaller groups.

I pulled forward just a smaller group of people. Twenty or so. When there were this few, I could see each of their brain patterns much clearer. And there was no question in my mind that they were all violently inclined. I thought, suddenly, with a vicious clarity, how wrong Kupier had been. This was not like he'd said it would be. This was not murder. This was Culling. I studied each of their brain patterns. There was no question that these were people who needed to be culled.

But the virus changes the images. It was a small voice in the back of my head, and I pushed it down.

I re-centered myself with that feeling of rightness. That feeling I'd had before. That Dahn and I were supposed to be here, together. Doing this. Together.

I pushed Kupier from my mind and concentrated on the group of twenty in my mind's eye. This was a dance, between the two of us. And I knew our next steps. I held those twenty in my mind. Held their brain patterns in place with such a tight hold, such rigorous precision, that there was no risk of making a mistake.

I held them. And Dahn culled them.

Their brainwaves simply blinked out of existence. There was just black where they'd glowed red.

Suddenly, something shook loose inside of me. If my heart had been a mountain made of stones, I would have felt a few of them shake free, tumbling down the side of the hill.

My eyes, my real ones, fluttered open, and I looked at the side of Dahn's face. His eyes were half open and I knew he wasn't seeing what was in front of him. He was watching exactly what his tech was showing him.

I felt a nudge at my tech and I realized he was focusing me. Damn. I was going off-track. He was already organizing the next group, and I nudged him away. I pulled forward thirty from the group this time. This way, we'd be halfway there. The thousand stood back in the line. Thirty stood forward. My mind circled each and every brain pattern, double-checking and holding them still.

Perfect. They were all perfect examples of citizens who needed to be culled. *Perfect.*

I held them still. Even while something inside of me trembled. Dahn culled. Their lights blinked out and I felt more stones stumble free, sliding down the mountain of my heart.

My palms started sweating and my vision tried to focus on the world around me. My feet in my shoes. The gray sky. Red dirt. The 360 view of the village.

"Glade."

I wasn't sure if he'd spoken out loud or through my tech. But he was calling me back. It wasn't unusual for a Datapoint to have to take a break during a Culling. But suddenly this didn't feel normal.

I felt like a dog on a leash. Dahn held the other end.

And he dragged me back in.

He'd lined up the next group. Just twenty of them. He'd already verified that they needed to be culled and my mind circled them again, just to check. He'd identified them. So it was up to me to cull them. I felt my tech tighten around each of their brain patterns. I held their lives in my hands as surely as if I'd held the string to a guillotine.

I imagined those red lights blinking into blackness. But they were still red. They were still red.

One stone tumbled down my heart.

And then another.

I held them in my mind.

Cull them, Glade. Cull them. This is natural. This is what you're here for. You and Dahn. This is what you've been training for. Cull them.

I pulled tight against their brain patterns. All I had to do was yank.

I released them from my hold. Their lights were still red. There was no blackness for them. All at once. And the relief of it had that mountain inside me tumbling all at once. My heart wasn't one thing inside of me. It was a thousand tiny stones, rolling out to every edge of me. Lost forever. My heart would never be put together again.

Dahn cursed beside me and I watched in detached horror as the citizens I'd released were culled.

I fell to my knees and tasted something. Blood in my mouth. Blood in the water. I wondered, insanely, if Dahn was coming for me like a shark after blood. He wasn't. He was still Culling. I knew, without having to confirm it, that he was sorting and Culling all of the rest of those we'd been assigned to at once. Doing all the jobs by himself. Because I couldn't.

It had been so natural, and I still couldn't do it. I thought of the horse. That black and glossy mane. The hooves pounding across the ground. There was no air in my lungs. I hadn't thought of that horse a single time since I'd come back to the Station.

Their lights were gone. I didn't let my tech sync back in to the Culling. To Dahn. But I knew it was over. I knew he'd done the whole thing by himself.

I've got you down there. I've got you.

Had he known?

I felt cold hands against my arm and I realized that I was still plugged into the power source. My arm was pulled up against the port and the rest of me was lying on the ground.

"It's over." That was Dahn's voice in my ears. Not through my tech. "But you have to get up. If you don't, they'll know something happened, Glade. Get up. Please."

It was the *please* that did it. In all my time knowing him, I'd never heard him say anything like that. Breathing deeply, still feeling like my heart had scattered to every edge of the solar system, I came up to my knees.

Dahn's hands were ice cold, but I let him drag me to my feet.

"It's over," he repeated. As if that made it better.

The next hour came in snapshots for me. I spoke to no one. And no one spoke to me. We'd been warned that although Datapoints were treated with reverence upon arrival for a Culling, they were often treated with fear, even hatred, during departure. Our case was no exception. Still, we had to exit the main hall and make our way back toward the landing dock where we could board our skip and head back out into space.

Dahn started to jog, and even though my teeth rattled with the movement, I followed suit. None of the citizens were outdoors. They'd all rushed back inside, the second the Culling had been over. Though, there was someone over there.... I craned my head to look back down one of the dusty streets and realized what I was looking at.

A pair of boots. Toes up. And arms spread-eagle. A mop of brown hair. Messy. Eyes open and unseeing. A body. One of the culled.

Black clicked over my eyes and I looked forward. I saw Dahn's back. And then a click of black. Dahn. Black. A home with a child peeking out the window. Black. Another body. This

202

one with a scarf over her hair and one hand over her heart. Black. Dahn.

"Dahn," I gasped.

He turned, and over his shoulder was another of the culled. A man who was sitting where he'd fallen, his body propped up by the wall behind him. His eyes were closed as if he were sleeping. But his legs were folded strangely beneath him.

Black.

Dahn's cold hands on my elbows. Dahn picking me up and tossing me over his shoulder.

Black.

———

Glade.

Dahn sat in his quarters on the skip that was currently skipping from one artificial blackhole to the next. As far as he knew, no one on the skip knew that anything had gone awry. Anyone who'd been overseeing the Culling from the Station would have seen Dahn take control, but they wouldn't necessarily have seen Glade's freak-out.

He wanted to go over to her room and check on her. Ask her what the hell had happened. But he knew that would draw attention from the crew. So, he sat on his tiny cot with his head back on the wall and called her through their tech again.

Glade.

They weren't trained to use their tech as intercoms to one another, except in battle situations. And he'd never intentionally invaded someone's personal space like this before. But sitting here, wondering and wondering, with no answers in sight? No. He couldn't take it.

Glade.

...What?

If Dahn had been someone who smiled, he might have smiled at the annoyed tone of her tech. It was just so her. And it sent a wave of relief through him. It meant that she hadn't been broken.

"Are you alright?" he wanted to ask her. But he didn't.

What happened?

...I don't know. It didn't feel like the simulations.

He paused. What the hell did that mean? The Culling had felt exactly the same as the simulations for him. In a way, it had been even easier. There'd been adrenaline. And not a hint of boredom.

They won't know. ... And I don't think we should tell them. He hadn't said the second part.

She was quiet for a long time. And then, finally: *...Don't worry. We'll keep your perfect record intact. I won't tell.*

He pulled back as if she'd slapped him. She thought that was why he didn't want to tell anyone about this?

Dahn sat and sat and didn't sleep. Sometime around the second day, when they were halfway home, he asked himself a question, finally. Would he still have stepped in for her if he'd known he would get caught?

He knew the answer immediately.

And he had absolutely no idea how to tell her.

CHAPTER FIFTEEN_

W e were back on the Station by the time Dahn and I spoke again. But to my surprise, it was through our tech.

Meet me in the simulation room in an hour. That was all he said before I watched him walk away toward his quarters.

Was this our new normal? Silent communication through our tech? I'd never heard of two Datapoints communicating this way. It was so... intimate. Strange and foreign and oddly sweet.

I stared after him, even after he'd disappeared down a hallway.

It had taken pretty much the full trip home for me to feel like myself again. At least physically. Emotionally, I had no idea what was going on. My heart still felt scattered to the winds. But it didn't make sense. Because I believed in the Culling. I truly did. I wasn't having second thoughts.

Even after seeing the bodies.

They'd been the bodies of violent, murderous people. And their communities were better off without them.

Kupier and the Ferrymen were wrong. I'd never been more certain of anything in my life. I was certain I'd have been able to sense a virus in my own tech.

So, why had it felt like murder?

I clamped down on the question like it was a snake I was trying to behead under a shovel. It had been sneaking into my brain every few minutes since the Culling and it was going to drive me insane. I had no answer for it. And I wanted to stop torturing myself. But I didn't know how. I didn't know the answer. I didn't know why the simulations felt so different from the actual Culling. I didn't know why Dahn was able to do it and I wasn't. I didn't know why I'd sensed something so, so different between the simulations and the Culling.

Unless the virus didn't affect the simulations, and it only affected the Culling... And what I sensed was the truth of things.

This thought was as snaky as the last. They'd chased one another's heads the entire way back from Europa. I hadn't had answers for either of them. I'd merely buried my head under my thin pillow and watched the stars lurch by out my port window.

Something wasn't right. And I didn't know what it was.

The only reason I thought that Kupier was right was because it was the only alternative explanation that I'd heard. There were probably tons of explanations for why I'd freaked out like that. The virus was just one of many. And I needed to stop torturing myself with it. I believed in the Culling. I believed in Din Io's teachings.

I cleared my throat as I watched Dahn walk off.

I believed in the Authority.

Dahn was right. I needed more training. The simulation room was exactly where I needed to be.

I jogged back to my bunk, ignoring the looks of the crew and the other Datapoints. Either they were still looking at me this way because of my time with the Ferrymen, or because I'd just gotten back from a Culling. Either way, I didn't care. I slammed into my bunk and tossed my bag down, quickly changing into a clean set of training clothes.

If I hurried, I'd have a chance to get something to eat in the dining hall before I had to meet Dahn.

I skidded into the dining hall, tossing food into the metal bowls everyone used, and scanned the area. Ignoring yet more looks, I spotted Cast sitting on his own and jogged over.

"Hey," I muttered as I sat down, already jamming some food into my mouth.

He jumped when he realized who I was and coughed around something in his mouth. "Oh. Hey. I didn't realize you were back."

"Just a few minutes ago."

Cast nodded, but I noticed the back of his neck going red, his eyes scanning around the room.

"You looking for someone?" I studied him.

"No." He immediately dropped his eyes to his food.

"Cast."

He didn't look up.

"Cast, what's going on?"

He cleared his throat. "She's just jealous that you and Dahn got selected for a Culling."

"Who?" My brows knit together in confusion.

He waited a beat, as if he didn't even want to speak the name. "Sullia."

My stomach dropped. Because Sullia and I hadn't so much as spoken to one another since we'd made it back to the Station two months ago. Which was fine by me. But that also meant that I had no idea what she'd told the tactical team. Our stories must have jibed enough, I'd figured, or else we wouldn't have both been alive. But I didn't like someone like Sullia with so much potential power over me.

I hardened my expression and Cast flinched away from me. "What did she do?"

"She's... just talking."

"Cast."

Finally, he looked up at me.

"Tell me what she's saying."

Cast dropped his head back and studied the ceiling for a second before throwing down his fork and turning to face me on the bench seat. "Fine. But don't kill the messenger."

"Duh."

"She says that you weren't loyal to the Authority while you two were with the Ferrymen. That they got to you. And that you're here as a spy."

I couldn't help but laugh. "Yeah. Well, I've got about three days' worth of interrogations under my belt that prove she's wrong." I took a bite of my food. "She's just trying to freak people out about the Ferrymen. Make them seem bigger and badder than they are. You know, that they're so bad, they even got me to switch sides. But that she withstood all that pressure. She wants to build herself up."

Cast nodded, but his eyes were on his food again. "That's – ah – just not what she's saying."

I waited, unwilling to prod him any further. This reticence thing he had going on was starting to get on my nerves.

He sighed again, like he really didn't want to do what he was about to do. This time, he kept his eyes on his food even as he spoke. "She says that you switched sides because one of the Ferrymen seduced you. That you two were sleeping together, and now you'll do anything for him."

Cast's cheeks got redder and his voice got quieter the more he spoke. I kind of felt bad for the kid. Or at least I would have if it hadn't been for the fact that my blood was boiling so hot that I felt like I could have breathed fire.

"Are. You. Kidding. Me?"

Cast must have sensed that it was a rhetorical question because he didn't answer.

I wasn't insulted at the idea that Kupier and I might have slept together. We hadn't. Not even close. But if we had, it wouldn't have been anyone's business. Least of all Sullia's. What upset me the most was the implication that I would bend over backwards, completely changing my alliances and my beliefs, all because I'd slept with someone.

But most of all, I was pissed off because rumors like this could get me sent straight back to interrogation. I shivered. I didn't think I'd survive another session like the one I'd gone through when I'd come back to the Station.

And, what was worse? I'd admitted to liking Kupier. My credibility to say that I hadn't slept with him was shot. At this point, if the rumor made it to Haven, he'd likely think I'd lied to him.

When I hadn't.

I was shaking as I rose up from my seat.

"Glade," Cast spoke very slowly. "Where are you going?"

"To kick Sullia's ass."

"Okay, no. Wait!" he called after me, and I heard his bowl clatter to the floor. "Let's just think about this! Let's go find Dahn real quick! He'll know what to do."

My blood went to ice as I strode through one hallway and then the next. She was usually in the sparring chamber this time of night. I knew I'd find her there.

Dahn was the last person I wanted to turn to right now. I thought of his voice in my head. His face, the last thing I'd seen before I'd blacked out. I thought of the brush of his knuckles against mine.

Yeah. I really, really didn't want to mix Dahn up in these rumors. He was the only person in this entire Station who didn't doubt me. He'd stood by me.

I've got you.

I couldn't lose Dahn, my credibility, and get tossed back into interrogation all because Sullia had added one more bit of subterfuge into whatever grand plan she was concocting.

I tossed my hair back over my shoulders as I stepped into the doorway of the sparring chamber. There. Finally. I thought of the horse. Proud and unstoppable.

"Sullia!" My voice rang out, and everyone who'd been sparring, ten or twelve Datapoints, turned to look at me. And then back to Sullia. And then back to me.

Clearly, they'd heard the rumors.

Sullia whipped around as if she'd been expecting me. And hell, maybe she had.

"What?" she snapped, adjusting the tape around her knuckles.

I stalked toward her. "I heard you might have some questions you wanted to ask me."

She'd looked as bad as I had when we'd returned from the Ferrymen, but two months back at the Station and she'd retained her natural glow. I noticed the streaks in her hair were dyed a deep pink now. It suited her. She looked like a queen, standing there, gorgeous and furious and in a fighting stance. For one horrible second, I wondered whether or not she would have stumbled during the Culling the way I had.

I pushed the thought aside. It didn't matter. She hadn't been chosen for the Culling. Dahn and I had been. And that was exactly why she was spreading rumors about me right now. She was jealous as hell. With nowhere to put the emotion.

Sullia scoffed. But she wasn't foolish enough to turn her back on me. "I have absolutely nothing to say to you."

"Funny." I took another step toward her. I could have reached out and touched her. "Because it seems like you have a lot to say *about* me."

Something flickered in her eyes, but it was gone too fast for me to interpret it. "The truth hurts, doesn't it?"

I scowled at her sickly-sweet tone. Even now, straight to my face, she was going to pretend like she wasn't lying.

I heard the telltale sounds of people gathering in the doorway behind me and I also heard a familiar 'Glade!', but I ignored it all.

"I'm confused. Are you trying to get me sent back to interrogation because you're threatened by how much better a Datapoint I am, or just because you're a sadistic psycho?"

That same thing flashed again in her eyes. She smirked. "You might have everyone fooled, Glade, including the Ferrymen. But you can't fool me. I know what you did." Her eyes landed on someone behind me and then came back to me. There was a knowing smirk on her face. "I know you slept with him. I know where your REAL loyalties lie."

People gasped and whispered behind me, and I continued to ignore it. "Sullia. I don't care what you say about me and Kupier. Who cares? But you wanna talk about loyalties? When all you did was suck up to the Ferrymen every chance you got? When all you cared about was avoiding any sort of pain or confrontation? When you're the one who passed up the chance to escape?"

That last part was the part that did it. I saw something behind her beautiful face snap. She was embarrassed that she hadn't tried to escape with me and Cast. She hadn't wanted people to know. And I'd just screamed it out in a gym filled to the brim with people.

I blocked the punch she sent jetting straight toward my face. And the next. And the next. The fourth caught me by surprise, right under the ribs, and I doubled over. Not before I kicked her knee out from under her, though. Sullia went down hard and I heard something crack against the mat.

A stabbing pain in my calf from her claw-like hand had me howling and kicking her hard in the ribs. Her face was a mask of rage as she rolled away from me.

I thought of the horse as she charged me, and my roll away from her was graceful and natural. I parried each of the combinations she sent my way. She was fast, but so was I. Let her tire herself out.

She got in two blows to my cheek and I got a good one in on her body before she fell to the floor on all fours, panting. I wondered, for a brief second, if she was done.

And then it hit me. The pain behind my eyes. White hot and blinding. Immediately, I matched her stance on the ground. I smashed my teeth together and screamed against the agony.

I heard her in my head. Almost laughing in pleasure. She was using her tech against me. She was – Jesus – she was trying to cull me. *Right now.* My brain held on, unwilling to be ripped from its socket, and I used my tech to smash her backwards.

The blow was mental, but she reacted physically. Flying backwards and holding the tech that sat over one side of her forehead. Infuriated, shaking from the pain, I pushed again, this time harder.

Sullia screamed, both inside of my head and in my ears. For a moment, her fingers dug into the tech on her forehead. I watched with sick fascination as she looked almost like she was about to tear it out of herself.

I pulled my tech back from hers because Sullia looked insane, and I had no idea what she was about to do next. But she didn't waste a second.

She was suddenly on me, knocking me to the ground and slamming one hand around my throat. I grabbed her throat right back and she gasped, the sound being my only warning before her tech was back and the pain became unbearable. I knew I wasn't breathing but I didn't care. I could only care about getting this horrible pain to stop.

I wasn't sure if she was trying to cull me or if she was attempting to fry my integrated tech, but either way, it felt like she was ripping my sanity away from me, pulse by pulse. My arms jolted when I didn't tell them to. My thoughts twisted with something dark. Something horrible and void. I tried to yank back, to get control of my tech, but her fingers squeezed down around my throat and things went spotty. The pain was growing in my head and that horrible, dark blankness was twisting with my consciousness again. I couldn't hear my own tech over it. Something was slicing into my brain like a knife. Something was tearing me open from the inside out.

I didn't have the energy or the power to attack her back. Things were getting fuzzy and blank. I couldn't even feel her fingers at my neck anymore. I was melting into nothing. This was how it happened.

And then I felt it. A nudge in my brain. Not evil. Not harsh. Not harmful. Just a nudge.

Come on, Glade. You can do better than this.

It was Dahn. In my thoughts. I felt the familiar bunching power of his tech. It was how he mentally stretched himself before a Culling simulation. And then I was stretching out with my tech toward Sullia, mixing my tech with hers. Dahn nudged me again, gathering my strength for me. The way I never could have done on my own. I slammed a wave of tech into Sullia and she howled, her hands leaving my throat and gripping her head-piece again.

Well. It felt so good that I did it again. Sullia rolled away from me while I coughed my breath back. I could still feel Dahn inside of my head. And that felt good, too.

Again. I'd asked it of him.

And one more time, the two of us together, both of our powers combined, slammed our tech against Sullia's. This time, she didn't howl. She didn't scratch at herself. She simply fell backwards. She was still and inert on the ground. The thinnest line of smoke curled up from the edge of the tech in her forehead.

———

I walked through the streets of Europa that night. In my dreams. The streets were empty. Not even Dahn was there. But the bodies were there. The sky was the deep navy that it was on Io. I could hear a volcano erupting in the distance, the way it did every day on Io. Wait, was this Io or Europa? I couldn't tell. It didn't matter. Because everyone was dead anyways.

I saw the man with the boots lying in the street. But look! He wasn't dead. He was rising up. He was smiling and laughing and asking me to come over to him. He wasn't a stranger after all. He was Kupier.

Kupier laughed and put his hands on my shoulders the way he always had. "DP-1, what did you do?" he asked me, and that was when he stopped laughing. "You killed them all."

"Not all of them," I said, lifting my hands in the air. "I didn't kill you."

"Yeah," he smiled, so sad. "You did."

I woke up with a start, sitting straight up in my bunk. I jumped again when I realized there was someone sitting on the edge of my bed. My tech told me who it was immediately. Dahn Enceladus, the reading said. Heart rate elevated. Unarmed.

"Dahn?" I whispered. "What is it?"

She's alright. He replied in my head. *Sullia. They just released her from the infirmary.*

I tucked my knees up to my chin.

Oh. I paused. I really didn't want to ask what I was about to ask. *We had to do that, right? We didn't have a choice?*

Dahn turned and looked at me, and in the dark room, everything was as gray as his eyes. *Do Datapoints ever have a choice?*

I shrugged. It was a good point. *What's going to happen to her?*

He paused, an uncharacteristically undecided look on his face. His shoulders fell an inch. *She's going to be confined for a while. For attacking another Datapoint. And for spreading treasonous rumors. But she'll have to go back into interrogations first. That's where she is right now, I think.*

I closed my eyes. Closed out everything but the feel of breath in my lungs. She'd had to go back to interrogations. God. I'd wanted to defend myself while she was attacking me. Hell, I'd wanted to do more than defend myself. But back to interrogations? I wouldn't have wished that on my worst enemy.

Hasn't she already proven she can be trusted?

Dahn shrugged. *She's a Datapoint who has recently been in Ferrymen custody who has attacked another Datapoint. It's suspicious, Glade.*

You could say the exact same thing about me.

You were defending yourself.

I sighed and dropped my head.

You won't have to see her anymore. Even when she gets out. His voice was soft in my head.

You mean they'll keep her away from me?

He nodded. *You're too important.*

I could feel his eyes on my face, but I didn't have it in me to turn back to him. *Glade.* He started and then stopped. *Is any of it true?*

216

I felt a tightness in my chest. *You mean what Sullia said about me? You want to know if she was telling the truth about any of it?*

He nodded, but his back was to me. He was looking at the opposite wall.

My loyalty is with the Authority. If that's what you're asking.

He nodded again. And this time he rose. I could just see his bulky outline in the dark room. He spoke the next words out loud, half facing me, as if they were too brutal to be spoken in our heads.

"Did you love one of them? Was she right about that part?"

I stared up at Dahn, shocked that he would ask me. Shocked that he didn't already know the answer. "Datapoints don't love, Dahn. That's why we get chosen to be Datapoints."

I think he looked down at me then, but it was so dark I couldn't be sure. "Right," he said. He took a step back and repeated, "Right."

———

The next morning, for the first time in my life, I was knocking on Haven's office door. It felt like a lifetime had passed since I'd last been in there. And I'd never before come willingly.

I entered when he called out, and I watched as surprise lanced over his face.

"Glade Io, what a pleasant surprise. Although, perhaps it shouldn't be so much of a surprise?"

"I'm sorry?" I sat in that same blue armchair as before and he sat in his.

He waved his hand. "Many Datapoints come to see me after their first Culling. Lots of questions come up. It's not unusual." His silver eyes followed the small movements of my hands and I stopped moving them. "I assume that's why you're here."

I nodded. Close enough. I was here for answers. "I've been syncing with the Authority Database. Like you told me to. I haven't been fighting it."

"I've noticed." He nodded. "And have you noticed how much easier the simulations have been for you?" He lifted a wry, smug eyebrow.

I resisted the temptation to lift one back. Instead, I chose my words carefully. "They definitely move more smoothly. And faster."

"And you're able to cull so many at once," he supplied.

I nodded.

"Something is wrong?" he asked, his silver eyes watching me so closely that I almost fidgeted. But I didn't.

I nodded again. I took a deep breath before I took the plunge and asked, though. I'd been around and around with myself. This was the only way that I could get the information I needed. I had to bring it up. "The Culling felt different from the simulations."

"Naturally," he said, crossing his legs and leaning his chin on one hand. "The same as the difference between a flight simulator and piloting a skip."

"Right," I agreed, watching his face carefully. "But this didn't feel like that. It almost felt like I was running a different program through my tech." Here went nothing. "I'm just curious, is the Culling identification program that we run on the sims the same as the one we run for the actual Culling?"

His eyes narrowed, just the tiniest smidgen, and nausea crept up from my stomach. "Yes, of course. They're exactly the same. I should know. I coded them myself."

The nausea doubled. I replayed that tiny narrowing of his eyes. He didn't want me to ask about the programming as I had. He hadn't liked it. And he'd admitted to writing the Culling program himself.

I cleared my throat again. "Then why did they feel so different?"

He turned away from me and, when he turned back, his eyes were narrowed again, but only for a moment.

"Perhaps you should consider the fact that you aren't a computer, Glade."

Ah. Yes. His answer for everything.

"You think that I was the difference between the simulation and the Culling?"

He nodded. "The programs felt different because you felt different. Datapoints are as close to emotionless as people come. But still, you must have felt something. Excitement? Ambition? Eagerness?"

His guesses at my emotions made the nausea curl and twist in my stomach. I said nothing, and he continued on. "It's hard to say. But there's a reason we cull with people and not computers."

"Why?"

"We cull *with* people, Datapoints, because it's *people* who we're Culling. We're not pulling the plug on a set of desktops. We're Culling people. Bad people, sure. But people. It's not embarrassing that you should feel some of the weight of that."

His words shocked and stabbed at me. He was admitting that I might feel a certain way about Culling. That, in some ways, it was the forced taking of human life. His eyes seemed more metallic than ever before, and I wondered, for a second, if he could somehow read my tech right now, even if he didn't have any himself.

"I was hoping, since I've been doing so much better, I could have a look at the Authority Database." I paused. "Like I asked before. I think it'll help me with my next Culling. If I understand—"

"Glade." Disappointment was so clear in his voice that I found an apology on the tip of my tongue before I could swallow it down. "I tire of telling you no. Never have I and never will I allow a Datapoint to dig around in a Database that holds the fate of thousands of lives in its motherboard. Any tiny mistake you made could throw off its programming! There's no chance I would risk innocent lives by letting you 'have a look at it.'"

I found I couldn't look at him.

"Besides," he continued, "since you're so curious, I'm shocked that you haven't spoken to your mentor about it."

"Dahn?"

Haven nodded. "He's the most knowledgeable Datapoint that we have, when it comes to the Authority Database."

My mind went blank for a second. "You're kidding me."

"Not in the least." His expression was startlingly serious. "Not every Datapoint resisted the Database from day one, Glade. Some of them, like Dahn Enceladus, accepted it immediately. He's been syncing with and working alongside the Database for years. He understands it in its entirety. Didn't you wonder why we paired the two of you together? A Datapoint who excelled with the program? And one who did not?"

220

I left his office just moments later, my head spinning. This entire time, Dahn has been an expert on the Database, and I'd been wasting my time sending puzzle games back and forth with him? I could have had the answers to my questions years ago.

I'd started to jog down the hallway toward his quarters when it hit me. What was I going to do? March into his room and ask him every question I had about the Database? He was going to know that I didn't trust it. I thought back on the questions he'd asked me the night before. He was worried about my alliances. There was no way he was going to answer outright questions. It would throw off every alarm bell he had. Best case scenario, he'd completely shut down on me. Worst case scenario, he'd turn me in to Haven and the tactical team for more interrogations. He was going to think that I was asking on behalf of the Ferrymen. Or worse, for a single Ferryman. One who everyone thought I was in love with.

I slowed and took a minute to look out one of the port windows. If I couldn't outright ask him, then how was I going to manage to get this information?

I needed it. I needed it from Haven or Dahn.

Because those snakes were still circling one another's tails in my head. Why had the Culling felt like murder? And why had the simulation felt so different from the Culling?

The thought struck me then, and I almost groaned in exhaustion from just the idea of it. There was a way to prove my loyalty to the Authority and to learn more from the Authority Database at the same time.

The same way that Dahn had done it.

By being the most efficient, statistically perfect machine of a

Datapoint of all time. He'd learned about the Authority Database through countless syncings. Through dedication. Through immaculate practice.

If I was excelling in the program, proving my dedication, then no one would question my ambition to learn more about the Database. It was only while I was resisting it that my questions would seem suspicious.

I cracked my knuckles as I turned away from the port window. If a perfect Datapoint was what they needed, then a perfect Datapoint was what they were gonna get.

CHAPTER SIXTEEN_

Jan Ernst Haven frowned as he watched the remote simulation screen. Through it, he could see all of what the participant saw. He could see the participant's vital signs. He could see the interface between the integrated tech and the Authority Database. He could see the effectiveness of the participant's sorting efforts. And he could see the speed and efficacy of their Culling, also.

What he was looking at both pleased and puzzled him. Glade Io was, once again, excelling. In the two months since she'd come to his office, she'd pulled firmly out of the middle of the pack. She was now the only Datapoint in training who could sort and cull over a thousand people in less than five minutes with one hundred percent accuracy.

She was interfacing with the Database with the same ease and trust with which she interfaced with her own tech. *And* she was listening to every bit of coaching her mentor was providing her.

It pleased Jan Ernst Haven because he'd suspected, from the first moment he'd seen her more than a decade ago, that she had these capabilities. It puzzled him because he didn't understand why she was suddenly pushing herself.

He'd seen her in the sparring chamber well after her comrades had gone to bed. He'd seen her taking apart one of the simulators and reassembling it – all within eight hours. He'd seen her studying with Dahn. Always with Dahn. The two of them with their heads together, studying the history of the Culling. Each and every one that had taken place. The parts that were hard for the Datapoints, the parts that were easy.

Haven wondered at this. Was she simply reaching her full potential? Was she scared that her sisters would become Data-points? Or did she, like so many others, simply believe in the Culling?

A message beeped on the bottom of the screen that Haven was currently watching. Another member of the Authority was contacting him. Yet another transport skip had been attacked. This one contained some new integrated tech prototypes that he'd been hoping to try out on the newest round of incoming Datapoints.

Nothing had been stolen, but the skip was badly injured. It was Ferrymen who'd done it.

Haven frowned. The Ferrymen. They were like the pigeons he'd seen videos of. So beautiful in the sky, so disgusting up close.

He could respect their determination. In fact, it was some-thing he wished more of his Datapoints had. But he got tired of swatting at them. The way a man in a lounge chair grew tired of swatting at a fly.

They'd tried to take his greatest accomplishment from him. And the worst part was that it had been seemingly random! They could have taken any Datapoint they'd put their grubby hands on. But it had been Glade Io who'd been whisked away.

Glade Io who'd been compromised.

And now it was Glade Io who was excelling in the program. Haven narrowed his eyes for a moment before casting the monitor aside.

It wasn't worth worrying over now. Things like this always revealed themselves in due time. The fly had to land at some point. It was in its nature.

And he would be ready.

———

"Dahn!"

He almost stopped walking when he heard her call his name. But he didn't. He couldn't. Not right this second.

"Dahn!"

She was getting closer to him. He could hear her footsteps behind him. And there. Her hand was on his shoulder, as warm and firm as ever.

Dahn.

This time she spoke in his head, and he cursed himself for ever starting that with her. At the time, he'd realized that it was the only way he was ever going to get into Glade Io's head. The only way he'd ever potentially solve the puzzle that she was.

But now, she was so comfortable using the same trick right back at him. Speaking through their tech to one another. It was like whispering in one another's ear. And it sent shivers down his back every single time she did it.

"Not now, Glade." He'd spoken out loud on purpose, trying to give her a hint.

"I came out of the simulator and you weren't there." Her brow furrowed and that serious mouth of hers got even more serious as she strode alongside him. Going wherever he was going. "Did I do something wrong?"

Dahn pulled up short for a second and looked down at her – that dark spill of hair, her dark eyes, that fierce expression she was always wearing these days.

"I'm bad at two things today," he muttered, half to himself.

"What? Dahn. You're good at everything and you know it."

He yanked one of her hands off her hip and pulled her into one of the exterior battle rooms. Datapoints were allowed to be inside them because the idea was for them to be comfortable with the spaces when it was time to go into battle. But right now, all Dahn cared about was the view.

He eased himself down into one of the reclining battle chairs and let his eyes wander out the window. He knew that if the window were bigger, he'd be able to see Mars. Like a red marble in the sky.

Dahn looked sideways and found Glade's eyes on the side of his face. She stared at him, waiting for an answer or an explanation. He hated when she did that. Considering that she never provided answers or explanations to him.

"What did you mean, that you were bad at two things?" she demanded.

He sighed. "I meant that I was a bad mentor for leaving you without an explanation. And that..." he almost couldn't say more. "I have to get used to not being the best Datapoint anymore."

Glade pulled back from him, her eyes narrowed, but he thought she looked surprised more than anything. "You think I'm better than you?"

Dahn let out a sharp puff of air. "Glade, you just sorted and culled two thousand citizens in fifteen minutes. Your vitals barely rose. You had one hundred percent accuracy. And it was your first time doing it. Yeah. I'd say you're better than I am."

She frowned at him for a minute. "I'm not, you know. Better than you."

He didn't dignify that with a response.

"I'm not!" she insisted, rising up from her chair to come sit on the arm of his. She blocked his view out the window. "I might have had some luck with Culling, but I have nowhere near the understanding of the Authority Database that you do. I'll never be as good until I do."

He frowned at her. "Everyone has their own style, their own path, their own way to cull. Mine is to lean hard via the Database. Yours is different. It doesn't matter how well you know the Database. The point is how well you cull. And you cull better than any Datapoint in history."

She frowned right back at him. "You really think the whole point is how well you cull? That's why you're doing all this? All your late nights in the simulator? Every conversation with Sir Haven? The years of pushing yourself to the brink? It's all because you believe so much in the Culling?"

She tossed her hair back at the end of her question, in that way that she always did. The way that reminded him of the horse they'd seen on video once. That horse had been beyond compare. He'd never seen anything like it before. Powerful, demanding, utterly unreachable. When he'd told Glade that she'd reminded him of the horse, she'd thought he'd only meant the hair toss. He hadn't.

One section of her hair remained in front of her and, without thinking, Dahn reached up and grabbed hold of the ends of it. *Like a paintbrush*, he thought, dragging it over the tips of his fingers.

No. Like a human's hair. She gripped it right back, tugging her hair out of his hand and tossing it over her shoulder.

He almost blushed. He hadn't realized that he'd pushed that thought toward her tech. He'd thought it was private. And that was what did it. What made him really tell her. He realized that, if they were sharing thoughts these days, well, it was only a matter of time until he slipped and she found out anyway. He might as well tell her voluntarily.

"I want to be a member of the Authority."

She rearranged herself, pulling herself halfway onto his chair so that her knee jammed into his outer leg. He found he didn't mind. She rested her chin on one hand and watched him.

"But all the spots are filled."

"For now," he nodded. "But three of the seven members are older. They'll not want to do it forever. They pick who is next, you know."

A light turned on behind Glade's eyes, as if she were finally understanding all the time that Dahn had spent with Haven over the years.

"Do you think they'd pick a Datapoint? I've never heard of a Datapoint on the Authority before."

"It's been done before, actually. Rand Europa – he was on the

Authority before Sir Haven was, and he was a Datapoint. And one other. Sita Enceladus. She wasn't on the Authority long before she died. But she'd gone completely through the Datapoint training."

Glade nodded. She'd obviously heard their names before. "You think they would choose someone so young?"

Dahn shrugged. There was his real fear. That he was running out of time in the wrong direction. That any new spots on the Authority would be filled before him simply because he wasn't old enough. "I don't know. Even if I were appointed in the next decade, I'd still be the youngest in history, besides Sir Haven." His gray eyes held hers. "I thought I'd have a better chance if I were the most effective Datapoint of all time. But. That's over now."

He leaned forward and dug his hands into his eyes for a second. "I just need a new strategy is all."

He could have sworn he felt something brush over the hair at the back of his head then, but when he looked up, Glade was sitting just the way she'd been a minute ago.

"Why is it so important? To be on the Authority? It seems like such a strange job. All work. All law. You won't even be able to live in your home colony."

No one knew where most of the Authority lived. There were seven members at all times and Haven was the only one who was known to stay anywhere in particular. The Station. The rest of them had highly secretive lives. For security reasons.

Dahn shifted, and the movement made Glade slide further into the seat. He'd never been so close to her before. Except when they were sparring, of course. But for some reason this felt different. Her listening so hard to him. Facing him. That knee of hers pressing against his leg. He could still feel the paintbrush of her hair. And maybe that's why he told her.

"I want to be in control of my life. I can't – I won't be at the whim of others more powerful than I am. Not for my whole life." His eyes grew distant as he looked past her and out the window again. He wished the damn window were bigger. "I was brought to the Station at a very young age. Did you know that? I didn't officially start training then. But I was first brought here, first met Sir Haven, when I was nine."

Glade's eyebrows shot up her forehead. "Most don't come until they're thirteen."

He nodded.

"Did you live here?"

"No. I just came here to meet Sir Haven. I traveled with him during the Culling. I – I'm still not sure why. I think he was testing me, trying to figure out if I could be a certain kind of Datapoint."

"But doesn't the testing do that?"

"Of course. But I think he was looking for something... even more than just that. I'm not sure." He didn't look at her. And he didn't tell her that he'd seen her. All those years ago. He'd seen her the day her father had been culled. He didn't tell her that, even then, he'd known that it was Glade who Haven was really looking for. Even then, he'd already been replaced by her in Haven's mind. "After the Culling was over, I went back to live with my grandparents. Until it was time for my training to start at thirteen."

Her dark brow furrowed now. "I didn't realize that you lived with your grandparents."

Now he did look at her. "You knew that my father was killed."

"By Ferrymen."

"By Luce. He was their leader for a time. The older brother of the one who leads them now. He was a Datapoint. My father, that is."

Glade sat as still as a layer of ice over a lake. She didn't speak for a long time, and Dahn wondered if this was where it ended, the longest conversation they'd ever had. It was strange to be so personal with someone. Thrilling and horrifying all at once. The same feeling as removing a long, deep splinter. Half of you wants to rip it out and the other half desperately wants to leave it in.

And your mother?

Dahn made sure not to wince. "Gone. She left me with my father's parents shortly after my father was killed. I've never seen or heard from her since."

He'd said it casually. As if it were something he'd talked about many times before. As if it didn't feel like swallowing razors to say the words out loud. He was strangely proud of himself for hiding his pain so well.

"No wonder you want to have ultimate control over your life." Glade's chin had found its way to her folded-up knee.

Dahn pulled back from her. Her words had scraped him clean like a knife over a stubbled cheek. He suddenly felt raw and exposed. Too tender for even her gaze to touch him. She watched him even now, with intense scrutiny. There wasn't malice in her eyes, or calculation. But there wasn't kindness either. Rather, it was understanding that he saw. As if she finally understood something she'd been trying to work out for years.

231

How could he have been so stupid? To tell someone all these things he should have never spoken aloud?

He was about to shove himself up from the chair, away from this room, away from Glade, when she reached out to him. He froze when her hands met his shoulders. Datapoints rarely touched. And she looked mildly unsure, as if this were the first time she was ever touching someone like this. Like she was copying a move she'd seen someone else make before.

"You know, Dahn. I'm not the best. Think about the Culling. I couldn't even stay conscious during that. I would have completely failed that test if it weren't for you. You were the only reason we survived that. Hell. You probably kept me out of another round of interrogations. So, no matter what I just did in the simulator, I'm not the best. *We're* the best. We're a team. Mentor and mentee. I would never have gotten this far without you, okay?"

He searched her eyes. He felt like she was trying to tell him two things at once. "I guess you're right."

She squeezed his shoulders in her hands, and for one tense second, he wondered if she was going to hug him. And then he wondered if he would hug her back.

But she simply released him, clapping those slender hands in front of her. "Okay. I say we get something to eat and then we go back to the simulation room. Only, this time? You're in there, okay? And I'm gonna watch your process with the Database and I'm gonna learn from you, okay?"

He nodded, a little mystified by her sudden energy. He felt completely rung out. Vulnerable. Exposed. And a little on edge. He could feel where she'd touched him on his shoulders, too. It burned.

CHAPTER SEVENTEEN_

I felt a weight at the end of my bed and, when I opened my eyes, I wasn't surprised to see that it was Kupier. He visited me a lot these days.

As usual, he made himself comfortable, stretching himself out beside me with one hand behind his head.

"You're the best, huh?" he asked me.

I nodded. "I have to know the truth. This is the only way."

"I told you the truth, Glade. You know I told you the truth."

"I don't know anything anymore. Why would I trust you, Kupier? You only wanted one thing, for me to help the Ferrymen bring down the Authority. You would have said or done anything to get me to trust you."

Kupier laughed. The way he always did. "You're funny, Glade. So smart and so dumb at the same time."

He held up one hand and there was his marble. Blue and dark all at once. Such a different shade than the slice of his eyes I could see. He held the marble up in the air, and when he took his hand away, it floated there before us. We both watched it as it expanded out from a marble and into a blue sort of cloud. It pulsed into a shape that I recognized. That had been burned into my brain. It was in the shape of the brainwaves of a person who needed to be culled. I tried. I reached out with my tech and tried to cull it. Over and over again, I tried.

And when I woke up, for real this time, I was alone. As always.

———

I also wasn't surprised when Haven came to me. It had been a long time since our conversation in his office. Truth be told, I'd lost track of time. It held no meaning for me anymore. The only thing that meant anything was practice. Success. Understanding.

I'd learned a lot about the Authority Database. With each simulated Culling and each syncing and there had been hundreds in the last month – I'd learned more. I was under-standing the culling program as a user. Every in and out. Every refiling of information it had to do, every hesitation. I wanted nothing more than to understand the program as a coder. But I'd take what I could get.

Throwing myself into excelling as a Datapoint had vastly changed my life on the Station. I barely saw Cast anymore. And Sullia had been moved to a different wing so that we wouldn't run into one another. We rarely did. But things were mostly different with Dahn.

I knew it both pained and thrilled him when I slashed through his records one by one. I wasn't *trying* to beat him. But the success was a side effect of my attempting to learn the Database. It annoyed me that everything I'd ever want to know about the Database was right there, inside his head, but I couldn't get to it.

He'd get suspicious, the more questions I asked about it. He'd already told me that the Database wasn't the point. Culling was the point.

Humans weren't computers. I couldn't code the answers out of him. So I kept going the only way I knew how. I interfaced with the Database every chance I got. Searching for any sign of a virus.

When I'd stepped out of my bunk that morning, Haven had been waiting for me. Hands clasped behind his back, his silvery hair almost transparent underneath the florescent lights.

Having mostly expected him to show up like this, at some point, didn't mean that I wasn't incredibly nervous. Either he was here because he was impressed with how much I'd improved, or he was here because he knew I was trying to puzzle out the Database from the outside in. One of those options sent me straight back to interrogations. Or to the executioner.

Suddenly, fifty / fifty odds didn't look so good.

I swallowed my words and my doubts as I followed him down the hall toward his quarters. Half of me wanted to ask if my mentor should be present for whatever we were going to discuss. I wanted Dahn's steely presence next to me. Steady. Reliable. But the other half of me wanted Dahn as far away from this as possible. He'd done nothing wrong. I would never want him to be connected to this.

"Well," Haven crooned when the second the door was closed behind us. "I won't leave you in suspense any longer, Datapoint.

I've been extremely pleased with your progress over the last few months."

My knees buckled, but it only appeared that I was sinking into the blue armchair. "Ah. I'm pleased that you're pleased. Sir."

He nodded, crossing his legs. "I always knew that we'd have to deal with questions from you. Questions that other Datapoints push aside in order to do their jobs. You've struggled with that, in the past."

"You – you mean my questions about the Database?"

"Among others. You remember that I told you I was there? The day your father was culled? I saw you. Observed you."

My mind skittered around like bare feet on unexpected ice. Haven had been there in my colony on the day of the Culling. Right. Hadn't Dahn said that he'd traveled with Haven during the last Culling? Had Dahn been there, as well?

"You had questions then. Even as a child of six. You didn't accept the Culling. Even as every citizen who remained did. Your mother told you to stop questioning it. I imagine she was fearful of you one day being culled. Especially considering your resemblance to your father."

Murderous.

Rogue.

I bit my tongue.

"She must have been so relieved when you tested into the Datapoint program," Haven mused. "It meant that you'd never be culled."

Relieved? My mother had wept for me. Becoming a Datapoint, torn from my home, put through the training, and learning to cull? It had been a fate almost worse than death to my mother. *Hide in plain sight. They can't find you if they can't see you.* She'd have been horrified to learn about my current strategy of standing out.

Again, I bit my tongue.

"Glade," Haven said as he came to stand up. "You must have noticed the Authority's interest in you. Even when you were a subpar Datapoint, we still had high hopes. You still had our attentions."

I nodded. I'd more than noticed it. I'd resented it.

He wandered over to the large blank screen that sat on one of his walls. It was black, yet he looked at it as if he were gazing out a window. "It's time to tell you what we've been watching for in you. What we've finally seen proof of over the last months."

He turned. "The Culling is a pillar on which our society stands. It keeps our citizens safe, it keeps our government strong, and above all, it is a tool for peace."

My time in the historical archives on Charon zipped through my head then, and I was infinitely grateful that Haven couldn't read my thoughts. Because I realized now that he could have said these exact same things – safe citizens, strong government, tool for peace – if he'd been talking about a completely different Culling program. One that culled the rogues and not just the violent.

I swallowed hard. Was I finding evidence, or was I just searching for it?

"But it's also a double-edged sword. It's made each of the cols a safer place. A happier place. This means that they've grown in population faster than we'd have expected. Originally, Culling every ten years was sufficient, when Din Io conceived of the model. But unfortunately, we've seen a rise in the occurrences of violence in the cols. Unhappiness, unrest, disobedience to local governments, murders." He sighed. "It's become very clear in the last decade that the Authority has been failing its citizens by not changing the model." He turned back to me now, and it was almost as if he was lit from behind. He seemed to glow.

"Starting with this year's Culling, we're going to cull annually."

I reeled back. A Culling every single year? I thought of Europa. The boots on the street. My stomach gave one quick heave. Would that mean even more people would be culled? Would it mean that we'd start to cull the young? It was such a huge upheaval to the system that there was no telling what kind of repercussions it might have. I thought of the boots on the street again. How many pairs of boots would there be? How many dead feet? Dead bodies? Dead people? Every year? God.

His eyes were tight on my face and I suddenly got the distinct impression that I was being tested for something. I had no idea what. I cast about for an appropriate response. What would a Datapoint say? I inwardly scoffed. That was a ridiculous question. I *was* a Datapoint. I just didn't exactly feel like one in this particular second. *Every year.*

"But, sir, you'd have to have thousands of Datapoints trained and at the ready to be able to cull every year. The existing group could never handle a workload that large. Are there even enough available candidates in the population?" I knew that, to be a Datapoint, you had to have an extremely specific psychological profile. We were rare. Very rare.

When I focused on Haven again, he was smiling. And the sight of it made me want to recoil from him.

"No. There aren't enough Datapoints to be able to handle that workload. But there is one who could handle it by herself."

Ah. So, this was what it felt like to have your life sucked away down a blackhole.

"Me?" My thoughts had come to such a standstill, I was kind of surprised I could even remember language.

His smile grew. "You, Glade Io. You're the one we've been waiting for. The safety of our solar system might rest on your shoulders."

I thought of the boots in the street. The woman with the scarf. Dead. Not murdered, but dead all the same. Alive one second and just a body, an object, the next second. The man in front of me didn't know about the experience I'd had there. He didn't know how badly I'd failed the one and only Culling I'd been a part of. He didn't know that it was only the simulations where I'd thrived. And then, it had only been because of the answers that I sought.

His smile grew even further, as if he were elated, like a child the night before his birthday party. "And we're not going to cull in portions anymore, either. You'll cull the entire solar system at once."

The universe buzzed to a standstill all around me. I swear, the sun stopped burning, blackholes stopped imploding, oxygen froze in the lungs of every living creature. "What?"

"We're changing the system, Glade. Because we found you. We've been waiting for you to reach your potential. And now I want you to show us what you can really do. The Culling is vulnerable. You see, every Datapoint has a different style, a

239

different level of skill. And sending them all over the galaxy to cull here and there leaves them open for attack from the Ferrymen, or even, in some cases, unwelcoming cols. We simply can't risk it anymore. Which is where you come in. A Datapoint who can cull all at once, once a year, from a protected location. Thereby strengthening the weaknesses of the system."

I sucked in a breath, realizing that I simply hadn't been breathing. There was no way that he was serious. How could I possibly take this sort of proposal seriously? He was asking me to cull alone, by myself, and everyone at once? That was damn near a hundred thousand people. I wouldn't even be able to *sort* that many, let alone cull the cullables.

"There is a chance," he continued, "that you're not capable of what we ask. So, we'll need you to do something for us."

I almost laughed. Just right in his face. A chance I wasn't capable? The man was asking me to cull an entire solar system at once. I couldn't even do twenty people on Europa. Of course I wasn't capable. Furthermore, no one was capable of this. This was an impossible task. A gross deviation from the system that I'd come to understand. To trust. A little worm of a thought wiggled its way through me. How the hell had Haven talked the rest of the Authority into this? And why? His reasons about weaknesses in the system seemed suspiciously thin to me. I searched his eyes and wished, recklessly, that Kupier were here. I wanted Kupier, with his huge, beating heart, to look at this man in front of me and tell me what he saw. Suddenly, I didn't want the logic of this situation. I didn't want the facts. I wanted intuition. Empathy. I didn't understand this. And I feared it.

"What sort of thing would I need to do?" My voice was steady. None of my suspicion, or fear, or reticence bled through, and I marveled at that. I felt, almost, like an android on the surface. A plastic covering over a human heart.

"You'll have to prove you can do it in a simulation."

The thought made my mouth go dry. But I supposed it wasn't any more ridiculous than anything else he'd just said. He wanted to change the entire Culling system. He wanted me to cull thousands of people at once, from a centralized location, and he wanted me to do it every year. "I – Sir Haven."

"Glade, I have seen your level of improvement in the last weeks alone. I'll be anxious to see what you can do in a simulation like this."

His words finally filtered down to me. What he was asking me to do. He was asking me to get in the simulator and try. To hook my tech and my brain and my*self* into that simulator and attempt to cull the solar system.

This simulation would kill me. I knew it would. And maybe that was his goal? I looked up at the man who'd come to be so familiar to me over the years. So familiar, and yet, such a stranger, as well. I had no idea what he saw when he looked at me. Was this his way of destroying me since I'd been abducted by the Ferrymen? Did he not trust me still? Or was this the ultimate show of trust? Putting the entire program in my hands.

"And if I can't do it?"

He sighed. "Glade, I don't think I need to make it clear that to succeed at this would put you on a level below only the Authority. You would answer to no one. You'd be the most powerful citizen in the solar system." Those silver eyes snared mine and I could have sworn my heart skipped. "A person of that stature would have everything she wanted. She'd have the answer to every question she'd ever asked."

I stumbled out of Haven's office ten minutes later. He'd said more. I think I'd said more, as well. But I hadn't been able to stop replaying his words in my head. I didn't understand them. Every question I'd ever asked. Was he offering me the truth? Was he admitting that there was something hidden within the program? Was he threatening me? Did he know that I was questioning the Database? Had he guessed?

I knew I didn't have a choice about whether or not I walked into that simulator. I was sure I'd be deemed a traitor if I didn't.

I sat down on my bunk later that night, completely unsure of whether I was walking into a trap or not. I didn't understand Haven. I had the strange feeling that we were playing a game with one another, but he was the only one who knew the rules. I wished so badly I had someone to talk this through with.

Kupier flashed through my head and I pushed him away. He was on the other end of the galaxy, and I knew exactly what he would have said to me. Dahn was next to come to mind, and I pushed him away, too. I couldn't drag him into this.

So, there I sat. Alone again.

CHAPTER EIGHTEEN_

N ews about my upcoming simulation was spreading. There were more whispers and stares than ever before. Even more than after I'd come back from the Ferrymen.

"How the hell does everyone know already?" I griped, slamming my food bowl down next to Dahn. "I haven't told anyone but you!"

He shrugged. "I didn't tell anyone. But I bet the simulator technicians told people. They had to reconfigure the entire operating system to handle that much data at once."

His voice was strangely blank, the same way that it had been ever since I'd told him what Haven was asking me to do.

A table of Datapoints whispered about me while glancing over their shoulders and I glared at them. Just what I needed. More rumors to follow me around. "It's not like I asked for this."

"Oh, don't act like you don't want it." The biting voice had come from behind me, and I didn't have to turn to know who it was.

"You're not supposed to eat at the same time as us, Sullia," Dahn replied to her in a bored voice. "In fact, you're not even supposed to be on this side of the Station right now."

"I couldn't resist the chance to come and congratulate our little chosen one, here, now could I?" She shoved herself into the seat across from us, and I could have sworn that the dining hall went quiet.

"I'm not a *chosen one*," I said, scowling at her. "They don't even know if I can do it. That's why they're putting me in the simulator first."

She eyed me. "If you don't want to do it, then tell them. Make it open auditions. Someone else can step up to the plate."

I scoffed. "You? Don't make me laugh. I don't think they want psychopathic traitors gaining access to every single person in the solar system."

Her eyes went glassy and hard. "I'm not the traitor between the two of us." Her eyes skittered to Dahn. "There's a reason Kupier didn't come for *me* that night, Glade. That night you went away with him."

I felt Dahn shift beside me. "That's enough, Sullia. You're going to get the both of you thrown back into interrogations with talk like that."

A muscle in her cheek twitched at the word 'interrogations' – but she otherwise ignored him. I'd never quite seen her like this. A little wild, a little out of control. When Sullia raged, it was always calculated, for a greater end. But this? With her eyes sparking and color on her cheeks, this was something different. I wondered what the last round of interrogations had really done to her, whether it had moved something that shouldn't have been moved. I wondered what another round of interrogations would do to me.

Sullia went on, seeming not even to hear Dahn. "You're not like us, Glade. That's why he chose you to be his little spy. You're not like any other Datapoint. And you're certainly not like me and Dahn. We may have motives, but at least they're visible." She was full-on sneering now, her eyes bright with disdain. "You don't care about being the best. You don't even care about surviving. You want something else. You're getting into that simulator for some *other* reason. Ask yourself if that makes you a traitor. Ask yourself that."

We didn't have to tell her to go. She got up and left.

I turned immediately to Dahn. "She's lying."

He seemed to soften a little bit, turning to me, his knee brushing mine.

"You're not anything like Sullia. She's lying about that. She just wants to get under your skin and pit us against one another," I told him.

He immediately stiffened again, turning away from me and staring down at his food.

"Trust me," I continued. "I've seen what the real her is like. She's a snake. You're not, Dahn. You're nothing like her."

"Yes, I am." He'd spoken so quietly I had to lean in to hear him, and I didn't miss that he immediately leaned away from me. "I'm exactly like Sullia. We all are. You're the only damn Datapoint who *isn't* like Sullia. She's right that you're different. And maybe that's the reason that you were chosen for this. Or maybe that's the reason that *Kupier*," he sneered the name, "chose you for whatever the hell it was he chose you for."

My mouth fell flat open. "Excuse me?"? I snapped immediately.

His mouth quirked to the side and he looked at me like I was
insane. "What?"

"Dahn, you need to apologize to me right now. I cannot
believe you'd say that to me."

I was certain that, in the six years he'd been living in the
Station, this was the first time he'd been asked to apologize for
something. Niceties and politeness were not something that
were valued in Datapoints. But I didn't care. Maybe I was
proving his point that I was different. I didn't care about that,
either.

Dahn said nothing. He just looked forward.

*You just accused me of being a traitor to the Authority. Thinking
that Kupier picked me for some sort of Ferryman mission. You need to
apologize to me.*

His eyes narrowed, but he still didn't look over at me. "No,
that wasn't what I was accusing you of." He spoke with his
voice, not his tech, and I didn't miss the callousness of that.

"Then what the hell did you mean? 'What he chose
me for.'"

Dahn laughed humorlessly and steepled his hands over his
face. "Christ, Glade, sometimes you're as dense as Cast is. You
wanna know what I meant? I meant that it couldn't be clearer
that the leader of the Ferrymen was trying to get close to you.
Why? Because you're pretty and honest and most people want
to get close to you. That's what I'm accusing you of. Not treason,
alright?"

I clapped my mouth closed and felt heat rise up from the
collar of my shirt. Dahn was furiously staring at his bowl of

food, his eyes anything but soft. When I didn't say anything, he jammed a bite into his mouth, shaking his head.

"Is it true?" Cast slammed his bowl down and I jumped an inch, my eyes still on Dahn. Cast sat in the seat where Sullia had just been sitting.

"Is what true?" Dahn asked, tilting himself a little further away from me.

"The whole simulator test you have to do tomorrow, Glade. Is it really the entire solar system? The Authority wants to find out if you can do it?"

I shrugged. "I'm not going to guess what the Authority's motives are."

Cast leaned forward, and he was almost trembling with excitement. "So, it is true. You're doing the simulation."

I nodded stiffly. Dahn hadn't moved an inch, and he still stared at the exact same spot ahead of him. His words from before tumbled in my head and made me nervous. He was acting this way because he didn't like that I'd struck up a friendship with Kupier. Kupier, brother of Luce. The Ferryman who'd killed Dahn's father. I understood now. God, I was so dumb. It probably made Dahn feel sick to his stomach to think of me as being friends with the enemy. Not just the enemy of our government, but Dahn's personal enemy.

Suddenly, I was just tired. So tired. There were too many things to juggle all at once. I couldn't balance Dahn's feelings at the same time. Maybe that made me a bad friend, but I was a Datapoint, after all. Nobody said we were good at friendship. I pushed away his sharp words from before. If I lived through the simulation, maybe we could talk about it then.

Cast's face went white. "But, Glade, it could kill you! Datapoints have died culling too much data at once! God. The whole solar system? Best case scenario, you lose your mind. No one can withstand that level of intensity. This is crazy! Why would they waste a good Datapoint like you on an impossible task?" He tossed his fork down. "And why would you accept?"

I was surprised by his concern. No one else had been concerned for me so far. But that wasn't what had my head cocking to the side. He had pretty much asked me the same question that Sullia just had. Why was I accepting this challenge?

The answers tumbled down so fast that my head spun.

Because I wanted the answers. I wanted to know if Kupier was lying or if Haven was. I wanted to know, for sure, why my father had been culled. Murderous or rogue? I wanted to know if the disjunct I felt between the simulation and the Culling was real. Was I sensing the virus? Did the virus exist? Had Haven planted it? Murderous or rogue?

"He's right." Dahn had softened again. His forehead rested in his hand as he pushed his food away. "You could end up dead or braindead from this. That's all that matters." He'd said the last part as if he were saying it to just himself.

"I have to do it."

They both looked up at me.

"I'm going to do it."

———

The next day, it was those two who flanked me as I walked into the simulation room. I tried not to glare at every single other person who'd come to watch me do the simulation, but I failed.

Miserably. I pretty much hated everyone at that moment. Or maybe that was my nerves talking.

It seemed like every Datapoint in training had come to see me make my attempt. And the room wasn't short of high-level Datapoints, either. I ignored Sullia skulking in the back corner, a frown on her beautiful face.

The one person who was noticeably absent was Haven. I didn't know why I'd expected him to watch in person when I knew he kept a remote screen in his office, but I had. It didn't matter. I'd step into the simulator, do my best, and hopefully step out. And then we'd all know.

"Alright," Dahn said in my ear. "It's just like any other simulation. You just walk in, hook your tech into the port—"

"I know how to do a simulation, Dahn."

"Yeah." His gray eyes searched mine and I felt the back of his knuckles against my hand. "I know."

"Don't die," Cast said from behind me, an unusual amount of worry in his tone.

I raised an eyebrow at him. "Yeah. Goals."

I didn't look at a single other person as I stepped into the simulator. Maybe Sullia was right. Maybe I didn't have the survival instincts that all of the other Datapoints had. Stepping into this simulation wasn't about greatness. And it sure wasn't me looking out for number one. It was about answers.

I blanked my mind as I hooked the tech on my arm into the port beside me. I felt the door of the simulator close, and I was plunged into blackness.

I expected a series of lights to open up in front of me, one for each colony. But that wasn't what happened. Instead, it was one solid line of light. I craned my head all the way around. It completely encircled me. I was surrounded by the colonies.

There was the icy blue of the frozen colonies and the baked red of the volcanic ones. Somewhere in there was my colony on Io, but I let my mind skip right over that. *Let's start before we finish, Glade.*

I'd learned in all of my recent simulations not to look hard at what was going on in each colony. No more close inspections of a grandma sewing in her hut. No more trailing a dirty mutt on his search for scraps. No more watching kids jump rope or play tag. This was not a sightseeing expedition. This was Culling.

Instead of searching out the individual brainwaves by using my own tech – the way I always used to – I instantly synced with the Authority Database.

Lean hard. That's what Dahn had said he always did. He leaned hard on the Database. I could do that.

I felt endless streams of information swirl and twist into my integrated tech as I synced up. I didn't understand how it worked, but the Database could organize insane amounts of data all at once. I watched in amazement as even a population of this size, the entire solar system's, didn't slow it down.

There were hundreds of thousands of people to sort and cull all at once, and the Database was careening through them. After the first ten thousand or so, each citizen's brainwaves were not an individual cloud of red. No, they melted into one another. It was line after line of red, all bleeding together. They were surrounding me. A 360-degree view inside the simulator. I could observe it with my actual eyes, because the simulator showed me the projection. But I could also close my eyes and see it in my head, as well. My integrated tech could show it to me there.

And that's what I did. I jammed my eyes closed and my tech showed me the mass of people, every one's living brain. An endless line of red.

A line of sweat trailed down my back. It was so many people. A hundred times the most I'd ever culled at once.

I could feel my tech scrambling to categorize all the information that the simulation was throwing our way. The image in my mind went completely black for a second as my tech skipped. It was overloading. I could feel the heat on my face and in my arm. This was too much data. It couldn't handle it.

Lean hard.

I accessed the Authority Database from another angle. I'd never taken both angles, both access points, at once. I was asking the Database to categorize each person in the simulation, and now, I was also asking it to streamline the data that it was sending through my integrated tech.

The program the Database was running shifted. And I actually *felt* it shift. Not just in my tech. But in my body. It shifted and my heart skipped; my hands tensed.

For a second, I was back on the operating table getting my tech embedded that very first time. My body. My mind. Everything fought the intrusion. I was me. I was just me. There was no room for anything else to control me.

The Database program struggled against me. I could feel it trying to complete what I'd asked it to do. In order to streamline the data to my integrated tech, it needed more access to that tech. It needed more access... to me.

Sync, Glade. I commanded myself to do it. Screamed it at myself. *Line up and sync. Allow it in.*

NO! My body screamed at me. My organic body. My fingers

251

and toes and throat and eyes. I thought of the horse. I could not be tamed. I was wild. I was free. I would not let an intruder into my brain. My brain was mine. It was my thoughts, my life. I was the horse.

But if I didn't sync, I couldn't handle the data. My arm tugged at the port and I realized that my knees were buckling. I wasn't in pain, but my energy was dwindling. So much data. My tech burned in my skin. I could smell smoke. It was going to overload.

A pain opened up behind my eye and I knew it was my own fault.

Sync, Glade! Sync. Sync. ... ... Sink. Sink. And then I *was* sinking. Down. As if into a pool of deep, clear water. It wasn't like syncing with my integrated tech. That had asked for my permission every step of the way. But with the Authority Database, I opened the tiniest bit and it shoved its own way in.

I think I screamed. And I think my tech did, too. Suddenly my arms were flinging out to the sides. My eyes were open and unseeing. I couldn't move, yet something was wiggling my fingers, opening my mouth. The Authority Database had my body. And it was controlling it like a computer program. From inside my brain, and there was nothing I could do. I'd invited it in.

This was worse than hell. Worse than death. No. No.

I struggled against the program for just a second, forcing my hand one way when the Database pushed it another. The movement scratched my own arm. A vicious swipe of a claw. The pain registered.

I felt it register in my tech and in the Database.

Oh, the Database seemed to say. *Oh. That hurts.* My hand fell.

I jammed it to my side and the Database let me. My hand let me, and the Database let me.

Blackness dissolved into the glowing red lines of just moments before. My integrated tech was digesting the data and showing it to me again. The sync with the Database had worked. It was organizing the citizens for me and chewing up the bites for my integrated tech.

My brain could see it all now.

I want to see them. I said it in my head, and I wasn't sure if it was to my own tech or to the Database.

But that was all it took for the citizens who needed to be culled to step forward in my mind's eye. There were now two sets of red lines. The one in the back held every citizen who needed to be left alone. The line in front, surrounding me, closest to me – those were the citizens who needed to be culled.

I tried to zoom in on the image, to check them. I wanted to see their brainwave readings myself. With my own eyes. I wanted to check and see who I was culling. I needed to see their patterns.

But something didn't let me. I felt the gears of the program grinding. My tech was *trying* to let me. But the Database wouldn't allow it.

I felt myself tighten against each and every brainwave that needed to be culled. I was about to do it. But I wasn't sure if it was me tightening in on them, or the Database.

I was about to cull without double-checking who was being culled. I was trusting the Database with the weight of the decision. I was trusting the Database to have done the sorting perfectly. I'd let the Database into my brain. And now it was going to use my brain to cull all these people.

No.

I tried again to zoom in, and felt a deep and striking pain in my head. Worse than my pain in the interrogation room. Instantly, I fell to one knee. I didn't care. I had to do this. I had to check and make sure I was culling the right people. The pain instantly struck again. It wouldn't let me.

I gritted my teeth and felt my tech grinding against itself.

Survive, Glade. Do what you have to and survive.

It was Dahn's voice. He was calling out to me. *Survive. Don't fight the Database. Let it in completely. Lean hard. Learn hard. The Database wants to cull. It won't let you see who. Learn, Glade. Let it happen.*

And I did.

I watched both red lines. My tech showed them to me in my mind. I watched that outside line shrink away, getting smaller. We left them alone, the Database and I. And then I watched that inside line get bigger and bigger.

Cull them.

My brain tightened against their brains. I used my mind like a hand on a plug.

I yanked. And I watched their light fade to black.

———

She was dead. Dahn knew she was dead. He'd never seen someone lay so still in his life. The simulator powered down, severing her connection to the Database, and Dahn carefully un-clicked her tech from the port.

She remained completely still. Her body was warm. No… it

254

was burning hot, and Dahn jumped back when the crystal-like tech on her cheek burned his palm as he grazed against it.

"Get a health tech!" he screamed to the crowd of Datapoints that swarmed the doorway of the simulator. "Get Sir Haven!"

"I'm here," came that reedy voice, and the Datapoints immediately parted for him.

Dahn swept Glade's hair off of her face, but even his concern for her wasn't enough to keep himself from doing a double-take when he saw Jan Ernst Haven. He'd never seen the man look like this. Wild and unkempt and with something akin to glee in his eye.

"She did it," Haven murmured as he stepped into the simulator.

"Yeah, and it killed her," Dahn bit out the words as he felt her neck for a pulse. He couldn't find one. "Oh God. Get a health tech!"

"She's not dead." Haven knelt, as well. He moved her head from one side to the other. "Though she may need to be resynced with her tech after this. It looks like she might have fried it."

When Haven's fingers touched the tech on Glade's cheek, her eyes sprang open.

"Oh God." Dahn fell forward onto his hands. "Glade, breathe. Can you hear me?"

She nodded and did as he said, taking a huge gulp of air.

Why wasn't she talking? Did she have a brain injury?

"Take your time, Datapoint."

With that, Glade's eyes flickered to Haven, and Dahn started when he saw something in her expression that looked almost like... fear.

"She needs the infirmary." Dahn's tone brooked no argument, though he was very aware of Haven analyzing him.

"Yes. Yes, of course." Haven rose, and his voice sounded almost cheerful. "The rest can wait."

Dahn didn't even address that comment. There was more? How much more was she expected to take?

———

I wasn't surprised to wake up in the infirmary. I was definitely surprised to see who was there with me.

Sullia and Dahn. They hadn't noticed me wake up, and their heads were bent down toward one another whispering.

"It doesn't matter, Dahn," Sullia was saying to him. "The only thing we know is that she's an unknown. She's not like us. She can't be predicted. It doesn't matter if she's Haven's precious chosen one. She can't be trusted. Not like you and I can. Haven will see that. He values the predictable. He'll see it."

I couldn't see Dahn's face, but I did see Sullia's hand on his arm. I didn't like that. I didn't like that at all. I shifted slightly in bed, my face scrunched in anger, but I wasn't the one who broke them apart. Cast was, as he came catapulting from the other side of the room to jounce my bed.

"You're awake!"

I winced at both his volume and the amount he was shaking me around. "I guess."

"Glade, you did it! Do you remember? You passed out afterwards so we weren't sure you'd remember. But you did it! You passed the simulation. You even culled sixty percent of the data. SIXTY percent. Can you believe it?"

I recognized this as happiness; I knew it when I saw it. But I couldn't tear my eyes away from Dahn's face. From his soft gray eyes.

Something moved behind him and I realized it was Sullia slinking away. It couldn't have been more obvious that she'd only come to my bedside to get to Dahn. My eyes went back to his and I tried to interpret what I saw there, but I couldn't. There was only that soft look of his.

"How are you feeling?" He sat on the other side of me and I resisted the urge to close my eyes and sleep forever. I knew that, as long as Dahn was there, I was safe.

"Ugh." I shook my head and pain shot behind my eyes. "Like I just culled the solar system."

"Yeah, well, you did." His tone was wry.

I cracked an eye and studied his face. "Has Haven said anything yet?"

"He made an announcement while I was carrying you out of the simulator. You'd passed the test. You're going to lead the next Culling."

I groaned, nausea rising from just thinking about it. "I'll bet Sullia loved that."

"I think she's organizing a parade as we speak."

I cocked my head. "Dahn, did you just make a joke?"

He shrugged, pink in his cheeks. "I'm happy that you didn't die."

"Yeah." I looked at the ceiling of the infirmary. Gray and brown. "Me, too. Hey. You'll be there, though, right? You're still my mentor? You'll be with me through the Culling?"

"I... don't know. None of us do. Everything's changing, Glade. You changed everything. And you're not exactly 'in train-

257

ing' anymore. That little show you put on was pretty much your graduation ceremony. You're a full-on Datapoint now. You won't need a mentor anymore. Besides, no one knows what the next Culling will look like now that we have a chosen one."

I made a face at him. "Don't call it that."

"He's right, though," Cast chimed in, his blond hair flopping in his face. "It's full steam ahead on the Culling. I heard that we're not even going to waste time training new recruits for next year. It's just us."

My heart leapt in my chest. "You're kidding! There won't be any new Datapoints admitted to the Station?"

"Well, except for your sisters. But I'm sure you already knew that." The smile fell from Cast's face as he watched horror shape mine. "What? You didn't know? Everyone knows."

"She's been asleep for two days, Cast. How the hell would she have found out?" growled Dahn. "I was going to tell you when you felt better."

I grabbed Dahn's hand, clutching it like a lifeline. "It's true?"

He sighed. "Yeah. It's true."

I dropped his hand and scraped my hair out of my face. "I have to talk to Haven. Now."

"No, Glade, you're not healthy enough." Dahn tried to hold me in the bed, but I slapped his hands away.

"Now," I repeated. And there must have been something in my voice that had him taking me seriously, because he fell back.

I knew he followed me to Haven's office. I knew he wanted to make sure I got there alright. But I didn't pay any attention to that.

There was only one thought in my head the entire way: what had I done?

THREE

CHAPTER NINETEEN_

I t only took eight minutes to finish my conversation with Haven. My sisters were coming here. Not yet, though, because they were still just eleven years old. They'd stay on Io while they matured. My genetic material was apparently too valuable to ignore. *But thank you very much for nearly killing yourself in our simulation. Now you can be in charge of the Culling you aren't sure you believe in. Oh! And I still won't answer any of your goddamn questions. Bye bye.*

It took one more day for me to get let out of the infirmary. And half that time to make up my mind.

It took two days to figure out the landing pad schedule so that I could sneak in and steal a com from the skip that Sullia and I had stolen. It took me a nerve-wracking five hours to construct a passable replica in the shop so that no one would notice I'd stolen it. And then it took me a day and a half to fix the damn thing.

The one perk of being the chosen one was that not a soul

bothered me in my bunk the entire time. Not even Dahn. Everyone was avoiding me. And, thank God for that.

Because I had a rebel leader to contact.

It was the sixth day after the Culling simulation when I snuck into the abandoned storage units in the bottom of the Station. Dark and dusty, orderly boxes towered everywhere, lashed together to form great crates.

I skittered around the back of a particularly large grouping of boxes. My back hit the wall and I slid down slowly, taking deep breaths. When I looked up, the boxes rose over me like buildings in a great city. No one would hear me down here. And if they did? Who cared? They could turn me in, and then we'd just all see what happened next.

I held the crappy, hotwired com in one hand, the battery pack that I'd rigged in the other. I sure hoped this thing could communicate over unknown distances. Holding my breath, I pressed the homing button. It blinked green for a moment before going back to its dull gray.

I pressed it again. Green and then gray.

Again.

And again.

"Damn it." I shoved at the box of uniforms next to me. I was cramped and dusty and someone could catch me at any moment, and this damn thing wasn't working. The homing button was supposed to alert its mother ship that it was lost. The mother ship would then contact back. Either the distance was too far, or I hadn't—

Beeeeep.

I almost dropped it when the com squawked at me. The homing button started blinking yellow. What did that mean?

"Mantis 5. Do you copy?" A loud, crackly voice sounded over the com and I scrambled to turn the volume down. "Mantis 5. Do you read?"

I took a deep breath. "I read. Patch me through to the Ray."

There was a long pause. Then, "This is the Ray."

Thank God. I'd thought for sure that the mothership would be the huge patrol skip that Sullia and I had stowed away on. But no, apparently our little skip's mothership had been the Ray. Okay. One hurdle down.

"I need to speak to Kupier."

Another long pause.

"Glade?"

I recognized the voice then, crackly as it might be. It was Oort. My heart squeezed down for a second and I gulped for air. "I need to speak to Kupier."

I dropped my head to my knees then, with the reality of what I was doing. What was I doing? This was insane. This was instant death if I got caught. I was reaching up to click off the com when I heard it.

"DP-1."

His voice, though crackly and distant, was just as deep as I remembered. My face hurt, and I realized it was because I was smiling. And that I hadn't smiled since I'd left Charon.

"Yeah."

"Long time no see."

Something behind my eyes was hot and tight. I gulped. Why was I still smiling? "Yeah."

"Soooooooooo?" I could tell he was smiling, too. I could hear it in his voice.

"Kupier, I need your help."

There was a long pause. "Glade, you stole my ship and left. And now you want a favor?"

"You kidnapped me!"

"Oh, right. So, then that makes us even."

"Kupier."

"… Glade."

I sighed. And now my eyes were even hotter and tighter. I'd been so focused on how to contact Kupier, I hadn't even stopped to consider what I should say when I did. I went with the truth. "They're coming for my sisters. Because of something I did."

There was a long pause. "Who is?"

"The Authority. Haven. They're going to make them Data-points. Because of this horrible thing that I can do. They think Daw and Treb will be able to do it, too. They're going to come for them. And they won't survive it, Kupier. Some citizens don't survive the integration process. Some kill themselves during training. Because it's so awful. It's terrible and painful and all you learn to do is cull. They won't survive it, Kup. You have to help."

"Whoa. Hey. Slow down, Glade. Take a breath." I heard him do the same. "What is it you're asking me to do?"

"To get my mom and my sisters from Io. They're in the Hera colony. Just get them. Syb Io, Daw Io, and Treb Io. They're small and blonde. Just get them and take them… somewhere. Anywhere. I don't care. Charon. Take them to Charon. Please."

There was another silence. The longest one yet. And then, "DP-1, you have to know I can't do that. Risk that."

A small noise escaped me, and it sounded like a wounded animal.

"Even if you were telling the truth and this isn't a trap –

which is, you know, doubtful – there's a hundred ways something like that could go wrong. I can't put my men in jeopardy like that. I can't put the whole movement in jeopardy. Not when I don't know for sure what I'd be getting into. What *you'd* be getting me into."

The noise from my throat happened again and I jammed my fist into my mouth.

"Glade, we're from opposite worlds. And when you left, I realized how big that gulf is. How can we ever really trust each other?"

"I trust you enough to put my sisters' lives in your hands."

He made a noise then. A groan. And the com caught the end of it. "If it were just me in danger, I'd already be on my way. I'd do that for you, Glade. You know I would. But it's my men that stand to lose here. It's Charon that stands to lose."

I didn't say anything else. I let the com fall from my fingers and I buried my face in my hands. I listened to Kupier call my name ten or fifteen times before he gave up. And then I just listened to the static crackle of the disconnected com.

———

Haven frowned across his desk at Dahn Enceladus. He found himself irritated with the young Datapoint.

For years, he'd watched the boy grapple with feelings for Glade Io without ever really understanding her. Haven had no problems with the ebbs and flows of youthful passion. Even young Datapoints were subject to the whims of their humanity occasionally. It was a part of life. But he did not want Glade Io to have any distractions. And the dark-haired boy who sat in front of him, with the purple smudges under his eyes, was a distraction.

"I understand that we can't risk losing the genetic opportunity of her sisters, but—"

"No. You must not understand at all, Dahn Enceladus, if you are here, in my office, trying to talk me out of it." It was practically the first time that Haven had ever had to reprimand Dahn, and both of them felt the sting of it.

"Sir, I only mean to give you information that you might not have."

Haven gestured for the young Datapoint to continue.

Dahn shifted in his chair in a rare show of uncertainty. "I think having her sisters here would be a distraction for Glade. She's connected to them on an emotional level. *Protective.* If they were here and undergoing the training, I don't think she'd be able to perform at the level that you're asking of her."

Haven was quiet for a moment before he leaned in. "And this is your opinion as her… friend?"

"As her mentor."

Haven was leaning back, a reply on his lips, when the small screen at his wrist beeped. A banner message zinged along the bottom. He frowned. Another Authority supply skip had been attacked. The fourth in a month. Again, nothing had been taken. He wanted the skip brought back to the analytics team here. He wanted to make sure no bug had been implanted in the computer mainframe or any spyware left behind. He didn't understand what the Ferrymen were doing, and he thought it might be time to swat back.

He typed off a quick reply, instructing the skip to come back to the Station for inspections. And then he was facing Dahn again.

"This has been a very exciting time for all of us, Dahn Enceladus. Everything is changing."

Dahn nodded tightly. "You mean to proceed."

Haven sighed. "You act as if I'm making this up as I go along, Datapoint. As if I hadn't been planning for this since the day you and I first saw her a decade ago."

Haven couldn't know that his words had just smashed something inside of Dahn, like a hammer to frozen glass. *Even then,* Dahn thought desperately, *there was never a chance for me to rise.*

CHAPTER TWENTY_

A week later, and I was sure I was losing my mind. No one had spoken to me in over two days. Dahn and Cast included. Cast was just busy – I understood that. Now that the Culling was going to take on a completely different form, everyone had new protocols to learn.

But Dahn? He was just plain avoiding me, and I didn't understand why. Something had happened and he wouldn't tell me what it was. I didn't mind giving him space, as everyone deserved that, especially Datapoints. But I hated giving him space when Sullia so obviously wasn't.

Every time I had sought out Dahn over the last two days, I'd found Sullia by his side. Sullia with one hand on his shoulder. Sullia whispering something intense and fierce just three inches from his face. And what was even worse, Sullia sitting silently alongside Dahn while both of them read. I didn't understand what was happening. And I didn't trust it.

I couldn't shake the feeling that I'd just lost my only real ally on the entire Station. And I wasn't even sure why.

And so I passed the time slowly. I spun unrealistic dreams of bribing one of our pilots to go rescue Daw and Treb. Or of stowing away myself, getting to them before the Authority could. Ripping out my integrated tech and disappearing with my sisters into the solar system.

Every one of those dreams ended up with me dead and my sisters in training. I couldn't do it on my own. There was no chance of succeeding.

That night, I pulled my curtains closed on my bunk and stared listlessly at the ceiling. I'd just have to protect them as best as I could when they arrived. It was all I could do now. I realized that Dahn had been right all along. Being a member of the Authority was the only way to be in control of your own life.

Kupier didn't come to sit at the edge of my bed that night. No, instead he slammed the curtain of my bunk closed behind him, breathing hard and looking wild-eyed. He squinted through the darkness as he put one knee up on the bed and brushed the sweat from his forehead. I'd had dozens of dreams about him since I'd come back to the Station, but this was a new one. I'd never seen him look quite so harried. Even so, I did what I usually did in my dreams. I rolled to the side so that he could stretch out and make himself comfortable alongside me, the way he always did.

This time, he didn't.

Instead, he flashed those white, white teeth at me through the dark, and he gestured at the strip of bed I'd just vacated. "Is that an invitation?"

His voice was ragged with the breath that still pumped his chest up and down like a bellows.

I stared blankly at him. I waited for him to ask me about the Culling, the way he always did. To bring out the marble and hold it in the air, the way he always did.

He didn't do either of those things.

"You don't look surprised to see me," he whispered, those electric blue half-moons bouncing back and forth between my eyes. He leaned forward, the knuckles of one hand pushing him up across the bed. He came close enough for me to catch his scent. "And actually, it's starting to freak me out a little bit."

"What?" I whispered back. He looked so clear, leaning through the shadows, the curtain of my bunk pulled closed behind him. "Wait." I sat up. We were just two feet away from one another now. "Wait," I repeated.

My hand shook as I extended it. I couldn't remember a single other time in my life when my hand had shaken before. When just the very tips of my fingers touched his warm cheek, I ripped my hand back like I'd been burned.

"Oh God." I let my breath out in a huff. "Oh my God. This isn't a dream. I thought it was a dream. But – oh my God."

Those white teeth flashed again, and he cocked his head to one side. "Been dreaming about me, huh?"

"Kupier," I gasped, my eyes hot and tight the way they'd been when we'd talked on the com all those days ago. I didn't think. I didn't hesitate. I lunged over the distance between us and wrapped my arms around him. My forehead jammed into his neck as I squeezed every breath of air right out of his chest. I heard him chuckle as his arms came around my back. He held me as tight as I held him.

"You smell like the Ray," I huffed, and the words came out on a wave of strange, loose laughter.

"I'm gonna take that as a compliment." He pulled back from the hug and the stubble on his chin scraped my temple.

"What the hell are you doing here?" There was something wet on my cheeks, and I thought it might be all of the anxiety I'd been going through this week. I thought it might be the pain of the interrogations. The raw fear and pressure of the simulation. I touched my cheek with my fingertips and pulled them away, astonished I was crying.

Kupier didn't seem to think anything of it. He merely pulled his sleeve over the heel of his hand and roughly brushed the tears off my cheeks. "I'd love to explain it all, but maybe we could go somewhere? Someplace where I'm less likely to get tortured and then publicly beheaded?"

I raised an eyebrow at him. "On the Station? That place doesn't exist."

"Luckily, I brought it with me."

———

Kupier snuck me through the Station the way he'd snuck in. Apparently, the Station had a hell of a ventilation system. It wasn't until we'd made it all the way back to the landing deck that I spoke again. My heart was thick and beating like a fist on a door. I kept looking over my shoulder, waiting for someone to spot us. It was craziness to be following him, but I couldn't help but think that I really didn't have any other choice. Kupier was my very last chance for saving my sisters.

"Kupier, where are we going? They're going to notice us."

"No…" he shook his head and tossed that grin around like he always did. "They won't even see us."

There was a huge supply skip that had docked earlier that day for some reason or another. I'd heard rumors that its computer systems were getting fully stripped and rebuilt. Even at this hour, technicians were circling it, taking notes and climbing on and offboard. It looked to me like they were finalizing the very last of the check. An alarm sounded briefly from one side of the landing deck. It was going to be taking off again soon.

Kupier and I kept to the shadows along the exterior wall. When we came around to the belly of the skip, where most of the supplies were kept, Kupier ducked from the wall through a small porthole that had been opened on the side. I was beginning to suspect that it was the same one that he'd snuck in on.

The second we were both fully inside the storage unit of the massive skip, Kupier grabbed my hand and yanked me down. It was so crowded with supplies that we had to crawl our way over the crates until we reached the very end of the skip, where the thrusters were.

The giant skip was as still and dark as the far side of a moon. It was almost like it was sleeping. I was sure he was taking me to whatever corner of the skip that he'd stowed away in. My stomach tightened uneasily. Just because he'd been able to hide there didn't mean it would be safe for us to talk there.

What the hell was I doing? I was parlaying with a Ferryman in the middle of the Station? This was insanity.

"Glade." He turned to me, as if expecting my sudden hesitation. "They won't catch us. I swear. I'm not gonna get you executed. But I'd rather not linger out here in the lion's den, alright?" He glanced behind him toward where the thrusters were.

I barely had to think about it. If we were gonna get caught, which I really thought was a distinct possibility, then I might as well find out why he'd come in the first place. "Let's go."

Kupier grabbed my hand again and swung me down into a cellar I hadn't noticed was there. Thanks to my Datapoint training, I landed on my feet like a cat. It was just seconds later that he was using some small, but very loud, tool to remove one panel and then another. I crawled after him through where the panels had been and glanced around at my surroundings as he reattached the panels.

My jaw dropped. To the best of my knowledge, we were currently inside of a thruster. Big enough to stand up in, the charred chrome of the mechanism made a long, skinny cave that opened up on the far end, where the flames exploded out into space. A chill worked its way up my back. The ship was off, sleeping, but knowing that I was standing inside a veritable fireplace was giving me pause. At any second, when they engaged the thrusters, we could be burned to a crisp, like a chicken bone in a bonfire. Standing inside the quiet thruster was like watching a murderer sleep.

I turned to Kupier, speechless.

He nodded behind him, that grin of his already in place. My eyes focused behind me and I saw a nine-foot-long steel capsule set snugly against the rounded inner wall of the thruster. It was so sleek, and charred so black that I hadn't even seen it before. You'd have to be looking for it to see it. It slowly registered, what I was looking at. A one-man ship. I'd heard of them before, and even seen a few pictures, but I'd never seen one in real life.

And if it was what he'd taken to be able to board this supply skip, then that meant it was flame resistant.

Kupier quietly jogged over to it and pressed on one side, and the door of the one-man skip pivoted open and he slid inside. I followed and the door closed behind me. There was very little room – we basically had to lie down to fit.

I looked around the capsule ship and shifted as best as I could. It was a true one-man ship. There was a pilot seat that was currently fully reclined, a control panel, and a huge windshield that extended over the top and front of the capsule. I assumed there was a small bathroom behind me and enough room for a few days' worth of food storage. But it really was remarkably small. Kupier and I both rolled to our sides to make room for one another, but even so, our feet had to stay tangled, and there was only an inch or so in between us.

"This is how you boarded the Station? You docked inside one of the supply skips?"

He nodded, a little smug. "Pretty cool, huh?"

"Yeah," I admitted, looking around the one-man ship.

"Why'd you come?"

Kupier sighed and rolled back just a bit so that he looked at the top of the charred black windshield. "Because I haven't given up on you." He tipped his head and looked at me. "If we're being completely honest."

I narrowed my eyes. "You haven't given up on taking me to Earth to hack into the Database and destroy our system of governance as we know it?"

His jaw tightened. "Dismiss it all you want, but you're a Ferryman at heart, Glade. The Authority just got to you before I could."

I opened my mouth to reply, but a yelp came out instead when the huge supply skip jolted beneath us. From all directions, there were sounds of the skip coming to life.

"Oh my God," I muttered, staring at him in shock.

"Shit."

"The ship's gonna take off," I breathed, pushing away from Kupier and feeling around for a way to disengage the door of the capsule ship. I had to get out of the one-man ship and get the hell out of the thruster before this thing took off into space. Otherwise, I was screwed. Royally screwed.

"Glade, stop. Don't—"

My hands found the release handles and the door of the capsule ship swung open. I flung myself out and into the smooth, charred cave of the thruster. I landed on my hands and knees and started scrambling toward the opening at the other end of it. It would be a fifteen-foot drop to the floor of the landing pad, but I didn't care. As long as I didn't get burned alive, I'd be happy. Thrilled. Ecstatic.

"Glade!" his voice whispered behind me, but I ignored it. I could hear other engines purring to life in the supply skip. It wouldn't be long until the thrusters engaged.

I was still scrambling when I felt two large hands grab me at my waist and start to yank me backward. I almost choked. Was he trying to kill me? Abduct me? Suddenly, everything that had happened to me over the last months weighed on my soul like lead. I was done with getting kidnapped and tortured and forced to be someone I wasn't. I was getting out of this thruster if it was the last thing I did.

I turned to the man grabbing me and I socked him in the face with every bit of strength and fury I had inside me.

His face whipped backwards. "Christ, Glade!"

But I didn't stick around for much longer than that. I was scrambling out toward the open end of the thruster. I had to get out of there, and fast, before these thrusters were engaged and I was a kabob.

I'd only scrambled a foot or two more when Kupier's hand grabbed the collar of my shirt, yanking me back. I choked and gasped for air as my teeth dug into the side of his hand.

"Stop!" he hissed. "Stop! Glade, you're gonna get us both killed if you don't get your stubborn, crazy ass back into this ship. NOW!"

He flung me around and let me go. I stumbled toward the capsule and heard the final set of engines engage. He was right. We were out of time.

The skip lurched underneath us again and I heard a second alarm go off. The thrusters were going to come on any second. Kupier's hands gripped my shoulders and he shoved me forward. The door of the one-man skip was still open, and he launched the two of us inside. I banged the hell out of my elbow and I heard him swear again as he landed right on top of me. He slammed the door down and locked it.

We were just letting out breaths of relief when the deafening roar of the thrusters exploded around us. The reinforced window of the one-man skip was already blackened and scorched, so it was still pitch dark, but the noise and the heat were enough to tell us exactly what was happening out there.

The supply skip lurched underneath us again, and this time I could feel that we were airborne. It slid out of the landing dock and slowly out into the blackness of space. Kupier's weight crushed me to the seat beneath me as we waited for the skip to orient itself. It was using the thrusters for small calculations, minor adjustments. But in a minute, it would engage its artificial black holes and it would skip to another part of the solar system. It wouldn't need its thrusters then.

Sweat beaded on our skin as the heat and the noise increased. I felt some roll down my neck and I wasn't sure if it was mine or Kupier's. It was just when I thought I couldn't take another second of the heat when the thrusters suddenly fell silent. The heat in the tiny cabin of the one-man ship didn't cease, but Kupier rolled halfway off of me and flipped a few switches. Cool, smooth oxygen pumped around us and I took a welcome breath. He flipped more switches and the windshield of the capsule skip cleared. I could see the night sky winking through the distant open end of the thruster.

"Good Lord," I mumbled, shifting so that I wasn't completely pinned underneath him.

"Man, you sure keep things interesting," Kupier laughed, but it ended on a moan as he tenderly tested the skin around his eye. "It's not gonna be fun explaining this shiner to the rest of the crew."

"Kupier, who the hell cares about your black eye? I just took off in a Ferryman capsule. I'm officially a rebel. Oh, Jesus." I leaned forward and clutched my hair. "If I go back, they're gonna kill me. If I don't go back, they'll enlist my sisters, no question. Shit!"

I wheeled on him — not that there was room to do much wheeling. "Did you plan this?" I demanded.

"Of course not! I thought we had more time!"!" He looked truly insulted. "Glade, have I ever actually put you in danger?"

I blinked at him. No. He hadn't. He'd had to do some brash

stuff, like kidnap me and dampen me. But he'd never really tried to hurt me or sabotage me. He wouldn't be Kupier if he'd done those things. "Kup, what am I going to do? God. I never should have gotten on this ship. I'm so, so screwed."

"Okay. Just give me a second. Let me think." He knuckled his eye for a solid thirty seconds. "Yeah, look. This really sucks, but I think I know what we can do so that you can return and not get executed."

I waited, breath held, for this plan. God, I hoped it was a good one.

"In a little while," he began, his blue eyes catching the flickering lights off the dashboard of our one-man skip, "they'll have to engage the thrusters again. We'll eject then and they won't notice. We can take this skip to a Ferrymen ship we have out on the other edge of Mars. That's what I was going to do anyways, before they took off five fucking hours early. But this way, you'll leave me there, on the Ferryman ship, and take this one back to the Station."

I stared at him blankly. "You want me to take this capsule ship back to the Station? But you'll lose it permanently. They'll dissect every bit of technology on board!" I didn't stop to think that maybe I shouldn't explain all this to him. "They'll learn a hundred things about your operation. Whatever you think about the Authority, there's smart technicians on the Station. You have no idea what they can learn from this skip, Kupier. Do you have any idea what they've learned from the other two skips we brought back?"

He shrugged, a small smile on his face. "So maybe we leave some breadcrumbs aboard all our ships here that aren't gonna necessarily lead to much. In case of capture. And this way, you'll get to look like a hero. You've commandeered a precious piece of Ferryman technology."

"They're gonna think it's suspicious if I'm just randomly *returning* to the Station in a Ferryman capsule ship when they didn't know I was gone in the first place."

"Say that you heard about the Ferrymen attacking the supply skips and you wanted to check out this one. That you'd heard of us doing the whole thruster trick before and you wanted to see. But the supply skip took off and you had to fly back in the capsule skip."

"Then they'll know that I held something back from them initially and they'll probably kill me anyways."

"God, I hate these assholes," Kupier grumbled, scrunching his eyes closed. "Okay, how about this...... Tell them you saw us practicing the maneuver while you were with us, but you thought it was only docking procedure, not a way of pirating an Authority skip. So you didn't think to mention it. But the pieces came together in the middle of the night and you had to come check it out for yourself."

"That might work."

"Or, Glade, better yet," he said quietly, "you can say fuck it, and fuck them, and just not go back at all. That's why I came to see you, after all, to ask you to do that. You can come to the Ferryman ship with me and throw in your lot with the bad guys."

I blinked at him. "Being around you exponentially increases my chances of getting killed."

My heart had slowed a little bit. I was accepting this reality. I'd have to return to the Station. I'd present this story, hope they believed it, and hope that my status as the chosen one would

279

carry me through the suspicion. Otherwise, I was damning my sisters to the Station. To lives as Datapoints. To *deaths* as Datapoints.

When had my life involved so many flipping dead-ends? I rolled my head to look at Kupier. So many questions. But only one made it to the top of the dog pile.

"You seriously came all this way on the slim hope that I could be persuaded to help you, Kupier?"

Kupier sighed, those slices of electric blue becoming sharper somehow. "I didn't hope. I knew."

"You knew? How?"

He looked up at me, and his expression was a curious mixture of surety and shyness. "Because you called me 'Kup.'"

"What?"

"When you called on the com. You called me 'Kup.'"

I wracked my brain, trying to remember. "Oh. Uh. So?"

He smiled then, a flash of white in the dim light. It was almost like he thought my answer was sweet. "So that means you trust me. And like me."

I furrowed my brow. "I'm not following."

He rolled his eyes. "Silly Datapoints with their stupid computer brains." He tapped one finger on my temple. "Nicknames mean you like someone. That they're your friend."

I thought of all the times he'd called me DP-1. My stomach tightened. The way it hadn't done since the last time I'd been with him.

"So you came all this way, risking your life over and over again, sneaking onto the Station, all because you think we're friends?"

He nodded and his eyes became serious. "Look, Glade, it's

no secret that I need something from you. You're a Datapoint, and the Ferrymen need a Datapoint. Not only to disable the Authority Database on Earth, but to get *onto* Earth in the first place. There's no way we can get around their shields without a Datapoint. Without this." He traced one firm finger over the tech on my arm, the tech on my face. His eyes bolted up to mine next, and it was then that we both realized that my tech wasn't dampened. For the first time, we were face to face and my tech was activated. I wondered how long it would take for them to realize I was gone. For them to start tracking my tech.

His eyes hardened and he continued on, like he was determined to ignore the fact. "I thought it was a lost cause when you left. That the one Datapoint, who I trusted, didn't trust me. So, we had to start from scratch."

"Is that why you've been attacking Station supply skips? You've been trying to find Datapoint technology without having to find a Datapoint?"

He nodded. "With little to no success. One look at the new integrated tech modules that they've been moving, and we realized it would take a decade to build the tools necessary to implant it in one of our own. We were pretty much back to square one when you commed me."

"And I called you Kup." I was just trying to keep up.

He nodded again. "And you called me Kup. And I knew that not all hope was lost. Because you trust me."

I tossed my hair over one shoulder and Kupier followed it with his eyes. "Kupier, I hate to disappoint you. But I don't think I really trust *anybody* right now. I mean, I trusted you to not murder my sisters if you went and rescued them for me. But you're implying that I trust you enough to ally myself with you.

281

To leave behind everything I know. To fight the Authority with you. Yeah. No. I don't trust you *that* much."

Kupier grinned then, smug and satisfied. "Trust me, you totally trust me."

I couldn't help but laugh, rolling my eyes. He pulled my hand down, away from where I'd been shaking my head into it. "Glade, you're a Datapoint, so you know how to fight. You know how to calculate. How to be logical and strategic. How to analyze data of all kinds."

I nodded.

"Well," he continued. "I'm just a regular guy. But I know emotions. I know feelings, DP-1." His eyes flicked over my face, trying to see all of me at once. I wondered how I'd ever thought of him as plain looking. That permanent smile of his, the shadow of stubble on his chin, his eyes so blue they glowed... all of it didn't seem plain at all. In fact, the way he looked was making it harder and harder to breathe.

"I know feelings," he repeated. "And you've got them for me."

He closed the distance between us, open eyes on open eyes. Kupier's nose brushed the side of mine for half a breath before both of his lips kissed my bottom one. "You missed me, Glade." Another breathless kiss, firmer than the last. "You like me." Another kiss. "You trust me."

This kiss lingered. And bloomed. I felt heat ignite in my cheeks, on the back of my head and my waist, where he gripped me. My heart pounded like the hooves of a horse. I'd never felt so wild in all my life. Our feet were tangled and his knee nudged in between mine. I was so warm, and half of me could barely believe this was happening.

FOOOM.

The thrusters fired on again, just as Kupier had said they would, and I jumped a foot in the air. I didn't get far before Kupier was pulling me back to him.

"Kupier," I tried, but his mouth momentarily distracted me.

"Kupier," I tried again.

"Kupier!"

"Hmm?" He pulled back from me, and his eyes were lidded and heavy.

"You said we had to eject when the thrusters came back on."

"What? When the – oh. OH! Crap. Hang on." He leaned forward and typed a quick sequence into the control panel. Our windshield was quickly blackening again as our capsule ship booted up. I held my breath, but it wasn't more than a few more seconds before we were jetting out in a stream of blue flame, rocketing off into space just as the giant skip we'd been riding on disappeared into a black hole.

The second we were safe from discovery, Kupier powered down the capsule's jets and let out a long, thin breath.

"Uh. Wow." He dragged a palm over his head, sneaking a look at me.

"Yeah." I turned and faced him, too. I wasn't surprised in the least to see a smile on his face. Though, this one was a little dopier than any I'd ever seen before.

"So..." he started. "I was kicking myself for not doing that before you skipped town."

"Oh." I gulped. "Really?"

"Yeah." With a flash of blue, I saw that he had the marble in his hands, and he was making it dance from one knuckle to the next. For the first time, I caught it up, held it between my fingers. The marble was warmer than I would have thought.

"All those things you said that I feel," I started slowly. "The missing you, the liking you, the trust?"

"Yeah?"

"You feel all that for me, don't you?"

He squinted at me. "I thought Datapoints weren't good at reading emotions."

I shrugged and tossed the marble back at him. "I'm good at reading information. And that," I pointed into the direct past with my thumb. "Was some pretty irrefutable evidence."

He grinned. "What can I say? I've got a thing for dark-haired girls who try to burn me alive using only the power of their scowls."

I rolled my eyes at him before looking out the windshield, absorbing the view for the first time. We were adrift and floating; Mars was coming into our view, filling up a quarter of the window. "Wow."

"Yeah," he agreed, following my line of sight. "Have you ever been down there? To the colony down there?"

I shook my head. "I've pretty much only been to Io and the Station. Well, and Charon."

He grinned at me. "You've never even been to Europa? That's just a hop and a skip from Io."

My stomach tightened as I thought of boots on the street. The body of the woman with the scarf over her hair and her hand over her chest. Oh yeah. I had been to Europa. I was just blocking it out. Instead of answering Kupier, I just shrugged.

I cleared my throat. "Have you been to all of the colonies?"

"Yup. It was kind of a personal goal of mine when I was

younger. Back before I became the leader of the Ferrymen. Before my brother died."

I glanced sideways at him. "Did you not want the job?"

"At that cost? No. No, I didn't." He looked more serious than I'd ever seen him before, and both of us watched Mars float almost out of view. "I wouldn't have wanted it anyway. Even if Luce had lived. I'm proud to be a Ferryman, but I never thought it would be ALL that I'd be."

"What did you want?"

"To be a frontiersman." He said it with a childlike grin on his face. It was the dream of almost every child in the solar system, at some point or another, to be one of the brave few who explored the limits of our territory, always looking for new resources, new places to live. Somehow, I didn't think Kupier was joking.

"An explorer."

"Yeah." He seemed to relax just the tiniest bit when I didn't laugh at him. "I was always curious about the cols; I wanted to know absolutely everything about any place that wasn't Charon. And then when I was old enough to start traveling with Luce, with the Ferrymen, I fell in love with that, too. The traveling part. I love all of it. The piloting. The on-the-fly repairs that are always inevitable. Navigating by the stars when the computer goes down. A few years ago, I was on board a ship that spotted an entirely new grouping of Trojan Asteroids. Never before seen or documented." He balled up a fist and banged it against his knee. "I'll never forget that. The way that felt."

He faced the windshield and I faced him. The warrior who wanted to be an explorer and the Datapoint who just wanted to be free. We were more trapped in our own lives than we were in the tiny capsule ship.

His face stayed forward, but his eyes slid to the side, and I caught just a flash of electric blue. "You keep looking at me like that, DP-1, and I'm gonna kiss you again."

I wasn't sure who reached for who then, but it was an hour or so before I noticed our view had completely changed.

CHAPTER TWENTY-ONE_

"They're gonna notice I'm gone. If I don't notify them of my whereabouts soon, they're gonna think I defected. And then it won't matter what I tell them about the capsule ship. They won't care. No story would cover it."

"Would that be so bad?"

"Kupier."

"No, listen." Kupier tugged at a length of her hair, letting it slip through his fingers like water. "You don't have to go back. I hate thinking about you there. About you on that Station with people who would do that to you."

She'd told him about the interrogations and he'd gone white with fury. It had instantly topped his list of reasons to burn the Authority to the ground.

She shrugged. "It's the way life is there. And more importantly, that's *my* life. It's the only life I know, Kup. I'm not going to just abandon it."

She had other people there that she loved. Who she couldn't

abandon. That was the only reason he could think of that she would stick to this so hard. Continue to ally herself with the Station. He couldn't make himself believe that the girl who'd just kissed his brains out could possibly have this much love for the Authority.

"Besides." She turned to him, her eyes flashing dark. "Do you have any idea what would happen if I threw my lot in with the Ferrymen right now?"

"Everyone would live happily ever after," he deadpanned.

She deftly ignored him. "Haven would come after you with everything he's got. I don't think he'd stop at just bombing the surface of Charon. He's resting all these dreams on my shoulders. At this point, the Ferrymen taking the 'chosen one,'" she almost sneered the word, "would be tantamount to war. I don't think there would be any line he wouldn't cross."

"Well," he started, figuring he should go for broke, "what if you came with me right now and we just threw the whole plan into motion? Got the Ray, headed straight for Earth, and destroyed the Database before anyone knew what hit 'em?"

"Yeah. I'm not doing that."

"Why?" He'd been joking before, but this question was deathly serious.

"Kup, I don't know what to believe. I... have questions about the Authority. Sure. Yes, I'll admit that. And I'm deeply scared of what will happen to my sisters if and when they get brought to the Station. But I don't believe enough in the Ferrymen ideology to put my life, and the lives of my sisters, on the line for your cause. You're asking me to not only turn my back on something I was raised to believe in, but you're asking me to *destroy* it. And I don't think the Authority is as squeaky clean as they say they are. And I have no idea if I'm going to go through with this Culling. But what if we get down there, send it up in smoke, and then realize that we were all better off when it existed? I don't know if I can handle that. I don't know if I can handle any of this."

She took a deep, shaky breath. It was the first time he'd ever seen her look fragile. But it wasn't because she was scared or tired. It was because too many people had asked way too much of her. Kupier bitterly regretted being one of them.

Glade turned back to him. "Not to mention that, if I die, that's just going to make things harder on Daw and Treb. Haven will just force them to be whatever it is that I am. And it almost killed me. The training. The testing. The simulations. My sisters are sweeter than I am. More tender. They wouldn't survive the training – I know it. I'm not going to completely abandon every-thing I've known."

Even for you.

It was unspoken. But somehow the words echoed on the air between them.

He leaned in for a soft kiss while he stroked a hot palm over her hair. His eyes were sad. "So, you're not ready to run away with me, huh?"

She rolled her eyes at him. "Yeah. No."

He shrugged and rolled to face the windshield. "Well. I guess that's fair enough." He turned back to her almost immediately, though. She'd never know how much rested on her answer to this next question. "But you're really just fine with going back to the Station and doing everything the Authority asks of you? You're fine, just ignoring all the parts that you have questions about?"

She hesitated, and he could have sworn he watched her get older in that second.

"No. I'm not fine with that." One hand played lightly with her tech. Her words sounded like they were almost impossible for her to get out. "I'm suspicious of Haven. And of this new system of Culling. He's given reasons for it. But even so... I don't like it. I don't want to just go back there and trust him, that what I'm doing isn't mass murder." She paused hard. "Genocide."

Kupier took a deep breath. Sometimes he wished that it wasn't a Ferryman thing to keep your head shaved. Because he really would have liked to tug at his own hair right this second. He settled for flipping the marble over his fingers. "Alright. Then why don't you go back to the Station. But this time, I'm the voice in your ear. Not Haven."

Sync or swim.

"You mean to be a Ferryman?" Her dark eyebrows were almost all the way into her hairline, and Kupier couldn't resist running one hand down the length of her soft hair.

"No," he laughed. "I think there'd be a mutiny if I unilaterally dubbed a Datapoint a Ferryman. But just think about it. The entire time that you were with us, on the Ray and on Charon, you had Haven whispering in your ear. Showing you the world from his perspective. Just let me do the same for you while you're on the Station."

He could see her considering his words. If she said no, if she just wanted to go back and bury her head in the sand, he wasn't sure what he would do next. The very thought of it exhausted him. The Ferrymen were quickly running out of ways to fight the Authority. And if what Glade said about Culling citizens every year was true? Well, then they were running out of time, as well.

Her face was so serious. That frown that he'd come to have such a soft spot for just deepened and deepened.

"Kup," she sighed, half resigned. "I'm pretty sure that would have been the case whether you'd asked it of me or not."

"Ha!" Kupier smacked his hands together over his head, startling a laugh out of Glade and making her grin. "Yes. Hell yes. Okay, that feels good."

"That I'm not just writing you off as a crazy man?"

"That I have part of your allegiance."

Her face grew immediately serious. "Yeah," she said in a quiet voice. "You do."

"Great. Because now that I know that, I can give you two presents."

She started out rolling her eyes at him, but pretty soon her mouth fell flat open when he grabbed up the tech on her arm and started to yank something off.

"Hey!" She tried to snatch her arm back from him. "You trying to get punched in the face again?"

He ignored her, his tongue poking out of the side of his mouth as he worked. It didn't take long for him to get one fingernail under the side of one of the crystals that lined her arm. He flipped off what looked like a two-inch-long piece of paper-thin glass. It had been completely invisible, pressed up against her tech.

Kupier held it up between them and Glade blinked, reaching for it.

"What is this?"

Instead of answering, he lifted up his hips from the seat of the capsule and pulled something out of his back pocket. It was the same as the piece of glass that Glade held in her hand, but it was a little bigger and a little sturdier looking. "It's a Ferryman's com. We've been using them for years. It's just messages, nothing by voice. And the messages can't be intercepted. We had to modify yours a little bit so that it blended in with your tech."

She turned it over in her hands, snapped it back onto her tech, and watched it go utterly invisible. She pulled it back off. "When did you put this on my tech?"

A look of chagrin came over his face. "Ah, right before we popped you in the dampener."

"Are you telling me that this has been here THE WHOLE TIME?"

He nodded again. "It has a locator in it, as well. That's how I knew where to find you in the Station." He held up the matching one in his hand. "I used mine to find yours."

Glade just blinked at him for a second, turning the com over in her hands. "So why didn't you use it to track us down when we left Charon?"

"I did."

She blinked up at him. "But you let us go."

He nodded. "I told you before, Glade. I can't force you to do this. To be on our side. I knew that if you wanted to go, then stopping you wasn't going to put you any more on the Ferry-men's team." He held her eyes for a second. "Here. Let me show you how to send messages on it."

He was sure she could have figured it out on her own, but he needed somewhere else to look for a minute. He typed words into his own and, a second later, they scrolled over hers, iridescent and purplish.

"Oh, that's cool," she noted. "Even though it's clear, you can't read the message from the other side."

"Right. So even if you get a message while it's on your tech, no one will know. The words will face in."

She fiddled around with it for a few more seconds and he watched the ethereal light of the com light up her face. He took another deep breath.

"You ready for your next present?"

"Hmm?" she asked, and he could tell she wasn't paying attention to him. Didn't matter. She was about to give him her undivided attention. He was sure of it.

"The Ray is on the way to get your sisters as we speak."

The com clattered out of her fingers and she stared at nothing in the air for far too long. "Excuse me?"

Kupier couldn't resist – he reached forward and tipped her chin up until she was looking at him. "I dispatched them yesterday."

"Before you knew where I stood? Before you knew that I was willing to be your ally?"

He nodded. "I couldn't just stand by and let them be taken. It's a long way to Io. So, it'll still be a week or so before they're safe. But we'll take them to Charon. Like you asked. We'll keep them safe from the Authority."

He barely got the words all the way out of his mouth before she was tackling him back onto the seat, squeezing the breath out of him.

"Thank you," she whispered. He felt her tears against his neck and wondered if she knew she was crying. "Thank you."

She popped up from the hug. "Then I definitely have to get back to the Station. If they think something is up with me, or that I left or defected, then my sisters will be the first place they go. And all of this will be shot."

"Right." He knew she was right. But there was a stabbing in his chest. Regret. Fear. He didn't want to let her go. And he definitely didn't want to send her back to a place that didn't care if she lived or died. That tortured her.

Sighing, he used his com to contact the nearby Ferryman's ship. The Ceph wasn't nearly as large or as fast as the Ray, but she'd do. "We'll be docking in ten minutes and then you can take off from there. You want to go over what to tell them at the Station again?"

She nodded, opening her mouth to recite her lines, but Kupier cut her off. He grabbed her hands tightly. "Tell me you've got at least one ally there, Glade. Someone who's looking out for you even a little bit. I don't think I can send you back in if there's no one."

Her eyes went just the slightest bit guarded, but she nodded. "There's someone. One person. My friend Dahn. I think I mentioned him a few times."

"You trust him?"

Her eyes fell now. "Things have been changing. But yeah. If my life were on the line, I'd trust him."

Kupier sensed something there. Maybe even something that Glade herself couldn't sense. And the words were like chalk in his mouth, but he said them. He had to say them. He hadn't been born selfish, and he wasn't about to teach himself how to be that way now. "Then stick close to him, Glade. Promise me that you'll stay as close as you can to him. Especially if," he swallowed, "something goes wrong on my end."

Her eyes were fierce when he looked back at her. "Are you saying goodbye?" She let out a frustrated growl and banged a fist on her own leg. "God! I hate humans! I can never figure out what they're really saying!"

He couldn't help but laugh. "I'm saying goodbye for now. And that I'll let you know when we have your sisters safe. And that we'll go from there." He kissed her one more time. It was meant to be soft, but it ended fiercely. He wasn't sure if he'd done that or she had. "And that I want you to take care of yourself. To *actually* take care of yourself."

She held his eyes and nodded. They sat shoulder to shoulder then, and watched in silence as the Ceph approached. They didn't speak again.

And he didn't look back when he jumped out of the capsule and jogged across the landing deck of the Ceph. She didn't look back when she launched off and into space.

They didn't look back. They looked forward.

CHAPTER TWENTY-TWO_

I knew that interrogations were a very strong possibility upon my return to the Station. There was a heck of a lot to be suspicious of. But in no way had I expected to get what I received.

I was applauded. Cheered for. Absolutely celebrated. Apparently, being the chosen one had some perks.

From the second I commed in to the Station to say that I'd recovered a one-man capsule ship that the Ferrymen had smuggled on to that supply skip. Well, it was like I'd announced that I'd single-handedly wiped the Ferrymen from the solar system.

The engineers were thrilled to have yet another piece of Ferryman equipment to study and learn from. The tactical team was relieved to understand what the Ferrymen had done to the supply skip.

And Haven? I think he was just glad I'd come back. I had no idea whether or not he believed my story, but both of us knew that throwing your 'chosen one' into interrogations was not exactly a good way to promote the new system of Culling.

It was nearly ten hours after I landed the capsule ship on the landing deck when I was able to track down Dahn.

Any guesses who was by his side?

I tried not to let it hurt that he and Sullia were running a simulation together. I tried not to let it hurt when I walked into the simulation room and watched as he bent his head over the same screen that she did. The two of them whispering about the things that had just happened in the simulator.

It was Sullia who noticed I was there. Her hair was mostly purple these days, and it suited her even better than the pink had. It was longer than it had been all those months ago when we'd been captive on the Ray. So much had changed since then.

I expected a biting comment from Sullia. But it wasn't what I got. Instead, I saw something much worse in her eyes. Hatred.

"You're going to get us all killed, Glade." She strode up to me, almost nose to nose. "You accuse me of being an opportunist. Of being a snake. But you're the one playing both sides. And don't even pretend that you aren't! I don't know what your end game is. But I know that you don't give a shit if we end up in a war with the Ferrymen. In fact, maybe that's what you're hoping for."

I crossed my arms over my chest and glared at her. "Get to the point, Sullia. This speech is high and mighty, but we both know you don't care about the fate of the Authority or the solar system."

I thought she might strike me, but she didn't. She took one step back from me and then another. "You're not the chosen one, Glade. No one is. I don't care who you are or what they think you can do. You don't have it in you to cull an entire solar system. It doesn't matter what happens with you or," she narrowed her eyes threateningly, "*to* you. Because I'm gonna be there. I'll be there to do everything that you can't do. It'll be me they're celebrating this time next year. Not some weak Ioan who never should have been selected to be a Datapoint."

"Take a walk, Sullia." Dahn pinched the bridge of his nose in between his fingers as if her speech were giving him a headache.

"Excuse me?" She whirled on him.

He raised an eyebrow at her. "You're being insubordinate to a superior officer. You're threatening the Datapoint the entire Culling is being reconstructed around. And you're just generally being kind of an asshole."

I thought for a minute that Sullia was going to throat-punch him. Not that she would have been able to get the hit in – Dahn was fast.

But after a few tense seconds, she just stormed out. "Screw you both."

Dahn and I looked at one another for a minute after she'd left. "Why are you spending time with her?" I couldn't help but ask him.

Immediately, I felt the awkwardness between us bloom again. I remembered that he'd barely talked to me since I'd gotten out of the infirmary after the simulation. After Haven had announced I was the chosen one. His eyes were flat as he started shutting down the simulator for the night.

"Because I understand her," he said after a minute. His back was to me. "Sullia isn't honest. She's not pleasant. You're right that she's a snake who would strike me down without hesitation. But I trust that she'll always be like that. I know what I'm getting."

I let out a long breath. "And you're saying that you don't trust me."

"Of course I do!" he snapped, turning on me. The insulted fury in his eyes went a long way toward soothing me. The tidal wave settled a little. "I just wish that I didn't. Because I don't know what you'll do next."

He stiffened as I crossed the room in three long strides. His body readied for an attack. It was with Kupier's voice in my ear that I flung my arms around Dahn's middle. It was like hugging a tree trunk. And it took at least ten seconds of sustained contact before one of his arms banded around me. But it was a light touch, as if he were worried he'd break me. Ironic, considering all the sparring we'd done, where he actually had been trying to break me.

"I was wrong," I spoke into the air next to his shoulder as I pulled back from our hug. Our lovely, stiff, Datapoint hug.

There was red creeping up Dahn's neck and he had to clear his throat before speaking. "About what?"

"When I said that Datapoints can't love. I was wrong about that. I love my sisters. My mother." I took a deep breath before punching him lightly in the arm. "And I love my family here on the Station. Who trust me against their better judgement."

Dahn's eyes held mine. They went from being soft to frustrated and back to soft. Some of his long, dark hair had come loose and he quickly tied it back, the tech at his temples catching the light. "I've said it before and I'll say it again. I don't understand you, Glade Io."

I reached out, and instead of touching him skin to skin, I did something I'd never done before. I gently clacked the integrated tech on my arm against the tech on his arm. Our computers shivered at the contact and I watched Kupier's hidden com catch the light.

"That's because we're human, Dahn."

EPILOGUE_

Four days after I'd returned the capsule, Kupier sat at the foot of my bed. It was the first night he'd visited my dreams since I'd last seen him. I knew it was a dream because he turned his blue marble into a blue blanket that covered us both.

"I found a planet that no one has discovered before," he whispered. "It's called Earth. You'll never believe how beautiful she is."

I laughed. "Kupier, the human race began on Earth. Everyone knows about it."

"No," he shook his head. "Not the Earth that I found. I can show you a different side that no one has ever seen before."

I woke up frowning. And I found that I believed him.

I didn't sleep any more that night, and it was almost time to get out of bed when I felt a strange tickle creep up my back. My tech was telling me something that I'd never felt before. It was the gentlest whisper.

The com. Suddenly, I knew it in my bones. It was the com

talking to me. I slammed the blankets over my head and flicked the Ferrymen's com off my tech.

Sure enough, words flashed across the screen.

DP-1. I joined up with the Ray. We're just hours away from Io. I'll let you know when we have Daw and Treb. Be safe.

I squeezed my eyes closed, just once. Something was rearranging inside of me. It was that mountain I called a heart. All the stones that had shaken loose during the Culling on Europa... I felt them gathering, finding their places again.

I knew that once my sisters were safe I was going to have some questions to ask myself. Questions I couldn't afford to ask while they were still in jeopardy. Questions about who I believed. And, more importantly, who I fought for.

For a brief, fantastical second, I imagined Kupier and Dahn standing aboard the Ray together.

Yeah.

Never going to happen.

I dragged myself out of bed. Dahn had agreed to keep training with me. More for something to do than for the practice. But I was glad for the reason to see him every day. And I was glad he wasn't avoiding me anymore.

It was when I got out of the simulator an hour or so later that I found Dahn frowning at me, a complicated expression on his face. It was like he didn't want to look at me, but he was making himself.

"Sir Haven wants to see you. He just called."

"Okay." I paused in front of Dahn. "I'll see you later?"

He hesitated for just a second, that hard look on his face slowly melting. "Yes. Sure. Definitely."

I knew he watched me go.

302

Haven was sitting in his blue chair when I got there. "Glade, I'll get right to it. I have good and bad news for you."

My brain shorted out as I lowered myself into the chair. For one, horrified second, I thought that Haven might be reaching out for my hand. But instead he just crossed his legs and leaned toward me.

"The good news is that your sisters are safe. I know how you worry for their welfare. They withstood an attack from the Ferrymen. They were almost abducted. But members of the Authority security had been assigned to protect them, and you needn't worry. They are completely safe, and in Authority custody on Io right now."

Kupier.

I could barely think. It had gone wrong. Kupier hadn't gotten my sisters. God. What had happened to Kupier? To the Ray? To the rest of the crew? My fingers itched to reach out to my silent com, but I restrained myself, knowing that Haven would track the movement.

"And the bad news?" I barely recognized my voice. It was like someone had coated my vocal chords in ice.

"I'm sorry to tell you that your mother perished in the course of the attack." He paused as if he were in genuine pain. "She was killed by Ferrymen."

———

I made it back to my bunk somehow. Maybe I crawled; maybe I floated. I'd never know. I knew just one thing while I lay there with the curtains closed, my com silent no matter how many messages I was sending to Kupier.

303

Haven was lying.

I knew, in my heart, that the Ferrymen hadn't killed my mother. I knew who had.

I slapped the com back onto my tech. Hiding it from the world. My heart shook in my chest as my body refused to absorb the fact that my mother had died. It was unbelievable, indigestible. Unreal.

I grabbed onto the only thing I could as my entire world shifted beneath me. The Authority had culled my father. Tortured me. Captured my sisters. And now they'd killed my mother.

I didn't care if there was a virus or not. I was going to destroy that Database. Yank it out at the root, burning it to the ground.

END OF THE CULLING_
THE CULLING BOOK ONE

Who gets Culled next?

Find out in book two of The Culling series.
The Authority is available at www.RamonaFinn.com.

THANK YOU!_

Thanks for reading **The Culling.**
I really hope you enjoyed it.
Please don't forget to leave a review!

Don't cull our relationship,
I'd love to stay connected.

•Sign up to my <u>Mailing List</u> at www.RamonaFinn.com

•Visit my <u>Website</u> at www.RamonaFinn.com

•Connect with me on <u>Facebook</u> at
www.facebook.com/ramonafinnbooks/

•Follow me on <u>Instagram</u> at www.instagram.com/ramonafinn/

MORE BOOKS BY RAMONA FINN_
WWW.RAMONAFINN.COM

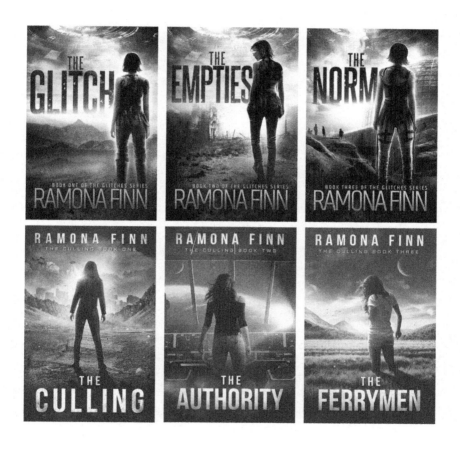